ISBN 978-1-331-35200-6
PIBN 10178086

1 MONTH OF
FREE
READING

at

www.ForgottenBooks.com

By purchasing this book you are eligible for one month membership to ForgottenBooks.com, giving you unlimited access to our entire collection of over 700,000 titles via our web site and mobile apps.

To claim your free month visit:

www.forgottenbooks.com/free178086

English
Français
Deutsche
Italiano
Español
Português

www.forgottenbooks.com

Mythology Photography **Fiction**
Fishing Christianity **Art** Cooking
Essays Buddhism Freemasonry
Medicine **Biology** Music **Ancient
Egypt** Evolution Carpentry Physics
Dance Geology **Mathematics** Fitness
Shakespeare **Folklore** Yoga Marketing
Confidence Immortality Biographies
Poetry **Psychology** Witchcraft
Electronics Chemistry History **Law**
Accounting **Philosophy** Anthropology
Alchemy Drama Quantum Mechanics
Atheism Sexual Health **Ancient History**
Entrepreneurship Languages Sport
Paleontology Needlework Islam
Metaphysics Investment Archaeology
Parenting Statistics Criminology
Motivational

MR. BRYANT'S MISTAKE

BY

KATHARINE WYLDE

AUTHOR OF 'A DREAMER,' 'AN ILL-REGULATED MIND,' ETC.

IN THREE VOLUMES—VOL. III

LONDON

RICHARD BENTLEY & SON, NEW BURLINGTON ST.

Publishers in Ordinary to Her Majesty the Queen

1890

'GOD help us and enlighten us for the future, that we may not stand in our own way so much, but may have clear notions of the consequences of things.'

CONTENTS

PART IX

PART X

PART XI

PART XII

PART IX

AN EXTINCT VOLCANO

MR. BRYANT'S MISTAKE

CHAPTER I

'I won't think,' Nannie told herself again next day; and really she did not think very much. She went about like a thing in a dream, conscious of a never-ceasing ache in her heart, but not probing it; another person from the resolute girl she had been yesterday. She could hardly believe she was not a phantom, while her real self was sitting docilely at Faverton by Maria's side—Maria, who no doubt was in a dreadful fright, even though unaware that her charge had run away in a carriage with a blushing young clergyman. 'I don't care!' thought Nannie; 'it won't hurt her to be anxious a little while. I have been anxious too, and I am alive still and very healthy. To-morrow I will write.'

To-morrow. Nannie was still disposed to defer everything till to-morrow. She heard in the morning of Mr. Randle's death, but the pain of bereave-

ment had not come to her yet; rather she had a
shocked feeling of relief. How could she have met
him again now she knew she was not his daughter?
To-morrow she would go to John and learn about it.
She could not meet John to-day.

And to-morrow—she must find some way of
giving his ring back to Sir Vincent. Ah no! she
could not give it up to-day! She was too sad to-
day. And to-morrow, perhaps, she would have
another message to send with it—a message to tell
him—

'Ah!' sighed Nannie, 'he will understand that
I *had* to do it. The ring must go back, and without
one word, one look—only not to-day, not to-day.'

And it came to pass that, unseen, Nannie saw
him when he was standing outside Tanswick station,
talking to Mrs. Bryant and Georgina. Nannie had
been wandering about, trying to get some authentic
tidings of Alick, and now she had strayed to Tanswick. There were trees about the station, and
Nannie hid among them and looked hungrily upon
the man she loved, and whom she was giving up for
ever. Her eyes filled, for she was lonely and miserable. Mrs. Bryant, who was not, it seemed, a good
woman, might talk to him on equal terms, and
shake his hand; and her rival might smile up in
his face unreproved, while she herself, whose lips he
had often kissed, was cowering away from his sight,

and would never feel the touch of his dear hand
again. And then Georgina jumped out of the pony-
carriage, and she and Vincent disappeared into the
station together. Nannie felt her heart tighten
suddenly. 'Yes,' she said to herself, 'the ring must
go back. It is all quite over and done with, and
she can do more for him than ever I could. And
he—perhaps *he* has *had* to do it.' For she had
caught a glimpse of her lover's face, and she saw,
alas! only too clearly, that, looking at Georgina (who
was all love and pleading, poor thing, as any one
could see) there was none of the rapture, the tenderness, the joy unspeakable, which she had known in
his smile when he had gazed at herself. 'He looked
at her,' said Nannie, with a great sob, 'as I shall
look at Alick—as I shall look at Alick!'

Much later on the same day, when she had
achieved nothing, and could hardly endure herself
for weariness and grief, Nannie was still lingering
about the cliffs, watching the fall of the twilight, and
wondering at the traces of the storm. She had not
in the morning visited that horrible precipice where
she had last seen Alick; but a spirit in her listless
feet turned her thitherward now, and with a sort of
dreary pleasure in reviving hateful emotions that at
least might waken her from the 'wan and heartless
mood' into which she had fallen now. 'If I could
even be angry with Alick as I was then!' she said to

herself. But it was not to be angry with Alick
that Nannie had come hither to-day.

'My God, my God!' said the girl, with a little
cry, carried away by the blast unheard into the
falling gloom, 'Alick is there!'

It had come suddenly at the last, the moment
she had been expecting; for which she had given up
lover, and home, and brethren, her hope, and her
happiness. She had found Alick; and she knew
only too well what significance the fact would have
for him. He was there on the dangerous, narrow,
little path below Dr. Verrill's house, overhanging
the sea. And a great repugnance and a great fear
overpowered her; she turned to flee noiselessly and
unperceived by the man she had come to save. At
any moment Alick might see her, and there would
be no escape. She looked round, but no one was
in sight. She had cut herself adrift from her lover;
had given him no knowledge of her extremity.
No rescue that was not too late could reach her now.
Vincent was not there; nor any one. Nannie crushed
herself against the rock, and looked fearfully at
Alick again.

Why was he there on the edge of the cliff where
it overhung a boiling flood lashed to fury by the
barrier which the crumbling rock still offered to its
advance? A fall there meant death. It had been
death to Dick Boulter's lass long ago; it had near

been death to Nannie herself not many days since. Such things were done at Everwell; the place was handy for drowning folk! Nannie did not know the part that overhanging precipice had long played in Alick's unbalanced imagination; but she realised at once that now, leaning over, his arms extended, his head thrown back, his eyes closed, he was at this moment in danger. Had not Nannie feared that deserted, despairing, distraught, his conscience seared and his courage gone, Alick was the man to destroy himself for grief? Thank God——oh, thank God, she had come in time!

Yet what to do? How to rescue without startling him out of all self-possession into the very evil she sought to avert? She could not tell what was going on in his mind—what thoughts he was thinking of herself even. 'He may hate me—think me a curse. If I call, if he sees me, he may flee, he may slip—and there on the cliff's edge—Oh, God, I should throw myself after him. I should not be able to bear it!'

Nannie crushed herself back into the shadow where he could not see her without coming away a little from the precipice. Her limbs were quivering, and she was white as any leaf; but she steadied her lips, and with voice harsh indeed but true and clear, she sang the first thing that came into her head—

> 'My Father's house on high,
>   Home of my soul, how near,
> At times, to faith's far-seeing eye
>   Thy golden gates appear!'

Alick moved his head.   He had heard and re
cognised the song—the voice perhaps.   He was
listening.   Nannie sang on, gaining confidence—

> 'Here in the body pent,
>   Absent from Thee I roam ;
> Yet nightly pitch my moving tent,
>   A day's march nearer home.'

The songs of Zion had become memories to
Alick; the gelden gates a dream, the body a
dungeon of torment.   With a long heart-piercing
groan, his arms crossed upon his breast, he sank on
his knees to listen.   Nannie could see his face now
—worn and wasted, his eyes lost in dark caverns.
She sang again, her voice stronger and sweeter
now—

> 'For ever with the Lord !
>   Amen, so let it be :
> Life from the dead is in that word,
>   'Tis immortality.'

And again the sweet, sad refrain, with its yearning
repetition at the close—

> 'Nearer home !   A day's march nearer home !'

'Nannie!' said Alick, in a soundless voice, which
yet reached her somehow.   She moved a little,

detaching herself from the shadow, her hands held out and a welcoming smile in her soft eyes—an angel of healing and hope.

'Are you there, Alick? Did you hear me singing our dear old hymn?'

He came to her then. Nannie took his hands in hers and led him to the quiet shadow. She sat on a low rock, and he sank at her feet, his hand still in hers. And for long neither of them spoke. The waves plashed sullenly at the foot of the rocks, and Nannie could see the fishing-boats putting out to sea under the wild clouds of a doubtful evening. After a time Alick stirred a little and let her see his face, already more natural in expression and hue. She smiled down at him.

'Hast thou forgiven me, Nannie?' asked Alick.

'Ay, dear lad,' said Nannie, all except that suffering face receding from her memory.

'Art thou my lassie?' he questioned, hesitatingly, but with a flush coming on his cheek and a flickering light in his dull eyes.

'Ay,' said Nannie. He raised himself on his elbow and looked at her.

'Thou wilt not leave me? · Thou art my lassie —my sweetheart?'

'Ay. Thou may'st kiss me, Alick, if thou wilt.'

Never was a more quiet, chastened kiss, but it meant her doom to Nannie, though not a change came to her pitying, steadfast face. And then again there was silence, and together they watched the cobles going out to sea under the stormy clouds.

CHAPTER II

'COME, Alick, let us go home. You are starved with cold, lad, and so am I.'

He rose without a word and stepped beside her. He looked fairly like himself now, and Nannie's fright had subsided.

'Thou art sure thou art my lassie?' he repeated, smiling at her.

'Yes, Alick,' replied Nannie, gravely.

'Then it were fitting I should thank God,' he said, stopping and uncovering his head.

'A deal can happen all of a moment, Nannie,' said Alick presently. 'I have been in darkness and sore trouble, but I have won out into His light again; and I have heard His voice saying, "Thou hast been faithful, poor sinner, in a few things, and now I have brought thee an exceeding great reward." And I had not heard His voice for many a day, Nannie.'

'Dear Alick!'

'I thought I saw a gleam of a white angel's

wing this morning. I might have known I was winning through. When I heard thee sing, Nannie, I understood then as He had brought me back.'

'From where, dear lad?'

'I have fared like my Master, Nannie. I have been driven into the wilderness to be tempted of Satan.'

I think you are sick and hungry, Alick. You have been starving in the wilderness. You may have a good plain loaf now and a butter pat, as a reward for not turning the stones into food.' But her smiles were a little too soon.

'There were worse temptations nor that,' muttered Alick; and she heard his teeth grating on each other. The gloom that suddenly enwrapped him, even as the stormy clouds had settled upon the sea, renewed Nannie's anxiety.

'What were the temptations, lad?' she said, thinking he would tell her the drinking story, and that she would be able to pronounce absolution. There was a long silence. Nannie glanced at her companion half nervously. At last Alick spoke.

'The devils drove me down the town, Nannie, where I had laboured and preached the Gospel, and they showed me the men I would have died to save, cursing me, and sinning, and cursing God. They never saw me; I was close to 'em many a time; and my heart was broke and bleeding.'

'Why do you say devils drove you? It would have been better to show yourself and speak to the men; but what you did had no sin in it.'

'Ay, it was devils. They kept telling me how the men had thrown stones at me, and had chased me from them, till I could scarce keep my hands from throwing stones at them. There was a little lad—Tim Laverick—I found alone one day asleep on the scar. I stood a long time over him, Nannie. He had led off in cursing me and throwing mud at me. And he had a little throat——'

'Don't, Alick. I don't like it.'

'The little lad never waked, Nannie. But I came away and did him no harm.' Again Nannie glanced at her cousin nervously. Yet this talk of devils was merely his old trick learned from the *Pilgrim's Progress* and his eye for making weird pictures.

'But the parson were the worst,' muttered Alick under his breath, looking round suspiciously.

'Who?' asked Nannie, frightened and not catching the name.

'The devil who moved me against *him* was mighty. I have followed him and laid plots against him. Nannie, have I not cause to hate yon man?'

'No, Alick, you mustn't go over it! I don't know what man you mean, but——'

'Him,' said Alick, jerking his thumb in the direction of the church; or of the Heights.

'Sir Vincent?' cried Nannie. Alick started as if he had been struck, and walked away a few steps. Nannie, aware of her folly, went up to him and drew his arm again round her.

'I have done with yon man, Alick! Never thou trouble thy head about him no more. It is thou I will have, and will be loving to all the days of thy life. There is no call for thee to be angry with Sir Vincent, or to make never a single plot against him. Alick, promise me. Oh, I love thee, lad. Kiss me as often as thou wilt, and promise me!'

She protested too much, and Alick saw through her. He laid his head on the rock and there was a groan in his voice as, after a long shuddering silence, he replied brokenly—

'I warn't thinking of thy Vincent, lass. Don't thou be fearful of me, Nannie; I have won through.' Nannie was no miracle of self-possession, and disabling and blinding panic was invading her, though she preserved her outward calm.

'Dear lad, I do think you have been very ill,' she said, 'and the first thing it is right for us to do is tó climb up that little path together and get Dr. Verrill to·feel your pulse, and say where we are to go, and what we must do, and what I'm to get for your supper. Come, Alick, come, my own dear Alick.'

'I will not go to Dr. Verrill,' said Alick, gloomily.

He sat down again and let her hand drop. 'I see Sir Vincent's horse go along the road towards Tanswick,' said Alick, under his breath; 'I'm thinking he'll be coming back from the train. And I will wait *here*, to see *him*.'

'What dost thou want to say to Sir Vincent?' cried Nannie.

'Thou canst go home, lassie,' replied Alick, bitterly; 'I can do my errand to Sir Vincent easier without thee, who art a darling to the two of us.'

'Oh, Alick, what do you *mean?*' groaned the girl. There was silence again; Alick's head buried in his hands, and Nannie praying for some one to help. Presently he resumed in a loud voice, of which the agitation sounded like fury to Nannie. 'I dragged myself to his house to-day to have it out with him. He was gone to Faverton, seeking thee, I'm thinking. I had to wait; and now maybe there's less need, now thou hast given thyself to me. But he's coming along this road, and before I dare take my happiness—it's maybe my duty—I will stop him and do it now. But I will not have thee by, Nannie. Go thy ways, lassie, and him or me shall tell you the end of it.' Nannie sprang to her feet, seizing his hands and pressing them to her breast.

'Alick! sweetheart—husband! I cannot leave

thee alone here with Sir Vincent!' she cried with terror-stricken eyes.

'Don't be hindering me, girl,' shouted Alick with sudden rage; 'it was not for that I told thee. Go and leave me to pray for strength.'

'Oh, Alick, Alick!' moaned Nannie. He turned from her and lay with his face on the ground, murmuring, 'Go, lassie, for kindness' sake. It will burst my heart to do it with thy sweet self by.'

It occurred to Nannie that her best hope was in running herself towards Tanswick to warn Sir Vincent. 'He will tell me what to do!' she thought; 'but oh! what a way of meeting him!' She left her cousin hastily, climbing up the steep path. But Alick, all his senses alive, divined her intention, and quick as thought followed and overtook her.

'Dost thou think, lass, I cannot run quicker nor thou along the Tanswick road?' asked Alick with a laugh, holding her trembling form with a grasp of iron, and swaying her backwards and forwards with a gentleness which at any moment might change to fury. Nannie turned obediently. Dr. Verrill was her only hope now. Then Alick went back to his lair in the shadow of the little path's turn, and Nannie, looking down, could see him crouching there, his eyes fastened on the narrow hemmed-in road above, along which she would have had to pass to give warning, and along which, in a few moments now, Sir Vincent would come trotting carelessly on the bay horse Pegasus. Nannie was too much frightened to know exactly what she feared. She made for the pink-painted cottage with the gaunt windows and the scientific garden.

Over the uneven ground sped Nannie, as fast as fear would suffer her; the three minutes seemed ten to her terror, and as she ran she cried aloud for help. It was nearly dark now, and the road was deserted. 'Lord have mercy, Nannie, whatever's the matter?' cried fat Mrs. Blake, the baker's wife, who was alone in the post-office. But Nannie heeded nothing; she dashed across the doctor's garden, pulled the door-bell, and rapped desperately with her knuckles. 'Doctor! oh Dr. Verrill, come out!' cried the girl; but there was no answer. Never, in an emergency, was a more useless man than Dr. Verrill. Nannie fancied she heard voices behind the house, and went round, edging her way rashly, for the pink cottage had little space between it and the precipice. She looked down, shuddering, to see that Vincent had not yet come, and that Alick was still waiting. But certainly, yes! two persons had appeared in sight, walking along the short cut towards Tanswick. The first moment of relief was so great that Nannie's eyes were blinded with tears, and she thanked Heaven aloud. Then she swept her hand across her eyes, and strained her sight to see who the people were, and if there were really good prospect of help in them. Ah! one was Mr. Bryant. Again she felt relieved; a gentleman like Mr. Bryant would know what to do, nor would he pass Alick without greeting. Nannie noticed without heeding it that the voices of the two men were angry, and that they were interrupting each other as if in dispute. Once— could it be possible?—her own name floated up to her. 'Who is that other man?' thought the girl; 'it is like the gentleman who spoke to me at the Heights. But oh! help has come!' She might have gone down again now, but to say the truth, repugnance filled her at the thought of returning to that miserable Alick. No; she would linger till Sir Vincent came; and she could watch and see what the gentlemen would do to her cousin.

But the two men were entirely engrossed in their disagreeable conversation, and they stopped to finish it instead of walking on past Alick and up into the road again. Nannie could see them plainly now; Mr. Bryant flushed and angry and agitated, his voice loud and his dignity forgotten; Mr. Kane angry and nervous too, but cool enough. And Nannie saw something more; that Alick had forgotten Sir Vincent, and, unobserved and stealthy, had crept quite close to the pair, and unseen by them, was listening to their talk. And they were standing just at the most dangerous part of that dangerous track ; the very place where she had found Alick an hour ago ; where the rock overhung and the angry waves of the rising tide boiled below. Some of the conversation reached her. Her own name again. Mrs. Bryant's. Nannie felt that for her to intrude now was impossible. Good heavens ! could the gentleman be telling Mr. Bryant *that ?* And then the waves roared again, and Nannie, who had heard nothing connected, heard no more. But Alick heard. Something intolerable,—some slandering lie about his Nannie, flung desperately from the clergyman's lips ; Nannie, spotless in her integrity and purity, but who was to be submerged now in the inky overthrow of her mother's shame ; Nannie, who was to be labelled ' worthless,' that none should soil his fingers by investigating her name, her history, her birth. With a yell that tore the air, Alick threw himself upon the liar.

Alas for Nannie ! What followed was never distinct to her memory. Mercy blinded her aching eyes and deafened her straining ears. She had no power of comprehension for the scene. ' Alick ! Alick !' she shrieked, but she was far above, and her voice was drowned in the roar of the billows, and the groan of the night wind storming round the cliffs. Mr. Bryant was a large and powerful man, but the blow had been too startling for effectual resistance. He fell upon the path, striking his head against the wall of rock with sufficient violence to render him for a moment helpless. Mr. Kane interfered; but it was an instant's work for the strength of distraction to seize the light slender figure of this man, who had confessed vile things in the hearing of the uncompromising prophet of righteousness. 'Alick! Alick!' shrieked Nannie from above; but the thing was done, and Frederick Kane's old sins had met their reward. He and his interference had disappeared, and Alick had turned again upon Mr. Bryant. The two men rolled together on that narrow ledge of rock; Nannie fled towards them, but her agony could avail nothing.

She was the first to see Sir Vincent, however. He had leaped from his horse upon hearing the cries from below. He had seen his uncle's fall had understood all at ·a glance, and was ready to act. But Nannie intercepted her lover. 'No— no—no!' she screamed, throwing herself across his way, 'not you! I cannot bear it! cannot bear it! cannot bear it!'

'Nannie, for God's sake let me go!' said Vincent, and then by force he unlaced her clasp upon his arms and flung her aside.

'Oh my own darling!' he said in a choked voice of Love's remorse, as Nannie tottered and fell.

But he left her and descended swiftly to the scene of struggle.

CHAPTER III

Mr. Bryant's strength was pretty well used up, and when Alick, unresisting now, had been securely bound so as to be altogether powerless, Vincent sent the clergyman to Tanswick for assistance. He had himself looked over the cliff and seen that Mr. Kane's figure, still moving a little, had rested on a ledge close to the seething waves, and in danger soon to be swept off by them. Vincent turned doubtfully to Nannie, who had crept down to his side.

'I must go and see what has happened to my uncle,' he said; 'will you be afraid to stay here for a few minutes? He cannot move, you know,' he added, in a low voice.

'I am not afraid,' said Nannie.

'You will call if you want me? Alick, listen; you will not say or do anything to frighten Nannie till I come back.' Vincent lingered, in his heart afraid to abandon the defenceless girl. Then Alick opened his hollow eyes and looked up. He had quickly given way before Vincent, recognising a master.

'I'm myself again now, sir,' he said; and added brokenly, 'God knows I was fearing something of this sort. Nannie will tell you I had gone this day to pray you to shut me up for fear. And I was waiting here. now to ask you to do it. God knows why it never came into my head to give myself up to none but you. And I suppose it's the gallows will be the end of it now,' groaned Alick. Vincent looked at him with the silence of great compassion. 'If you had come five minutes sooner, sir ' murmured Alick again; 'I was waiting to give myself up to you. I had told my Nannie. And I sent the lassie away, lest I should falter for the love of her.'

'Oh, Alick, and I did not understand you!' mourned Nannie, laying her hand on the poor bound, shaking fingers.

'We'll soon have you yourself again, Alick,' said Vincent, gently. 'Yes, I wish I had been five minutes sooner, my poor friend! But we mustn't be too downhearted. I daresay my uncle is little the worse. Will you and Nannie take care of each other, while I go and help him up after his tumble?' He left them unwillingly, climbing down to the edge of the waves.

'Nannie,' murmured Alick, 'if the man isn't much hurt, wilt thou forget it, lassie? They was saying evil things of *thee*, Nannie, and I could not bear it. And thou hadst just kissed me of thine own free will and given thyself to me. If the man isn't much the worse, Nannie—Nannie—wilt thou be my lassie still?'

'I will, Alick,' said Nannie, sadly.

He closed his eyes again, and Nannie sat beside him while the darkness descended and folded them in its wild embrace. It seemed long before Sir Vincent returned, looking himself now much agitated and shaken.

'Is he asleep?' he asked, glancing at Alick.

'I don't know. Well? The gentleman——'

'Is *dead*,' said Vincent, in a low voice.

It was raining, and they sat together drearily without speaking, and watching Alick, who had opened his eyes as the last words were uttered, and who kept them open now with a strange expression of dumb anguish. Vincent took off his coat and wrapped it round Alick's starved and quivering form, but no one spoke again.

When at last the sound of help from Tanswick was heard above, Vincent touched Nannie's hand for a moment and raised her to her feet.

'Leave us now,' he said; 'there is no more you can do.' Nannie looked at the stricken Alick with grieving eyes. Then she pressed his cold forehead with her lips. As she moved slowly away, she stopped and looked back at her lover, who was leaning over Alick and speaking to him; but feeling her glance, Vincent raised his head for a moment, and for the first time his eyes and Nannie's met.

Vincent never told any one till long afterwards, the full detail of what he had witnessed down there on the edge of the waves; for the wretched sufferer had died in his arms, but not without involuntary and uncontrolled horror at the roaring waves encroaching upon the narrow ledge which had checked his fall. The place and the manner of that end were appalling, even without the few semi-conscious sentences, which were surprising and revolting to Vincent yet the germ of explanation and wild hopes for Nannie and himself. And when the Arch Fiend had suddenly ended the final struggle, and the corpse had been with difficulty sheltered and secured from desecration by the waves, Vincent stood shuddering and looking at the dead man, alone there on the margin of the storm, hardly daring to avert his eyes from the ghastly sight, or to induce himself to abandon it to the rain and the spray and the din of the obstructed waves. But he remembered dear Nannie waiting with her no less fearful charge above; he was getting dizzy himself here on the edge of the precipice, so close to the whirlpool; and a great longing to be with the woman he loved surged up in his mind. He

covered the dead face and made his way up the
steep of the rock again.   Once, half-way, he fancied
he heard a movement below, and paused to look
back at the still figure he had left, half expecting
to see it stir, or hear it cry.   But it was an illusion;
and another minute brought him to Nannie's restora-
tive presence.   He longed to take her natural,
beloved frame in his arms, and warm his heart
against the beating of hers; but there were those
woe-struck, deeply conscious eyes of the grieving
Alick to restrain him.   He could only sit by her
side and feel her near and know that they were
suffering together.   That silent watch with its un-
spoken sympathy drew their souls nearer together
than all their half playful courtship, with its
mingling of sighs and smiles, fancies and fears.
Now, if never before, the very depth of their being
was stirred; and for Vincent at least nothing could
ever undo the force of this hour and these surroundings; and there was no question of gentleman and
lady with him again, but simply of man and of
woman whose souls had been wedded by irresistible
affinity.

And then Nannie had kissed Alick's forehead;
and she had looked at Vincent with a strange en-
treating, despairing gaze, in answer to the restrained
passion of irrevocable love in his.   And she had left
him.

CHAPTER IV

'THERE is one question I wish to ask,' said Vincent, looking at John Randle, 'about a matter which seems intimately connected with all this—Who is Nannie?'

The two young men and Mr. Bryant were in the library at the Heights, and on the sofa lay the white covered form of the dead man, Frederick Kane.

Mr. Bryant was in a condition of trembling nervousness, easily attributable to his share in the scene upon the cliff, but caused in reality by a conviction that the long-dreaded moment of exposure had come. He had locked Emma up in her room for the present, but so unstrung was the miserable woman that he knew she could no longer ward off suspicion, even if her unhappy history had not already passed into other people's knowledge. For himself he was agitated, shocked, terrified; had had no time to get up a plausible version of affairs; had no idea how much was known; could not even remember his own words and deeds, so as to be sure all or any had been consistent with a mere knowledge that Emma had once had a daughter who had died at a year old. Mr. Bryant was so

conscious that he hated Nannie—the memorial of
his meanest action—that he thought every one must
know this hatred. Would not everybody ask him,
'Why?' And he had no satisfactory answer ready;
while he was hesitating and blundering some one
would say out the truth.

Mr. Bryant, however, had no intention of confessing one word more than was necessary. Like a
whist player, he had entered upon a game moment-
ous to himself and others, with no knowledge of the
cards of his fellow-players. From their play he
would have to guess their position and to shape
his own; and every card he laid down would be
irrevocable and would be remembered against him.
From his youth up Mr. Bryant had been skilful
and fortunate at whist; the recollection gave him
courage at this supreme moment; though of a truth
his mere nerves were so shaken that, like a drowning man ready to catch at any straw, he was in a
mood to be rash from desperation. Mr. Bryant was
still surveying and sorting with dismay his hand of
miserable cards—never an honour among them—
when the game began. Sir Vincent led with the
question, 'Who is Nannie?' It was fortunately
not yet Mr. Bryant's turn to play.

John Randle, after a pause, replied that he had
heard nothing to prevent his believing that Nannie
was his sister.

'But you have heard something?' said Vincent.

'So it seems, sir; have you? If you choose to say it out, I can't help myself, but it appears to me a stirring of mud to no purpose. It don't bring Nannie no nearer to you that I know of,' he said, insolently.

'We are all too nearly concerned to attempt impossible mysteries,' said Vincent; 'besides, Alick will not spare us to-morrow.'

'Then, sir, you had maybe better ask Mrs. Bryant. It's little I know of the matter; and if my father washed his dirty linen at home, I don't feel inclined to send it to the laundry. I suppose he had a right to bring up Nan as his daughter if he chose? and if he hadn't mentioned the matter in the morning, it wasn't likely he'd volunteer it in the evening.'

Vincent looked inquiringly at Mr. Bryant; but that gentleman, who had marked every word of and every inference from the young farmer's speech, merely said, leaning his brow on his hand, 'Spare me, Sir Vincent. Surely you must conceive that this is the most painful hour of my life.'

'It appears to me, sir,' repeated John, 'if you want to get at the truth you'll have to question Mrs. Bryant herself, for she's the only one left who knows much about it. My father's dead and buried, and his knowledge with him. This corpse here might have told you part of the story, but it's little you'll get out of him now.'

Vincent still looked at Mr. Bryant, as if expecting him to speak. The clergyman felt himself suspected. He rose, and said with dignity—

'Insult the dead, if you choose, John Randle; but not one syllable shall be uttered in my presence against my wife.' Reseating himself, he resumed his attitude of dejection.

'I take it, sir,' said John, in a stage whisper, 'putting two and two together, what I've heard from the Governor (precious little) and so forth, that the parson was never informed of the true state of affairs between his wife and her former husband, as she called him.'

'I think,' said Vincent, addressing the clergyman, 'that we must ask you to speak. Mr. Randle and I have some claim to be put in possession of the facts. When my uncle alluded to the matter to me he was past speaking distinctly; but he certainly seemed to assert that Nannie was his daughter and that Mrs. Bryant was her mother. He appeared to have had some wish to claim her. I remember to have heard accidentally from Miss Bryant or from my mother, on your daughter's authority, that Mrs. Bryant had been a widow. Am I to understand that my uncle—'

Mr. Bryant pulled himself together. He had

been annoyed by Georgina's tattling about her step-mother. Perhaps after all she had played his game. 'My dearest wife,' he said, calmly, 'passed as the widow of an American gentleman named Grant who was drowned, as we all believed, in the wreck of the *Philadelphia* a year before our marriage. Investigation had revealed to me that Mr. Grant had deceived her, and that there had been no legal marriage. She was childless, and I never conceived it necessary to distress her or her brothers with the knowledge of my painful discovery. Her innocence from first to last was complete.' Mr. Bryant was pleased by this speech. It sounded almost well. It showed Emma in a harmless light; himself in a generous one; and it was very nearly the truth.

Vincent merely raised his eyebrows. John Randle, however, who had no patience with great delicacy of feeling or speech, burst into a laugh.

'It's a wonder she took the trouble of concealing her child then,' he exclaimed.

Mr. Bryant swept his brow with a pained expression. 'I have not yet,' he said, 'dared to question my beloved Emma as to the meaning of that rumour. A child? She had no child. I never heard of a child until this evening.'

'Mary Smith they called her,' said John; 'she was reared in our house and is buried in Faverton churchyard.'

'*That* child?' exclaimed Mr. Bryant; 'what a strange confusion! Oh, I can explain it now. The child you speak of was daughter of a woman named Matilda Smith, who died at her birth—a cousin of my wife's.'

'Anyhow, sir,' repeated John, turning to Vincent, 'no proof has come up that Nannie is her, and I cannot for the life of me see what we'll gain by seeking proofs at this time of day. If the brat's mother was ashamed to own her at first, I guess she'd be so still.' Vincent was not listening apparently.

'Grant, you say?' he said to Mr. Bryant; 'the man Grant then, it appears, was my uncle?'

'So, to my unspeakable horror, I have learned to-day,' said the clergyman.

'From Mrs. Bryant?'

'From Mr. Kane first. Then from my wife.'

'But she was an innocent woman,' sneered John.

'Entirely innocent. Injudicious in her silence, no doubt. My poor Emma! I saw she had some cause of distress lately.'

'Pardon my pressing you on such a painful matter,' said Vincent, still thinking of Nannie; 'you are convinced there was no marriage, Mr. Bryant?'

'I am most thankful, as it turns out, to be able to say I am.'

'Will you oblige me with the facts?' Mr.

Bryant stated them briefly. He was on firm ground here. (Confirmation of this part of the history being subsequently found among Mr. Kane's papers, Vincent was obliged to relinquish the sudden and cherished hope of leading to his mother a welcome niece bearing her father's name. Even Nannie would have come into favour in that position, as Vincent easily surmised. But the hope was illusive and short-lived.)

'You still think her an innocent woman,' sneered John again.

'You will not repeat that remark, if you please,' said Vincent.

Mr. Bryant volunteered the information that he had been intimately acquainted with Benjamin Randle and with Emma till within three or four years of his marriage with her; they were simple people, of whom it was easy to conceive their having been deceived; to imagine conspiracy on their part, especially on Emma's, was impossible; there was total and absurd misconception in this story of a daughter.

For Mr. Bryant intended to terrorise his wife into denying the child altogether. His ready wit had surely saved both their characters, now that the kind grave had removed Ben Randle. Evidently the young Randles knew nothing distinct; and Mr. Kane's investigations, which he had asserted to have been successful, but had never had time to report, remained unsuspected, except by Mr. Bryant himself.

But John still held a trump. He turned impatiently to Sir Vincent.

'Well, sir,' said the young farmer, 'I don't wish to offend you, but whatever Mrs. Bryant says now, she confessed it all to Nan a few days ago, and went down on her knees to the girl, to persuade her not to tell the parson, because he held the opinion, as we see ourselves, that she was an——'

'Who told you this?' interrupted Vincent.

'The lass herself.'

'Nannie! Perhaps I should inform you,' said Vincent drily to Mr. Bryant, 'that Alick has a different story.'

The clergyman was in a great predicament since John's last item of information. But now he only smiled sorrowfully and said, 'That unfortunate madman!'

CHAPTER V

To Mr. Bryant's annoyance John Randle contrived to linger behind with Sir Vincent. There was a sort of quarrelsome sympathy between these two. John said with awkward friendliness—

'You are pretty well done up, I take it, sir, by

this day's work. The best of us has to put limited liability to the prospectus of his strength.'

Vincent smiled, and admitted that he had been rather more active than he had intended, considering that yesterday he had still lounged on the sofa.

'I went to Faverton to look for Nannie,' he said. 'You have told Mrs. Randle that she is here? Your wife was anxious.'

'Sir,' said John, 'I hope you'll remember what I said just now, that nothing we have heard to-day makes me give up Nannie for my sister, and in all your dealings with her you'll have to reckon with her brother. Maybe that silent gentleman in the room with us didn't understand that his sweetheart had a brother too; maybe my father, who is silenced also and can't explain himself, didn't defend his sister like he ought. But we'll have no mistakes in our generation.'

'I think you and I understand each other pretty well,' replied Vincent, his eyes resting thoughtfully on the dumb companion to whom John had alluded. 'One thing I am sure of—that Nannie is a different person from Mrs. Bryant, and your sister's best safeguard is in her own character. It is a trite saying that a man is what a woman makes him. Mind,' he added, 'I am not hinting at any palliation of my uncle's conduct. He does not appear—so

far as I can see at present—to have done his part
with even ordinary fairness and generosity ; nor, to
say the truth, from my knowledge of him, am I altogether surprised. He found a pleasure in trampling
upon weakness. But, Mr. John Randle, that is a
game which gives no pleasure to me ; and I repeat,
Nannie is not Mrs. Bryant. You may trust us both
unreservedly. It may be a satisfaction to you,' he
added, smiling, ' to know that I got no opportunity
to-day of speaking to Nannie.'

'And to-morrow,' said John, ' I mean to send all
my three sisters to Faverton. You will oblige me,
sir, by letting the girl be till she has got over this
shock. It's enough to upset a young creature, and
prevent her knowing what she's about on any
matter.'

'Well, said Vincent, 'will you tell Nannie,
that as soon as she wishes to see me I am at
her service ? Stay, I will write it.' He took a
pen—

'My Darling—Your brother promises me that
you shall not be persecuted or distrusted. When
may I come and speak to you ? '

He handed it open to John to deliver. They
shook hands at parting, and John delivered this
love-letter punctually.

For to-night Nannie was with Alick's mother.

Mrs. Leach was the woman thoroughly to appreciate a tragedy. It pained her immensely, but then it afforded such magnificent opportunity for displaying her qualities that she could hardly wish the occasion away. Her performances could not be called affectation, for she went through them also when she was alone. But she dearly loved a spectator; and when she could get no other, she pressed one of her children into the service. Lizzie, impelled by a fascinated horror, was the most available. She could sob beautifully to order, and when her mother pulled her long lank hair pathetically down, she did not fly into a passion like Polly, or at once plait it up again like the unromantic Sarah. But when Nannie came in, Lizzie would clasp her hand convulsively and whisper between the acts of the drama, ' I am sure mother is crazy. I do believe mother is crazy. Oh, Nannie, I am so afraid we shall *all* go crazy.'

Nannie, and Sarah who obeyed her like a dog, got supper as usual, and gave the children treacle with their bread, and encouraged Mary Anne and Jimmy to squabble as to who got the most. Meanwhile Mrs. Leach sat by the window with a cup of tea at her side, in which she suffered neither milk nor sugar, her Bible open on her knees at the Lamentations of Jeremiah. She had removed her gown and robed herself in a black shawl; the sun-bonnet which she usually wore indoors and out, was thrown on the floor and her long gray hair was hanging down. It was an admirable tragic instrument. Now and then she twisted long wreaths of it distractedly, and wound it round her head, or her throat, or carried it across her brow like a sabre-cut; with masses of it she wiped her streaming eyes; now she would throw it all violently behind her and clap her hands to her temples; and then she would tear it out in handfuls and fling them on the floor at her feet, very much vexed when Sarah swept them up in a dust-pan and burned them in the fire.

'Nannie, Nannie,' sobbed Lizzie, 'she acts like the girl Alick cast the devil out of, who tore her hair and made faces. If mother begins to make faces I shall scream. I know I shall.'

'Take Jimmy's fingers out of the sugar-bowl,' replied Nannie, calmly.

She sent the children off as soon as she could, and wished she might get away alone to be silent under the great woes that had come upon her. Standing at the window looking out at the stars and trying to think, a shudder passed down her frame, and she saw the whole horrible scene over again. And she thought of the dumb anguish-stricken eyes with which Alick, now come to himself, had gazed helplessly and hopelessly at her, as she sat between him and Sir Vincent, who was her lover too, and afraid to look at her in the presence of that silent sufferer. But every minute Mrs. Leach called her niece, and Nannie had to put off her own woe to help and strengthen the distracted mother.

'That it should come to this!' wailed Ann Leach, bowing herself on the girl's kneeling form; 'my blessed boy! who was filled with the Spirit and taught the way of salvation to his poor, unholy, untruthful mother; to be reviled, and spit upon, and punished for a thing as it stops my heart-throbs to think of.'

'Oh, aunt, no—no—you must not say it. It was *not* our Alick's real self who did it. And the man provoked him, aunt! saying things against *me*— Alick's sweetheart—and them belonging to me!'

'Oh, my dear, my dear! whatever have you been doing to let folks get speaking against you? Oh, Nannie, Nannie! I have been a sinful woman, and I have suffered pangs, and I've buried two husbands, and I thought I had wept more than any woman above ground. But what is loss of husbands and sorrow for sins beside this? My blessed boy, who had spoke God's truth of thousands, and now he's ruined himself for ever!'

She tore off her two wedding rings and other movable articles and flung them disconsolately on the floor, and then she sobbed and sobbed till even Nannie grew frightened.

'Let me read to you, aunt. Dear Alick's favourite chapters in the Revelation——'

'No, Nannie, the Lamentations. There's words in the Bible meant for every one, and Lamentations is meant for me. I am not angry, my dear, if you cannot feel it like me. He was only your sweetheart. He was not the son of your womb; he never sucked at your bosom, and learned his prayers first at his mother's knee. He never was the hope of your life, and twice the stay of your widowhood. Read from the Lamentations, Nannie; there's nothing else could be fit for a woman like me.' But just then Mr. Bryant came in, presumably on a visit of consolation.

CHAPTER VI

ALAS! poor man! no one could look more wretched and downcast than he, whose worst sufferings were perforce unconfessed. Nannie's gentle soul pitied him, and she would have lingered out of pure sympathy, had he not dismissed her with some unnecessary harshness. Always this hateful girl in his way! He was in no condition to endure her intrusion to-night. 'It is you who have been at the bottom of all this,' he said ; and was glad to see that the words stabbed her to the heart. But the girl went, and he turned wearily to Mrs. Leach.

'No farcing, Ann, I must beg; any one can understand that Alick's crime is very painful to you. I feel it and all its accompaniments too keenly to require any stirring up of the feelings.'

'Oh, dear me, sir! It ain't crime. It's his poor head.'

'That is what will be put forward as an excuse. Sir Vincent Leicester fortunately concluded long ago, from your son's religious extravagance, that he was insane. I, and other persons acquainted with fanaticism, did not share his opinion. Alick is no more mad than I am, or than I should be, had I accustomed myself to obey every impulse of my fallen nature, under that most blasphemous delusion that I was inspired. Do you follow me, Ann ?'

'Oh dear, sir, let me call Nannie to argufy you! What do you mean by fallen nature ? Alick never had *that* anyhow—'

'Come now; his inspirations were always synonymous with his inclinations, weren't they ? For instance, he was a clever speaker, with a love of notoriety.'

'No more hadn't he that! He was a signboard of modesty !'

'A love of importance then; so he believed himself inspired to preach.   Again, take this matter of
his marriage.   He was in love with an unsuitable
young woman; light in her conduct and certain to
bring misfortune—as she has—upon one so correct
and severe as Alick.'

'Lord bless us, sir, what are you saying of
Nannie?'

'I have no doubt—in fact, I know—that your
son remonstrated with the girl; if he had not been
possessed by that monstrous delusion he would have
recognised her worthlessness.'

'It ain't true!' began Mrs. Leach, but he checked
her.

'Allow me to speak, Ann.   Alick is not the
first man who has been led astray by a thoughtless
woman; he considered himself inspired to reform
and marry this girl, and he has pursued her till she
has achieved his ruin.'

'It ain't true!' said poor Ann again; but he
continued remorselessly—

'Again, circumstances of various kinds, many
of which I regret extremely, have contributed to
render Alick unfriendly to myself.   Still possessed
by this notion of inspiration, he did not struggle
against the sinful feeling.   Unfriendliness ripened
into hatred.   That hatred spread, and cankered his
whole nature.   He took upon himself to judge me

as a minister of religion—wished to remove me. That was not so easily accomplished. Then the idea of murder presented itself. My dear Ann, you start at the word. Remember the deed was attempted; only prevented by accident; and a second murder, not, I believe, deliberate, has been actually committed.'

'Oh, my poor, poor boy! Oh, his poor, poor head!' groaned Mrs. Leach.

'I can conceive,' pursued Mr. Bryant, 'how the idea appalled him when it came to him first; I daresay he tried to put it away. But it recurred again and again, until—alas! for human nature—it began to seem attractive; he found himself considering plans for its accomplishment; and there were times when he fancied he had a commission from Heaven to do this wicked thing.'

'Law, Mr. Bryant—to kill you?' said the woman.

'Exactly; and proofs that the crime was premeditated will, unfortunately, not be wanting, Ann. Singular purchases that he made at Uggle Grinby; singular gestures; singular lyings-in-wait about my house when he had given the impression that he was far away. One evening he forced his way threateningly into my study; I thought him intoxicated and turned him out; but he had a knife in his hand. He was a clumsy and cowardly criminal, poor wretch, about this his first crime.

But in a legal sense, Ann, I cannot admit that your son was insane. Now, if I tell all I know of Alick, and give the melancholy history of the religious presumption which has led to his fall, those who know anything of human nature—and remember he will be tried by sensible men, by strangers, uninfluenced by his popularity here, or by Sir Vincent's ignorant prejudices—will not hesitate to pronounce him accountable for his actions, and to bring him in guilty.'

Mrs. Leach for once was affected beyond the consoling power of any posturing. She looked helplessly at her visitor, her face ashen and her eyes staring and expressionless. Then she burst into a groan. 'Oh, sir!' she cried, 'I'll go to dear Sir Vincent and all of 'em, and say what I have known since his babyhood, sir, of his poor head.'

'Ann,' said Mr. Bryant, sitting down and taking her hand with a kindness that was not altogether insincere, 'do you remember, a week or two ago, how Sir Vincent brought a doctor—a specialist—here to examine Alick's condition, and he asked you many questions about your son's health, and about his head, as you call it? Do you recall your replies?'

'Mr. Bryant, sir, I am a sinful woman. Alick told me many a time that I was an untruthful sinner, and I'd be punished. The Lord knows

I've repented of my sin, and I'd take the pledge against lying if any one would minister it to me. Mr. Bryant, when I answered yon specialing doctor, God knows I was lying half the time. It seemed to me a wicked and a shocking thing for 'em to want to make out my blessed boy a madman, and to come to his mother to baptize' (she meant confirm) 'such an ugly notion. I couldn't bring my tongue round the right answers; and no more couldn't Nannie, who never spoke a lie in her life. But now, Mr. Bryant, I'll up before all the world, and I'll tell the whole truth about his poor head, and the trouble it's been to me all along!'

'And who will believe you, Ann?' questioned the clergyman.

'I'll say,' said Mrs. Leach, rising in a magnificent pose and stretching out her hands to heaven, "Oh, men and women, who have blessed children of your own, and know you would damn yourselves to save them, I lied to preserve my son from the madhouse; but I speak the truth now to save him from the gallows-tree."'

'My poor woman,' said Mr. Bryant, 'they will say that, with your small instinct for truth, you were more to be trusted when there was no such tremendous issue at stake.' Mrs. Leach fell on her knees and prayed aloud.

'My God, my God, I will never lie again!

Only save my boy—my blessed, innocent, suffering boy, who is Thy servant through it all.'

'Ann, for Heaven's sake, rise !' said the clergyman; 'this is blasphemous. God's name must not be dragged into this miserable tissue of crime and fraud,' cried Mr. Bryant, covering his face with his hand.

Mrs. Leach dragged herself to his feet and knelt before him. 'Mr. Bryant, ask Emma how a mother's heart feels. You won't come forward against my boy ? '

'I must state facts.'

'Facts can be stated so as to mean and make folks think what you choose. That ain't lying anyhow ! You can tell the facts you talk of, and make folks think they mean the poor dear was wild when he acted so. Man !' cried Ann Leach, 'I have kept a secret for you, and it's only common justice, if you know anything as would harm my boy when he might be saved—it's only common justice as you should keep it secret for me.'

It was the point at which Mr. Bryant had been aiming. Yet now that it had come, it shocked him. He was playing with a man's life, for the purpose of saving his own character. Hardly even that, for Ann Leach's unsupported word would not be sufficient to blast his character.

Mr. Bryant hesitated. He was playing a part

intolerably mean and base; and hardly even necessary. Should he give it all up, even now at the
eleventh hour, and let the whole truth come out?
Mr. Bryant hesitated; enamoured of repentance, and
far more moved than he had intended to be, by
Ann Leach's grief.

He walked to the window and looked out
on the night, dull and black like his own erring
soul; the one short flash of moonlight quickly
swallowed again in the murk and gloom of cloud.
If he came away without bribing Ann Leach
to silence he knew he would repent his weakness
on the morrow. After all he was frightening rather
than hurting her; for in his heart he expected
Alick's acquittal, and had little intention of insisting
on the points against him.

'Have you kept our secret, Ann?' he asked
suddenly; 'it has gone about.'

'I never told no one nothing,' cried the woman
with indignant emphasis, 'till I saw the bitter grief
of that poor, childless woman, your wife, Mr. Bryant;
and I did give *her* a hinkling about Nannie.'

'You did very wrong in saying one word to
Emma. She has blundered grievously. A suspicious person would form most evil conjectures
from her conduct. She has compromised herself
altogether, and in a way that is compromising to
me also,' said Mr. Bryant with emphasis.

'Well, I never heard you go on at your wife before!' cried Mrs. Leach.

'She has led me into a most horrifying trap. I have learned to-day only, that that miserable man——'

'I knew that long ago!' exclaimed Ann, delighted; 'and you didn't, Mr. Bryant?'

'I? What do you take me for—you and Emma —that you allowed me to come into his vicinity for a moment?'

'Maybe Emma didn't know he was here,' interrupted Ann, frightened for her sister-in-law by his indignant gravity of utterance.

'Know? She refused to meet him; invented a headache—what not; I believe she deceived me. You too, Ann—you have been treacherous from first to last.'

Mrs. Leach never flew into passions; when others became heated, she was cool and wily. At the present moment she smoothed her apron, neatly twisted up her hair; recovered her wedding rings from the floor and put them on. 'Maybe,' she said remorsefully, 'I *was* a bit stupid to tell him all about Nannie.'

'You told him about Nannie!' exclaimed Mr. Bryant. There was a silence.

'Come now, Ann, you have been false; and you and Emma herself owe me some reparation. I believe I can be of assistance to your son, but if so you shall pay me for it.'

'Well, may be,' said Ann, not discomfortably. Even then it took him some time to get the words out; they sickened him.

'Emma has shown one spark of generosity. She has not dragged me into this scandal. Very well. You, Ann Leach, shall not contradict her.'

'Lord have mercy on us!' ejaculated Mrs. Leach.

'Woman,' said Mr. Bryant, in great agitation, 'your nature can have no conception of what the naked truth would entail for me; the suspicions, the inferences— Besides the mere truth is damnatory. You led me into a piece of cheating which I have never ceased to curse. You changed those children and—you fool—you made me aware of it.'

'I never see such a man! Whatever was the harm, Mr. Bryant?'

'No harm, in a sense, if you had carried it through properly—if you hadn't taken to drink and put people on the scent. I speak folly. There was this much harm, Ann Leach; if that transaction were known, my character would be gone for ever. Harm? Of course there was harm. It was a vulgar fraud; unworthy of a man, heinous in a clergyman, impossible to a gentleman.'

'I never *see* such a man!' repeated Mrs. Leach, in dismay.

'Now listen to me. You shall pledge yourself, here and now, no matter who asks you, when or where—you shall pledge yourself to say what Emma says, and what I intend to say; and what there is no one left to contradict: That I married and lived with Emma in ignorance of her previous history; that I never knew of her daughter till to-day. If the children were changed, she did it herself; or you; or Sarah; or Ben. *I* knew nothing of it. I married a childless widow. And I will do all I can for Alick.'

Half-an-hour later, Mr. Bryant left the house. He was ghastly to look at, and he trembled from head to foot. But he was victorious. He had the woman's oath. Surely this time—for her son's sake —she would be true!'

'My God, my God!' he groaned, 'into what utter degradation I have brought myself! But it is nearly over. How thankful I am that Georgie's match is off. We must flee from the place, and Heaven grant I may never see one of these people again. God knows I will act no more in this sort. And I will make it up to my poor Emma.'

CHAPTER VII

BUT his work was not yet ended. There was a lower depth yet into which he must descend. He had still to silence his wife.

Inconceivable though it seem, Mr. Bryant loved his wife. Her very helplessness appealed to him. He never could keep up his wrath against her without an effort. And now that he came in, bruised after the campaign with that dreadful Ann Leach, and found poor Emma crushed and heart-broken, he would have given all his wealth to be able to take her in his arms and show her that their troubles were for ever at an end.

On the contrary, he had to mete her a cruelty that a week ago he would have deemed impossible.

He seated himself gloomily by the table, looking at her, his head on his hand. She cared for and understood little except that he was displeased.

'Ned—Ned,' she said, tremblingly, 'I did try to tell you, and you stopped me. You were angry. You wouldn't listen.' Mr. Bryant was silent. 'He said he was going away—never to come back.'

'Emma, it was horrible.'

'You were so taken up about Georgina and Sir Vincent——'

'Say no more. Each word makes it worse. You have brought about a crash.'

'Let us go from here.'

'We must.'

'It was—for Nannie,' she began, timidly.

'Exactly ; you have sacrificed me to her.'

'Ned! how sacrificed *you*. It is only me. No one will think worse of *you*.'

'Nonsense.' He walked up and down the room impatiently. He was exasperated by his fate ; by the turn events had taken, which made some sort of escape possible for himself by the sacrifice of this dear, gentle woman.

'Ned, how could any one think ill of *you* for it ? you, who were so kind, so generous to me— so——'

'Good heavens, don't speak of kindness and generosity,' he burst forth. 'We won't have any more high faluting and tall talk. We will give up trying to be better than our neighbours. We will strive after nothing higher than practical sense and worldly success.'

'Do you mean——'

'Why look you how it ends !' cried the clergyman ; 'look at your nephew : this Alick Randle, who is spending the night in prison. I swear to you he

was an honest man—more honest than ever I was;
a religious, God-seeking man, more than ever I was,
though, to be sure, I knew the way of God more
perfectly. But extremes meet. He sought to be
too good, and he has ended in imposture and in
murder. I tell you Heaven itself does not smile on
too much goodness. The wise man found it out,
and is not he with his sarcasms reckoned one of
the inspired writers? " Be not righteous over
much; neither make thyself over wise: why
shouldest thou destroy thyself? " It is what we
have done, Alick Randle and I. We have strained
to heights impossible; and failing, ruin stares us in
the face.'

'Dear Ned, I do not understand.'

'No; you never understand. You have lived
with me all these years, Emma, and you do not
know me in the least. You have not gauged my
limitations, my shortcomings. Fool, why did I not
recognise them myself? Why did I make myself
a priest, a successful and applauded one? righteous
overmuch—when all the while this moral crash,
which has come to-day, was possible to me? I tell
you, Emma, it is as much ruin to me as Alick's
frenzy and police-cell is to him. I cannot meet it
I am bankrupt. It will bring degradation to me.
The limitations of my nature are such that if I am
robbed of responsibility, cast from my position, dis-

honoured, pronounced a cheat and a liar—I shall be powerless to begin life again ; to go aside humbly, and repent and accept my chastisement meekly. I could not live in that position. I should defy Heaven, and from righteous overmuch, I should grow apace to evil abominably. Don't trouble, Emma, to say you do not understand me. I know it. I talk to you in the bitterness of my soul, because there is no one else I can talk to.'

'And it is all my fault?' said Emma, mournfully.

'I don't know. Yours or mine, what matter does it make ? Yours or mine, or neither's ? Enough that it has come, and that the days of my righteousness are ended.' So he raved ; and then he let her talk in her gentle, foolish way.

'Oh no, Ned, no. Is there nothing we can do to turn this aside from you ? *You* have done *no* wrong. You have sacrified a great deal for me. It was my fault. The beginning and end of it was my deserting the child. God has punished us for that. But it is over now. The world knows about it. I have her. I will do my duty to her now.'

'Emma, Emma, will you never have done ? Always back to this ? Do not madden me about the child to-day. She is well provided for. She has not suffered. But disgrace is confronting *you*,

Emma, and myself; and my daughter, who is absolutely unconnected with these events. She will be disgraced and shipwrecked too in the scandal— my poor, innocent, ignorant Georgie!'

'Oh dear, Ned! why ever did you marry me? I would not have injured Georgie for all the world. I always tried to be a mother to her. How ever will she suffer?'

'If *I* lose my reputation.'

'And all along of me? But what can we do, Ned? You can't cut me off from being your wife.'

'I am not sunk so low as that, Emma,' he said, with a bitter smile. 'No, no, we are gray-headed, almost old. I suppose we don't seem much like lovers. But we love each other, do we not?'—he took her hand and drew her to him—'with a love, Emma, that would survive even great blasts of misfortune?'

'Oh, Ned, yes—yes. Your true, lasting love has been the best thing in my life. I wish I had been more worthy of it, Ned. Will you forgive me, now?'

'Forgive *you?* My God!' He rose, putting her from him.

Presently he spoke again in a different tone. 'You do not, Emma, sufficiently consider the remarks which will be made on that acquaintance you

had allowed me to drift into. My love, it is inconceivable that the truth will be accepted. Your folly
there was monstrous; it would not be believed possible; at least not on the supposition that we were
open with each other on that whole frightful chapter.
It freezes my blood to imagine what may be
suspected. The man hanging about here, day after
day, for no ostensible reason! Vincent disliked
him; Lady Katharine and he had not one taste in
common! Will it not be asked, if he was not re-
newing acquaintance with you? Good heavens! if
you had perhaps kept up a clandestine acquaintance
with him all along?'

Mrs. Bryant turned very pale. 'Ned, I'd die
rather than have you or any one suspect that.' He
drew his arm round her again.

'*I*, Emma, suspect you? Never. But, my love,
if it were supposed that we were *not* frank with
each other on that affair; that you or I—one of us
—had believed you his wife—would not your
hòrrible perplexity—your hesitation—your silence
—be partially understood? I don't wish to dwell
on that, Emma,' he said, hurriedly, shocked at himself; 'it only just occurred to me. Let us dismiss
the subject.'

'I am sure, Edward—unless it was to hurt
Nannie—I would do, I would endure *anything* for
you; and Georgie,' added poor, unreasoning Emma,

with an effort. He was silent, and Emma waited patiently. She did not understand his suffering, but it moved her. His anger was what she dreaded; what she felt unable to brave, except very occasionally for her child's sake.

'Emma, we must leave this place immediately, and go to another where we are not known. If possible, you shall take your niece, Nannie, with you——'

'Nannie!'

'——and the whole object of my life shall be to make up for what I have made you suffer, to deserve the good opinion men hold of me. We will go abroad, I think; and if I can save my reputation we shall be happy still. Alas! Emma, I cannot prevent your sad history from being known *here*. Thank Heaven, it is an innocent one! But there *is* a way in which *you* can save *me;* which means, in a sense, saving us all.'

'Only tell me, Ned.'

'You shall have your Nannie, if I can get her for you,' he repeated.

'Oh yes, Ned. Only tell me.'

'So long as we are here, you would have seriously to lie a little.' She paled.

'Is that what you meant about righteous overmuch?'

'I have to be disgracefully frank with you,

Emma. But you seem to have lied already accidentally.'

'Dear Ned—how ?'

'You told the girl that *I* did not know of your
child ; that *I* had believed you that brute's lawful
wife.'

'Oh no, Ned. I never said so.'

'I have it on Nannie's authority.' Mrs. Bryant
pondered.

'I told her not to speak of it to you,' she cried
with agitation, 'for I knew you'd be mad with me
for telling her. It was to help her against Sir.
Vincent.'

'She understood you in the way I said. It is
what they all think. Leicester, young Randle,
Nannie, Alick.'

'Think I took you in about it ?' she cried, indignantly. He nodded.

'Well, Ben knew better than that !'

'Ben is dead !'

'Ann then !'

'Ann is a notorious liar.'

'But is every one going to turn against me like
that ? You, Ned, didn't you tell them ?'

'*We might say the same,*' said Mr. Bryant in a
low voice.

Presently he told her all. 'Emma, I must confess what I have done. I was asked suddenly. I

was ignorant that you had disobeyed me, that you had spoken of these matters to any one. I thought I could spare you much remark; much suffering. I said it was nonsense about a child; that your infant was still-born. I had always told you Mary Smith could not be acknowledged. And then, to my dismay, I learned that you had confessed to Nannie. Emma, you disobeyed me, and secretly. You were wrong there.'

'Well, Ned? Ned, we cannot help it now.'

'No; but if I am not to admit to Sir Vincent and to young Randle that I lied—my love, you do not know all it would entail!—you must fall in for a week or two with what *I* said; with what they have all understood from your own words: that I veritably *was* ignorant of that wretched child's existence; that I was unaware, or that you believed me unaware, which comes to the same thing, of the illegality of your marriage with Mr. Grant.'

'I couldn't bear any one to think I had used you so, Edward,' she whimpered.

'Pshaw! No one will care a pin how we used each other. *I* know the truth—isn't that enough? And if there is a bit of a cackle, you sha'n't hear it.' He was adroit at making the worse appear the better reason, at least in addressing a helpless, affectionate woman, who had little foresight for consequences, and was used to trusting him implicitly.

'I cannot explain the whole thing to you, my poor
Emma, nor the misfortune for us all which I wish
to avert. It can be done in this way and in no
other. I should not propose it, if you had not
yourself accidentally done the thing already. My
love, in a month we shall be far away, and honest
and happy again. Is it so much to ask of you?'
Then changing his tone—

'Or—or would you torture me into betraying
you? Good heavens—on the spur of the moment,
with the idea of protecting you, Emma, I have
pledged myself to that statement! and if you do
not fall in with it— Good God, I am a moral
bankrupt; I have no power of truth left in me!
I might say you lie! and, Emma, it is I who would
be believed—not you. I beseech you, Emma, do
not put me into that temptation. Have I not
humbled myself enough to you? I tell you solemnly,
I have no power of truth left in me. I am bankrupt.'

'I will say whatever you wish, Ned,' said Emma,
at last, aware that she only dimly understood his
motives; aware too that he was her all in life;
'only,' she pleaded, 'let us come away from here, so
we need never have to be false again.'

'Oh, Emma, forgive me!' groaned the miserable
man, on his knees before her.

'You have to forgive me too, dear Ned! I have
been such an unlucky wife to you. I never was

fit for the grand folk,' said Emma, already falling back into trivialities. 'We sha'n't go no more among grand folk, Ned, shall we? I can't help wishing Georgie was married, and then you and me could go back to our old ways; and Nannie would be a daughter to us.'

Poor Emma! to the last nourishing Hope on Illusion.

CHAPTER VIII

ALICK was committed for trial at the approaching Assizes, much to the distress of all the people with whom we are concerned; Mr. Kane's family, with the exception of Lady Katharine who mourned for her brother, being less dismayed by the man's tragical end than by the publicity and scandal to which it had given occasion. The circumstances, with all their romantic accompaniments, got into the newspapers, and the case attracted a good deal of attention. Mrs. Bryant's history, greatly exaggerated and blackened, became public property. It was horrible to her husband, and far worse than he had expected, but he had gone quite too far to draw back now. He opened all his wife's letters and forbade her to look at a newspaper, so she was never aware of half the terrible things said of her. Housed in a dream, she suffered comparatively little.

The only conversation she had with any one on the subject was with Sir Vincent, who came to her one day and asked her bluntly, but not unkindly, if all these things were true.

'Nannie's mother?' he questioned.

How often she had said the words tenderly to herself and had longed to acknowledge the fact. Truly she had been a deceived and innocent woman, and she had come by the child innocently enough! She had never felt very guilty about it. When Vincent, without sign of agitation, or loathing, or contempt, such as she had been bidden to expect, asked her that simple question, she looked up quite frankly and answered, 'Yes.' He was silent for some time, studying her. Was it possible she could be the guilty woman she was represented?

'They tell me,' said Vincent, 'that there is no proof that she is not Nannie Randle in fact as well as in name. Is that so?'

'Mr. Bryant says so. But I know it. She is like——'

'She is like my mother,' said Vincent, with a smile. He was so friendly that poor Emma talked on of it.

'It must have been some dreadful mistake of my brother's wife. I cannot think any one meant to deceive me.'

'That is less difficult to imagine,' said Vincent,

'than some things that have been asserted.' He had stared at her in astonishment; she was certainly incurably stupid, but could mere stupidity account for her extraordinary innocence of manner?

'What things?' asked Mrs. Bryant, rather alarmed, for she knew she had a part to play, and was always afraid of forgetting to do it.

Then Vincent said the blunt thing, for which his manner atoned: that she had deceived her husband.

The poor thing grew pale and would have fled; but with an effort restrained herself and repeated her lesson.

'It had not seemed to me exactly probable,' said the young man, drily. Mrs. Bryant was alarmed, for his manner betrayed incredulity.

'Oh dear, Sir Vincent,' she said, with agitation, 'do ask Mr. Bryant how it all came about, and he'll explain everything to you. It is dreadful to have to say such things, but it would be worse to have any one think ill of Mr. Bryant, who has been so kind and so generous to me, and is such a really good man himself,' she ended, indistinctly. What she meant was not very clear, but Vincent was touched.

'I will accept whatever you say, Mrs. Bryant,' he replied, 'only if there was anything you would let me do for you——'

But Emma gave him no further explanation or even hint.

Mr. Bryant, in fact, established his case, or by judicious hints and silences, got it established for him without the smallest difficulty. No one had any claim to pry into the details, to test the links in the chain; to demand, as it were, chapter and verse for his quotation. Old Lord Henslow, indeed, who was very angry with Vincent about everything, complaining that all the misfortune and all the scandal were his fault, had repeatedly asked what he had meant by putting such a man as Bryant into the living. He undertook to visit the clergyman and find out every fact of his history. 'No one can deceive me, you know,' he said; 'I am not a boy to swallow everything I am told.'

But he came home with his tune completely changed. Mr. Bryant had taken him very coolly, making him feel inquisitive and impertinent. Still the clergyman had not absolutely refused to speak, and all his utterances were entirely credible and consistent and plausible. And he was so evidently a man of refined feeling; honourable to an excess, and guileless; so much attached to his inferior wife, and really, it seemed, unable to believe in the fact of her monstrous conduct. Under cross-examination, Mr. Bryant's story would probably have broken down; but it completely deceived the self-confident old gentleman. He was quite taken with Mr. Bryant, and having a distant view of the clergyman's wife, saw in a moment the miserable sort of person she was.

'I tell you what, Katharine,' he said to his daughter, 'Vincent wasn't such a fool as I thought about that parson. He's a fine fellow, and a chivalrous fellow, and a clever fellow; and I'm monstrously sorry for him. Not a gentleman by birth, of course —he confesses that at once; but I have a prodigious respect for any man who has made his way upward. If some one would poison off that odious wife of his, I declare I'd present him to a living myself; something better than this savage place. And what a fine girl his daughter is!'

'Poor dear Georgina!' sighed Lady Katharine.

It was a great thing for Mr. Bryant to have got Lord Henslow to credit his statements. Everybody saw at once that no other view of the case was even possible. In fact, no one but Vincent dreamed of doubting the clergyman. Why should they? Mrs. Bryant, it seemed, told the very same story. Nannie had told the same story. Ann Leach told the same story—with variations, of course; no one expected her to give precisely the same account of anything twice. Alick alone, who had overheard the talk between Mr. Kane and Mr. Bryant about Mary Smith, declared that the clergyman was lying; but Alick had sunk now into a condition of gloomy taciturnity, and would not, or could not, explain himself.

Alick was proved to be either mad or desperately wicked, and no one would have thought of minding him, even if he had cared to tell all he had heard. And he did not care. The conversation had not been important in his eyes; it was not sufficient to excuse what he had done himself, and it faded now, if not from his memory, at least from his thoughts. *He had killed a man.* Alick could think of nothing else at this time. He was as Cain; *he had killed a man.* What else could possibly matter?

At this time Mr. Bryant went about in the parish with his usual industry, his usual kindliness, and more than his usual almsgiving. He preached weekly in the schoolhouse, and in a simple, hearty style, which the people liked. One address was about poor Alick's fall; and he spoke of the wretched deposed prophet without disrespect but with pious horror, showing up ruthlessly his errors and charlatanism. The greater number of his hearers had been all along in passive opposition to Alick, and were much impressed; a few from among the fallen prophet's converts were in a state of abject bewilderment, and hoped they were now doing well in allying themselves to the authorised minister, while they offered timid prayers for the man whom they had trusted to have been he who should have redeemed Israel. Mr. Bryant dealt tenderly with these wounded souls, and made them feel his sympathy.

He did not at present attempt much with the uproarious restoration crew, who were still drinking themselves drunk in the beer-house, and had abjured all religion,—a vain thing which led to murder. These were a difficult problem, and Mr. Bryant's chief desire at present was to irritate no one. He imported the young curate from a neighbouring parish to preach for him on Sundays in the church nave, the chancel being screened off and under repair. In too great distress of mind was the vicar to do anything very public himself. Poor Mr. Bryant! It was easy to understand his sorrowful air, his retirement, his pale and suffering face. Every one knew his attachment to his wife; what a love match it had been; how unswerving had been his loyalty to the uninteresting woman, whose inferiority he must have perceived. It was shocking to think of the blow these revelations must have been for him. From very intimate friends he received letters of delicate condolence. The delicacy of his own expressions in reply was beyond all praise. It was touching the way he identified himself with the poor woman's disgrace,—never allowed himself to be betrayed into hints of censure. He stuck to it valiantly that in the matter of her main offence she had been merely innocent and deceived. He could get no one to believe him, but he stuck to it—publicly at least. To a clerical brother (of some importance) whom he was able to see, he expressed himself apparently with less reserve.

'Surely,' he said, passionately, 'the general character must be taken into consideration in estimating a fault! I will never again preach the common doctrine, of a little leaven leavening the whole lump. It is not so; repentance may be genuine, sanctification may be progressing, while yet there remains some one sin unconfessed, unforgiven, unabandoned. Oh, my God!' said the wretched man, 'tell me that it may be so; tell me that His long-suffering forbears even with such.'

The brother clergyman was much affected. 'Unconfessed to *man*—unforgiven by man,' he said, correctingly.

'Yes,' responded Mr. Bryant with eagerness, 'who can ever know what has passed between the soul and its God? what agony of confession—what redoubled energy against sin in other directions. But to abandon the one sin—the fatal sin—may be impossible. Human nature is weak—which of us knows how weak? God knows, and God's compassion and long-suffering are boundless. It is so. It must be so. I shall never again dare to be positive about the wrath of God.'

'My friend,' said the other, 'I feel sure it is not with wrath that the King of Mercy hears you at this moment. But,' he added, being a man of great

sincerity, 'it is inconceivable that such secret con-
trition as you suggest, would not, if accepted by
God, be followed by open abandonment of the
transgression.'

'Oh, my dear friend,' said Mr. Bryant, 'if it
involved ruin for oneself and for one's best beloved?'

Had that church dignitary had one suspicion of
Mr. Bryant he might have given him the moral
assistance he so sorely needed. But he was hitting
in the dark, and he could not drive the nail home.
He took up a quite erroneous impression, and, I
fear, spread it. Poor Bryant's concern about his
unhappy wife was greater than the occasion justified.
What they had heard of her was bad enough; he
was convinced there was more which had not
come out. Wretched woman! It surely would
have to come to a separation. Even if her repentance was assured, how could she continue in the
position of a vicar's wife? Who, knowing her
history, would wish her acquaintance? How could
Bryant foist her upon ignorant people? He was
not the man to act in that hypocritical way. Nor
could it be in any sense justifiable. And to tell the
truth (remarks always ended in this way), she was
a very vulgar woman.

CHAPTER IX

ALAS! the vulgar have few friends. Emma Bryant
had never attained to her husband's easy deportment
in society, and it was her punishment that now
every one turned against her with a feeling of
relief.

'I always said,' confessed Lady Katharine, 'that
I disliked her. There is some satisfaction in knowing there was good reason.'

'Mother! mother!' expostulated Vincent. 'I
wish you'd go and see her,' he said, impulsively, 'and
talk it over with her.'

'My dear boy!' was Lady Katharine's very
decided refusal.

'Why do you take such an extravagant interest
in her?' asked old Lord Henslow; 'the ruggedness
of the place seems to have developed an extraordinary mildness on you.'

'Why should we gibbet the woman?'

'I certainly consider she should be punished,'
said Lady Katharine, stiffly.

'"Few have a right to punish, all to pardon,"'
quoted Vincent.

'I am always glad to pardon,' said his mother,
'but if to decline further acquaintance with Mrs.

Bryant be to punish, I think I have that much right.'

'Is she never to speak to a respectable woman again?' asked Vincent.

Lord Henslow put on his spectacles. 'She appears to be a great friend of yours, sir. Pray, what have you done to express your sympathy?'

'I went to see her. She seemed to me much as usual. What good could *I* do? Do you suppose she would talk to me? If my mother went to her with some sisterly compassion, she might get something out of her.'

'Sisterly!' echoed the lady.

'What do you want to get out of her?' asked the grandfather.

'Oh, I don't know. I have a strong feeling we haven't got to the bottom of it all yet.'

'So have I. This tri-weekly *Uggle Grinby Record* kindly stirs the mud for us. Has this paragraph anything to do with your interest in Mrs. Bryant and her belongings?' said the old man, stuffing the newspaper with its column of county gossip before his grandson's eyes.

Vincent's hair stood on end as he read the thinly-veiled assertions.

'Dear! dear! What have they put in this time?' said Lady Katharine, seeing her son's flush, and divining that it was something about Nannie.

'That is a lie,' said Vincent, returning the newspaper, 'and I will have it retracted.'

'My dear boy,' replied Lord Henslow, 'we have become public property. There will be no end to it if we begin denying the slanders our kind friends are putting into circulation. They are the penalty of greatness. Don't, for decency's sake, get into a controversy with a halfpenny newspaper. It is not such a very abominable suggestion, is it? And it will be forgotten in a month.'

Vincent made no reply.

'Did you ever see this girl, Katharine?' asked Lord Henslow as the grandson left them. The sharp young ears caught the question, however, and Vincent put his head back into the room and called Lady Katharine to him.

'Mother, you will kindly remember that what I told you of myself and Nannie, I told you in confidence. I do earnestly beg of you not to repeat it without adequate reason.'

'But, Vincent, if, as you say——'

'Mother, remember that Nannie has not accepted my proposals, nor authorised the coupling of our names in the only way that is warrantable or creditable. Until she does so, talk of a relation between us may give rise to atrocious suspicions. I am determined that Nannie shall be subjected to no annoyance that I can prevent.'

'I wish I could think you had given it up, dear,' sighed the widow.

'I shall never give it up. But I don't wish to *force* her consent, if I can help it. Don't assist this infernal gossip and slander to put us into that position.'

'Oh, Vincent! you forget to be civil even. This girl has come between you and all your respect for your family.'

'Mother,' said Vincent, 'I love you, and you know it; and I have a respect and an affection for all my relations; but I seriously tell you, I should rather never see one of you again, than lose my wife. That will give you some notion of her importance to me; and if I lose her after all, it will not be without suffering that my mother at least ought to respect.'

For a little note had passed from Vincent to Nannie; and a little one from her to him, in which she had said, 'No—no—I have given it all up, entirely and for ever. Don't ask me again. I will explain as soon as we can dare one little last talk. But I have no strength for it till this dreadful waiting time is over. Please forgive me, and bear with me till then.'

And so, though Nannie was still in Everwell with Mrs. Leach, she and her lover had not met. Nannie was shy of criticism; for as she wasn't a

lady, none of her friends and neighbours hesitated
to ask her questions or to intrude their comments.
And she heard of the slander in the Uggle Grinby
newspaper, but happily not till in its next issue she
was able to read Sir Vincent's angry rejoinder.
After this she hardly went out at all. To be
catechised on that matter would be unendurable.

It was wonderful, considering that by Mr.
Bryant's precautions the vicarage ladies were kept
in ignorance of the scandal that had arisen, how
successfully Georgina (on the dear Baroness's authority) defended her father's cause. Mr. Bryant
shivered when he heard of the thin ice she had
skated over in talking to Lord Henslow for instance,
and could not conceive how the Baroness had unconsciously told Georgina so many untruths most
serviceable to him now. Perhaps he perceived that
his daughter was his partner (and a very clever one)
in this horrible game he was playing; but such was
his high opinion of her, that he never guessed she
had peeped at his cards; had listened at doors,
questioned the servants, read the *Uggle Grinby
Record*, and otherwise made herself perfectly informed of the true state, not only of what was said,
but of what Mrs. Bryant had long ago really done.

Lord Henslow, perceiving her entire ignorance of
these horrible exposures, was quite touched when
she ended her artless tattle with a half tearful apology

for repeating all this that the Baroness had told her. It was natural to her to talk of her dear father; he was so devoted to his simple wife! But it was a pity his Emma had so lost her beauty; her ways were not always quite— Georgina would never be able exactly to make a companion of her. Oh yes, she and her stepmother were on excellent terms; Emma was such a *good* woman, it would not be fair to be angry with her because she and her relations —well, were not *quite* what Mr. Bryant had supposed at the time of his marriage. And poor Mrs. Bryant had evidently *suffered*. Perhaps her first husband had been unkind to her. Georgina knew very little about *him*. Mrs. Bryant always seemed so *nervous* if any allusion were made to Mr. Grant. There was a sort of mystery about him. But papa himself had told her a little once; enough to show what *he* had thought of Mr. Grant; and how highly he valued and respected the poor woman who had been, it seemed, somehow ill treated. Oh yes; Georgina was quite content to look at Emma with her dear father's appreciative eyes, and to *love* her for his sake; even if personally Mrs. Bryant was a little——

Old Lord Henslow was quite captivated by Georgina, and almost forgave her for having, fortunately without success, set her cap at his grandson. Then Georgina confessed her utterances to her father, who listened aghast.

'You have done no harm, my dear, in repeating that much,' he said, 'but do not, I pray, discuss my private affairs again.   It is—my dear child, I may as well tell you there is an anxiety connected with this unhappy affair of Alick Randle, which I may never be able to explain to you fully. .You will oblige me, my love, by not at present exhibiting curiosity, nor by speaking of it to any one.'

'Why mayn't I know, papa, if it concerns you?'

'Some things, Georgie, are unsuitable for a young girl's ears.   But if at any time I think it advisable, I will tell you myself.'   For Mr. Bryant felt that Emma had to be protected from this splendid step-child.

'You are quite off with Vincent, Georgie?'

'Quite, papa.   We had a few plain words, and he knows why I have dismissed him, and what I think of him,' said Georgina, tossing her head. 'We have really quarrelled, you know,' she continued, 'only there is no good in letting that show.   I could never forgive him his conduct, and I daresay he will not forgive me for telling him so.   I must say, I should be glad to leave this place.'

'We will arrange it, Georgie,' said Mr. Bryant, with a sigh.   He had detected allusion to Nannie in this speech, and did not inform Georgina that Mrs. Bryant wished to take the girl into the family.

CHAPTER X

VINCENT was vexed to find his grandfather on the scent about Nannie, and enslaved by the attractive clergyman and his charming daughter. 'I have no sooner got rid of Uncle Frederick,' he said, 'than here comes another of the family. I won't stand it.' He expostulated with his mother. 'Why has my grandfather taken up his abode here? I don't want him. He'll be tumbling into the sea some day, and then we shall hear it is all our fault! I really can't fence the cliff all round on his account! If people can't suit themselves to Everwell, they had better stay away.'

'He is such a support in this trouble,' said Lady Katharine, sighing; 'why, Vincent, have you taken such a dislike to all your relations?'

'I don't dislike one of them in their proper place; but why, because I am a youngster and my grandfather is a peer, should he come and live in my house without an invitation, and tell me what to do about every trifle? I declare to you, much as I value the dear old gentleman's bones, I won't fence the cliff all round to preserve them!'

'How can you laugh, dear, on such a subject?'

'Laughter is a safety-valve.'

'You and I never can talk now, Vincent, without bickering.'

'That is a gross exaggeration, mother. We
are very pleasant together between times. But,
mother dear, I cannot resist a desire to go to
the devil, or on the return journey, in my own
way. I am not intolerant of advice, generally,'
laughed Vincent; 'I like what you say very much
indeed, as a rule; I greatly prefer my grandfather's suggestions to Uncle Frederick's. But Job
would have lost patience, if, whenever he tried to
think out the answer to Twice two, his whole family
had bawled out, Four! Of course it's the right
answer, but that is a singularly uncomfortable and
inconclusive method of arriving at it. And suppose
Job had had a secret suggestion that it was five?
I have my own opinion about Alick; I have my own
opinion about Mr. and Mrs. Bryant; I have my
own opinion about Nannie. They may be faulty
opinions, but I do honestly believe they have
deeper foundations than those of my grandfather,
who never heard of one of the persons named
till last week, and who has no motives of affection or self-interest to make him careful in his
judgments.'

Lady Katharine had no idea how to set about
ejecting her father; she only became exquisitely
uncomfortable whenever he addressed his im-

patient grandson. Vincent bore it for a day or two longer; then proceeded to act upon one of his opinions at once.

'I am sorry to hear, grandfather, that you were troubled with asthma last night. Do you think it possible that the air of Everwell at this time of year is perhaps a little asthmatic?'

The old man stared. But he took his lesson to heart beautifully, and even defended the boy afterwards when Lady Katharine apologised and lamented. 'I tell you what it is,' said Lord Henslow (they were in his house by this time, for the old man had not only relieved his grandson of his own presence, but for a few days of Lady Katharine's also), 'Vincent has a good spice of *our* character. If I were you, I wouldn't sugar his tea for him as you did his father's; I'd hand him the tongs. And you'd better turn out when he marries, Katharine.' She sighed.

'I am not allowed to ask your advice on the thing I am really anxious about—the thing which has really *changed* him,' said the poor lady, despairingly.

'What, have you been reading the Uggle Grinby paper? Depend upon it, Vincent will manage that affair for himself,' responded the old man, impatiently. 'Let him alone, my dear. Upon my word, I like him better than I did. This business has brought out his qualities. He has temper, self-possession, pluck. What more do you expect in a lad of his age?'

Meanwhile, to the great relief of every one, Nannie had been unanimously decided to be herself; daughter of the deceased Benjamin Randle, and not the unnecessary Mary Smith, whatever had really been the parentage of that long-forgotten and fever-slain infant.

'It was a mare's nest. Take my advice, Nan, and never think of it again,' said John, very kindly; and the poor child was grateful.

'It's nice to have brothers and sisters, John,' she whispered; 'if I had ever heard any one say I was like mother—*your* mother, John—I'd be happy.'

'Well, the parson says so,' said John, reserving his own opinions. He felt very keenly that the name of Randle had been disgraced in more ways than one, and now announced his intention of carrying out an old wish, to sell his household gods and join his wife's brother in Australia. Patty and Caroline were quite ready to emigrate, for Patty was a woman of energy and Caroline on the look-out for a husband.

'Nan also,' said John, 'she'll find a husband quicker than you, Carry, my girl.'

But Nannie said little beyond coaxing for a promise that her dear troubled Sally, who was sick of life at Everwell, should join the party. Maria consented, as she wanted a nurse for her little boy; and the great girl, who had the vaguest idea where Sydney was, became uproariously jubilant.

CHAPTER XI

VINCENT had twice been to X—— to visit Alick. The first time, having leave to see him in his cell, he was alone with the prisoner for twenty minutes, most of which time passed in silence. Alick had pushed his stool over to the narrow casement, and sat with his chin on his arms, looking away at the north-eastern sky in the direction of Everwell. In this posture he would stay for hours without moving. There were a few books and tracts on the little table near him, but they had not been opened.

'Well, Alick?' said Vincent's pleasant voice.

The man looked round for a minute, and then back at the sky again, without a word. His face had the same suffering expression as when Nannie and her lover had kept watch over him in the gathering darkness after the tragedy. Vincent waited.

'You look better, Alick. I hear you have learnt the way to sleep again.' The prophet broke silence rather suddenly——

'Ay. There's times when I think you are right about me, for no one but a madman could sleep with a burden of thought like mine. But I do. I sleep in the starlight with never a dream, and the street noises wake me of a morning like a christened child. I shall sleep to-night when the darkness comes, for all the waking and the burning in my soul now. It makes one wish,' said Alick presently, 'there was a long sleep under the grass, on and on, too low for the street noises to come, and never a dream, nor a wakening more.'

'It may be so, Alick,' said Vincent.

'No, sir, no!' replied the sufferer, sitting up straight and facing his visitor, 'there is no wakeless sleep for me, nor for you. I used to think I'd waken in the New Jerusalem with the pearly streets. Maybe you'll get there, sir. But there's a many who have been within sight of the walls, and have sung the songs of Zion with an honest and a true heart, and who have been castaways at the last,' said Alick, resuming his dejected posture.

'The future is a mystery,' said Vincent, gently; 'then or now, Alick, we can only be men, and meet our fate as boldly and as calmly as we can. But what else besides the future do you think of when you sit here in this cold window?' A smile broke over the worn face.

'Sir, was it you asked 'em to give me a window looking towards Everwell?'

'You like thinking of Everwell and your old friends there?'

'Ay. I used to suppose,' reflected the ex-preacher, 'as Paradise, the garden Adam and Eve was in, was one particular place. But it was a state, not a place; and one man has it in one country and one in another. Maybe every man gets it once. It was at Everwell for me.'

'Paradise?'

'Ay. I was only there an hour. I cannot think there's a many who's there for so short a while! The cherubim flew swift when he came to turn *me* out! I'm thinking he thrust at me with the fiery sword, which turns every way, or I should not have started on my exile so sore hurt and wounded.'

Vincent chose to wait till Alick spoke next, and there was a long pause, in which the woe-struck eyes gazed unfalteringly at the morning sky over Everwell.

'Go away,' said Alick, curtly, looking round for a moment. The visitor rose at once. He held out his hand, but Alick pushed it away angrily.

'There is blood on my hand,' he said; 'the blood of your kin. Go.'

'Yes, he was my kin. You and I, Alick, are friends.'

'No, sir; you and me never was the same sort of man. It was a dream as we could be friends. I have dreamt many dreams, and I have seen 'em all roll away like the wreaths of a thunder-cloud. I care more than you for the ways of life, and of the heavenly city, and the blessed ones in it; but it's like *you* who'll get there, and not me; and I have sinned sins you would never have sunk to, not for all the devils in hell. You and me are different men, sir. I do not want you, staring at me in my misery. You don't say nothing to comfort me.' Vincent felt indeed that his utterances were miserably inadequate. Expression was not easy to him, as to this wretched Alick.

'At least, your friends have not forgotten you,' he said; 'we are doing all we can. Those who knew you and—loved you best, Alick, do it still.'

'There never was but one as knew me,' murmured Alick. But he seemed touched, and his look came slowly away from the sunny clouds till it rested on his visitor's compassionate face.

'Do you think I am mad now, sir?' asked Alick, quietly.

'No, I don't. I think you have recovered.'

There was a pause, the man's features working under the influence of some wild emotion. Suddenly he flung himself on his knees at Vincent's feet, and seizing his hand, clutched it violently.

' Ah, God !' he groaned, ' perhaps I am mad *now*, and you are not real, and the prison-house is not real, and none of the things I think have happened, have happened, and the man is alive yet ; and Nannie is my lassie ; and I am not a castaway.'

' Alick ! My poor friend !' said Vincent, ' my poor friend !'

After this Mr. Bryant also thought it well to visit Alick, and it was half hoped by those who wanted to prove his irresponsibility, that the sight of his enemy would rouse him to some show of unreason. But beyond a momentary purple flush, the sufferer betrayed no agitation. Mr. Bryant felt embarrassed, but apprehension and discomfort were no novelties to him in this man's presence. He tried to speak kindly of Alick's kindred, and of what was doing in his workshop ; but he got no answer, and was not sure if he had been heard. Then of Nannie. Alick looked round for a moment.

' Stop that,' he said ; and Mr. Bryant dropped the subject.

' You are not the only person in trouble, my poor fellow,' said the clergyman. ' I could wish, for my beloved wife's sake, you had not revealed the subject of that conversation you overheard. It has brought a terrible retribution for sins long repented.' His tone was dry and hard, masking his torture.

' Man, have *you* repented ?' asked Alick, sternly ;

'I heard your talk with yon ill-lived traitor. Your own mouth condemned you.'

'My poor fellow,' said the clergyman, 'your memory deceives you. I hear you impute to me expressions which I never used; which I could not have used, because they are incompatible with facts. You were beside yourself that day.' He was merely warning Alick of the course he meant to take, and had no thought of trying either to persuade the man or to purchase his connivance. He knew well enough there had been no bathing in Lethe for poor Alick. And then, the latter keeping silence, he went on to speak sacerdotally of the man's awful deed, its fearful consequences to the victim and to himself, of the religion he had professed, and of God's mercy, upon which he should rely. Alick heard him out without interruption or movement. Then he spoke.

'I am in my senses to-day,' said the prophet, rising to his feet, 'and I tell thee I am a castaway, a vessel of God's wrath, who have murdered men, soul and body together, and who would have murdered thee. But I am holier than *thou*. Get thou out of my sight.'

When Mr. Bryant returned home, his wife and even Georgina exclaimed at his pale looks. He called Emma to him and threw himself on the sofa, motioning her to a chair by his side. Presently something like a groan burst from his lips.

'Emma,' he said, 'if it is any consolation to you, I tell you I would give the world we were out of this business. I tell you, Emma, I would give the world I had the courage to walk up to Sir Vincent Leicester, or to any one, and say, "I have cheated you all, right and left. I have been a liar, and a swindler, and a traitor, to you, and to myself, and to my wife. But I will be so no longer."' Yet he looked round and listened nervously, with a dread that some one besides Emma might have heard.

'Dear Ned! but you have harmed no one!' cried Mrs. Bryant.

'I have harmed you, Emma. And the sting is that it has all been so paltry; for such little objects, such little sins. They were little at first; but they grow—they accumulate. And the sum total is appalling.'

PART X
GIANT DESPAIR

CHAPTER I

THE hours moved slowly on the day of Alick's trial.
There was a large concourse, for the case had provoked attention, and the fame of the fallen prophet
had spread through the county. People strained
their necks to look at him, and marvelled at his
inoffensive air and suffering eyes. There was no
sign of insanity about him now, and the general
feeling was that the plea would not be established.
The trial was not really long, and the side issues
so painful to the prisoner and the witnesses were
not, after all, dwelt upon much. Mr. Bryant had
a few distressing questions to answer, but they did
not throw much light on Alick's case, and only
provoked sympathy with the popular clergyman.
For the rest, he did his best for the accused,
making light of Alick's hostility to himself.

Mrs. Leach was fanning herself with her pocket-
handkerchief, and once she exclaimed audibly, 'Don't
he keep his promise beautiful!' Now and then she
tried to make suggestions to the witness, having

from the opening of the proceedings established
her character as the always welcomed 'funny person.' She was specially indignant at a suggestion of
Alick's intoxication. In a mood of profound contri-
tion herself, she cried out, 'Tell 'em, Mr. Bryant,
it never was from *him* I inherited my sad ways.'
And though she was hushed up and threatened
a dozen times already, it was less severely than if
she had omitted the word 'inherited,' which seemed
to every one killingly droll. Vincent, and perhaps
nobody else, caught her ejaculation about Mr.
Bryant's promise.

But Mr. Bryant's examination did not come off
till Alick was able to listen without exhibiting, perhaps without experiencing, great emotion. It had
been quite otherwise when the tale of his career as
prophet and teacher had been sketched by the counsel
for the prosecution. That was almost more than he
could endure. It was exactly what he had dreaded;
by reason of his sin, God's work was evil spoken of
and had come to nought. Those watching him saw
his white face grow whiter, his eyes and lips
agonised, a strong shivering establish itself through
his frame. But the only time his self-control failed
him through the whole strain of the day was at
the assertion that of his converts, no one had remained true to his profession. 'Is there no one?'
he cried aloud, in his sonorous and startling voice;

'*not one?*' and was silenced instantly; but it was less easy to silence Mrs. Leach, who started up from her place, with her arms extended, and her face beaming—

'I, my blessed boy, I. Your mother is converted. She shall show before the day is over that she has crept out of her sins, as a caterpillar out of a chrysalis.'

And she sat fanning herself, and smiling, and trying to think what sensational thing she could do, to show the whole world that she was repentant, and that her poor boy, for all his poor head, had been a true, Israelitish, inspired, and efficacious prophet.

Nannie, of course, when her turn came, made an exceedingly favourable impression. Beauty does that easily, and Nannie was more than beautiful. Terrible though it was to her to appear in any sense against Alick, she was nerved to magnanimity by feeling that with her, if with any one, it lay to show that Alick at the time of his terrible deed was out of himself. The jury were unanimous in the opinion that they had never seen so fair a creature. Her first answer, clear and firm, made a sensation. 'My name is Nannie Randle; I am the defendant's cousin; and *I am promised to be his wife.*'

Sir Vincent Leicester raised his eyes for a moment and looked at the pale, steadfast face of the young girl. And Lord Henslow, the only person who remembered

to observe the young man whose namé had been dis-
agreeably coupled with Nannie's, saw the look, but
could detect no change of expression on his grandson's
face. He took a pinch of snuff, and decided that,
granted a flirtation between Vincent and that lovely
young woman, this absolute imperturbability betok-
ened the still waters which run deep. John Randle
had started at his sister's assertion, and muttered
frowningly to himself; but Mrs. Leach stood up and
cried aloud, in jubilant tones, 'Amen, Amen. Praise
ye the Lord!' waving her handkerchief, and then
wiping her eyes with it, and subsiding into her seat
again, murmuring movingly, 'My precious! my sweet
daughter-in-law! my grateful and noble and loving
beauty!'

And Alick had thrown himself back in his place
with his eyes closed: I doubt if he listened to another sentence from his Nannie or from any one.

Nannie told her story quite simply and touch-
ingly. She had been walking with her lover. He was
very strange, and she saw that what she had been
fearing was the case; his mind had given way.
And she described the unhappy Alick's wild words,
her own terror, the dread that he was meditating
something against Sir Vincent, the terrible scene
which she had witnessed. And then she told of the
great woe which Alick had endured in the failure
of his holy work; getting through it all very well.

But in cross-examination poor Nannie found many subjects brought forward which she had not at all expected, and which seemed to exhibit her as a person undeserving of any trust, who had roused in her sweetheart feelings of perfectly reasonable fury.

Had she known Alick long? Had she kept company with him long? She had had other lovers? Only one other? She had been a long time making up her mind between her two lovers? Was Alick jealous? Who was her other lover? Nannie looked round helplessly and was silent. Was it Sir Vincent Leicester? 'Come, answer, if you please, Yes or No.' Nannie appealed against the question, and it was dropped. She was blushing scarlet, however, and every one guessed the answer. John Randle stamped his foot with all his old feeling of displeasure and disgrace; and Nannie gained little by the dropping of that question, for the matter was gone into farther. As a matter of fact, however, she sustained the ordeal well, and no one carried away the impression that she was even an ill-behaved coquette who had ruined her lover's temper. Her account of Alick's holiness, his delusions, his terrible grief and reckless despair, impressed every one with a sense of pity, and of belief in her truth and her affection for her unhappy lover. The counsel for the prosecution himself raved about the brave, gentle girl for a month to come.

And then Sir Vincent Leicester was called; and if he was not quite such an interesting witness as Nannie, still people craned their necks to see him, because he was young and popular, was nearly related to the dead man, and, it seemed now, the hero of a love-story. His evidence was, of course, short and very much to the point, and unembarrassed by hesitation or mixed motives, or any sort of sentimentality. He described as much as he knew of the tragedy; he had for some time believed the defendant out of his mind, because of so and so, and so and so, and so and so. He had had him examined by Dr. Simpson. He had seen Alick in a brain fever more than a year ago. He admitted that Alick and he had, at times, been on somewhat strained terms. Was not the defendant jealous of him? Yes; it was partly jealousy which had unhinged his mind. The witness was jealous himself, perhaps? Reasonably so. His acquaintance with last witness? He knew Miss Nannie Randle; he had had the honour of seeking her as his wife, before she had engaged herself to the defendant.

At this piece of information Lord Henslow became purple with horror, and took no further interest in the proceedings.

CHAPTER II

MR. BRYANT had left his two ladies at home, and no
other arrangement had been even suggested. Himself, he had spent the night at X——. But in the
morning Georgina came down to breakfast in a dress
she had never worn before, and announced her intention of going to the town and being present at
the 'very interesting trial.' 'You will have to
come with me, Mrs. Bryant,' she said; 'papa would
not be pleased for me to go alone.' She was putting
on her bonnet as she spoke, and over it a very thick
gauze veil. Evidently she wished to disguise herself.

'My dear Georgie,' said the stepmother, much
agitated, 'I couldn't *think* of going to such a place,
and no more must you. Your pa would be most
awfully vexed. I am quite positive, my dear.'

'I will take the responsibility,' said Georgina;
and, resolved to prove Mrs. Bryant an openly 'impossible person,' she carried her point.

In the train they encountered Patty and Caroline;
Mrs. Bryant was still crying, and Georgina began to
think that after all she could effect her purpose with-
out dragging the woman into the court. It seemed that
Caroline was dying to behold the proceedings, so Miss
Bryant put her pride in her pocket and took the

farmer's daughter with her for a companion. The moment was a proud one for Caroline, who had long copied Miss Bryant's dresses and attitudes, and was ambitious to be seen in her company.

Emma went with Patty to the inn close to the court, where John had taken a room for the day and where his wife received them. Mrs. John gave 'that woman' a very cold shoulder indeed, and reproved Patty for bringing her. Emma shivered, and sat alone in the corner of the dusty, empty, little room, hearing without heeding what seemed the heartless talk of the two respectable, well-to-do young women. How angry Edward would be, she thought, at her having let Georgie come! The girl seemed to have a genius for embroiling her with her husband. And Emma knew she was entirely out of place herself this morning at X——. Had she been a woman of energy she would have fled home again by the earliest train. Oh, how dreadfully angry Ned would be!

The hours moved along very slowly, till at last John appeared, leading the broken and agitated Nannie. 'Get the girl something to take,' he said, 'and look after her.' John had grown very fond of his youngest sister. But he went away again, and the women, of course, wanted to know all that had taken place. Nannie was too much upset to talk.

'No, no, it isn't over; only they have done with me. Let me alone, Patty, do. I will sit here with my aunt,' said the girl, fleeing to Mrs. Bryant, who, at least, was silent. Nannie sank on the floor by her side, her head on Emma's lap. And the poor mother took comfort; for the first time the child wanted her. Nannie was not comforted; but the rest and the relaxation of the great strain was a boon. Somebody was caring for her, just for a few minutes; she had no need, for an interval, to exert herself in any one's behalf. For an hour, at least, Alick's fate was beyond her control; and she was not responsible for Mrs. Leach; and Sarah and Lizzie were not clinging to her and saying, 'Oh, Nannie, Nannie, what will be the end of it? Whatever are we to do?' But more than an hour passed, and the room grew dark, and silent but for the loud ticking of the clock, while the four women waited and trembled.

'We shall have a job with her if there is bad news,' thought Maria, noting Nannie's white face, which seemed shrunken and faded with care, the sweet eyes lost in dark hollows.

'Did you mind giving evidence, Nan?' asked Mrs. John, thinking anything were better than letting the child go on thinking in this feverish way.

'Mind? Mind speaking out before all those people and about such dreadful things? And with *him* listening? How can you ask, Maria?'

'Now, Nannie, don't be cross,' said Patty, cross herself with nervousness; 'if you hadn't been a naughty, disobedient girl, you'd never have got mixed up in such doings.'

Then Emma herself had a pin to stick in the wounded spirit. 'Darling,' she whispered, 'was there anything said about—about you and me?'

'Oh, I don't know,' said Nannie, wearily; then rousing herself, 'no, nothing about you and me; but there was a little said about you and that gentleman. It wasn't said to me. It had nothing to do with me. Do you mind so very much, aunt? *I* had to bear it too. They said every one knew *I* had gone wrong. It isn't true; but I suppose all the world will believe it. It isn't so bad as the things they are believing of Alick.' And she hid her face and was silent again, while Mrs. Bryant stroked her hand timidly and caressingly.

And at last steps were heard coming down the silent street, and some one entered the inn. There were voices and a little commotion; and the four wearied women knew that tidings had come. Mrs. Bryant effaced herself in the corner, and Maria and Patty rose nervously, holding each other's fingers.

Nannie sprang to her feet and stood with her back against the window, pressing her hands against her heart while her eyes gleamed with terror, and she had difficulty in repressing a scream.

Sir Vincent Leicester entered. He walked straight to Nannie, not seeing the others.

'What is it? Oh, what is it?' she cried, in a voice of agony, her frame shuddering and retreating before him, while her breath came in quick, hard pants. 'Tell me—quick—quick.'

'It is not the worst, Nannie,' said Vincent, slowly. It required a great effort for him to remain calm and cold, with his Nannie gazing at him in this weakness of agony—agony, too, for another than himself.

'Tell me,' she said, more collectedly, stretching out shaking hands. Vincent held them between his, for indeed she seemed too nerveless to stand unsupported.

'Nannie,'—he spoke slowly and distinctly; '*Acquitted—on the ground of insanity: to be detained during Her Majesty's pleasure.*'

She withdrew her hands then, and covering her face, burst into soft weeping. And the other women wept too, none of them daring to speak, nor to interfere with these two, whose relation to each other was a mystery.

Vincent stood before her with compressed lips

and hungry eyes, till she was somewhat calmer.
Then he turned slowly to go away. She had, it
seemed, no words for him. Nannie uncovered her
face and watched him as he retired. He opened
the door; then paused and looked back. Nannie
crossed the room totteringly and followed him.
She took his hand, looking up at him—

'Will you meet me—to-morrow evening at
sundown on the shore?' she said.

'I will, Nannie.' They were silent for a moment,
looking at each other, their hands clasped.

'To say Good-bye,' she added, soundlessly, though
he heard her. Another pause; and a slow, painful
flush rose upon Vincent's features and then died
slowly away, leaving him pale almost as was she.
He gently raised her dear hand to his lips and left
her. They heard him stumble as he descended the
stair.

CHAPTER III

MRS. LEACH'S appearance in the witness-box had been
the signal for universal attention. It was a great
occasion for her, and her very genuine anxiety to
rescue her poor boy was only equalled by her
anxiety to distinguish herself. She wore her dis-
carded widow's weeds, and having brought her

youngest child with her, was vexed that the posthumous darling was not allowed to be in her arms while she gave her evidence. ˙She was at all times a buxom, handsome woman; and excitement, which was almost delight, was becoming to her, in spite of her crape and the melancholy occasion. I am afraid her family blushed. Nannie alone appreciated her humorous qualities, and even Nannie was distressed by them to-day.

Nannie was away and Alick was tongue-tied; there was no one in the whole assembly able to control Mrs. Leach. To keep her to the point was impossible, and she was given, or rather took, license to expatiate and to talk such as was never permitted to witness before. Her description was wanted of her poor boy's poor head; but it was not to be had without parenthesis about his sweetheart, the state of souls at Everwell, and her own two husbands, both named Jim.

Now Mrs. Leach, to use her own expression, had been 'fit to be tied' when she had heard the assertion, so calmly made and apparently so undisputed, that her son was a religious impostor, and that not one of his converts had been genuine. Why yes, *she* was genuine. *She* had been converted; she had suffered pains of remorse; she had signed the pledge and wished to give up lying. She racked her brains to think how she could demonstrate all this to the public.

She felt herself the most important of all the witnesses, being there to testify not so much to the badness of her son's head, as to the Divinity which had spoken through his lips, and turned men's souls from darkness to light. Could she establish his inspiration, of course the charge against him would fall to pieces. No one could be absurd enough to suppose that one taught of God could have committed a murder.

The train of Mrs. Leach's thoughts was not intelligible to her hearers. No one understood why she took this opportunity of confessing her sins, and avowing her wish to forsake them. No one distinguished her as the witness to Alick's spiritual supremacy—the one genuinely reformed penitent. But there was no stopping her. Whatever the question, she told how she had tippled and had nearly driven her blessed boy wild by that; and how she had prayed all night; and how she had been a poor deceitful body, fond of inventing and juggling and bamboozling every one. And finally she flourished her handkerchief before her eyes and screamed out something in a voice so loud and stammering with excitement, that nobody could exactly understand what she was saying, except that it was wholly irrelevant and somewhat unseemly, to be waved aside and hushed up as quickly as possible. 'I wanted to please Mr. Bryant, but I'm a converted woman now, and done with lies for him or myself, all through my blessed boy's praying for my poor soul. I buried her, I did, for Nannie, for Mr. Bryant; and she's Mary Smith!'

Mrs. Leach had no idea that agitation had made her unintelligible. She looked round triumphantly, expecting to have made a great sensation, and to have altered the whole complexion of the affair. But she only saw a few persons near her in fits of laughter; and she was got out of the witness-box as quickly as possible, and the matter of Nannie's parentage was never once even alluded to. Her strange information never got into the newspapers, and could not have been taken in by the reporters. No one appeared to place any more credit in her veracity, nor any less in the clergyman's, nor was Nannie's name ever disputed, nor Mr. Bryant troubled for the smallest explanation. That gentleman smiled composedly when Lord Henslow asked him how he had been unlucky enough to offend that madwoman.

The madwoman; exactly; Mrs. Leach had after all done a great deal for her poor son. Every one perceived that unsoundness of intellect ran in the family.

And so the whole thing was over, and people went away smiling, for the verdict was approved. Alick Randle was soon forgotten by the world, and

Frederick Kane was spoken of in his family no more. The tragic note had been sounded but not sustained, for the victims of tragedy have imposing funerals and marble monuments under lofty domes; but here was a case for mere whited sepulchres and the conspicuousness of silence. Let Frederick Kane be buried, and Mrs. Bryant, as she could not be thought of without him, disappear. And hide Alick in a madhouse perhaps for the rest of his days; no one could possibly want him again, and if he were a torment to himself—well, fate had still dealt kindly with him, for he had escaped disgrace, and charity was ready to cover the multitude of his sins. The world had had a nine days' wonder; it had not had a tragedy. Yet even a nine days' wonder is always apt to prove a tragedy for some two or three.

CHAPTER IV

MR. BRYANT had caught Ann Leach's words well enough, for he had their clue. And he was as uncomfortable in his heart as ever deceiver could be. If others heard? understood? if—one or two —they believed? And why was Vincent looking at him in that insolent way? 'Positively insolent,' said Mr. Bryant to himself, maligning his young friend who was merely wondering.

But Lord Henslow shook hands with the clergyman, and every one regarded him with respect, silent sympathy, and admiration. 'Thank Heaven it is all but ended now,' he murmured, as he left the court, his terrors subsiding. And then he felt a hand laid upon his arm, and beheld, Georgina. It is needless to say that Mr. Bryant was speechless with indignation. Lord Henslow and several other acquaintances saw her, and observed that she was struggling with tears.

'Papa,' said the daughter after a while, when his first anger at her intrusion had subsided, 'it is absolutely necessary that you take me to some place where I can speak to you alone.'

And Georgina explained that Mrs. Bryant was in the town.

'Emma! For God's sake, you don't mean to say *she* was present?'

'No, I am thankful to say, *I* prevented that. I suspected some allusions to her, and I insisted on her having the decency to stay away.'

'Georgina, your coming has displeased me more than I can express,' said her father.

'I am sorry.' Then she said emphatically, looking him full in the face, 'It is fortunate I am not so indignant with you as I have a right to be.'

Mr. Bryant trembled, for he feared his daughter, that too clever partner in his game.

'I warned you, Georgie, of a mystery, which I intended to explain to you myself.'

'Yes,' said the girl, 'and I suppose to garble the truth to me as it seems you have done to others!'

'Georgina! I, garble the truth? What do you mean?'

'*I heard what Mrs. Leach said*,' replied Georgina. He was silent for a moment. Then Ann had been less unintelligible than he had hoped!

'Is my daughter thinking of taking that woman's statement against mine?'

'Oh! Was it not true what she said?'

'Certainly not. You are making yourself ridiculous by asking. Be quiet now, Georgina, and tell me where my wife is. We must return home at once.'

'Papa! Have you no compassion for me in this sudden ruin? I cannot return with Mrs. Bryant.'

'My dear, I have the greatest possible compassion for you, but I cannot and will not make a scene in the middle of the street. Come now. The Ball Inn? This place here?'

'I never make scenes, papa. But I think you are insulting me, dragging me into this public-house, and forcing me into the company of that wicked woman.'

'Hold your tongue, Georgina,' said Mr. Bryant. But he had heard her, and he feared his daughter still.

Truly the inn, which had filled with people now, had very much the appearance of a public-house· At the bottom of the stair they encountered Sir Vincent, who was standing with one hand pressed to his brow, and a countenance of sharp anxiety ; for Nannie had broken down, and he would not leave the house till he knew her restored. Mr. Bryant did not reflect that the young man's presence in the public-house was almost as remarkable as his own ; his one sensation was annoyance at being detected seeking his wife in this kind of low place, by the man who was suspicious of him already. However, he marched on up the unsavoury stair, dragging Georgina after him.

Nannie was just recovering a little ; and, surrounded by all manner of officious people, she was turning to Mrs. Bryant for defence, when the clergyman entered.

'Emma, our train leaves immediately. You must come away at once.' He was too much exasperated to speak kindly, but he was really anxious to get her away instantaneously. Anything else would be capitulation to Georgina.

The tension of the day made every one's nerves irritable. John Randle, delighted to have something to do, jumped up and pushed Mr. Bryant from the room.

'Get out of this,' he said; 'my sister has turned sick. I won't have her bothered by your d—d interference.'

Always that detestable Nannie in Mr. Bryant's way when he tried to do his duty ! Mrs. Bryant and the Randles waited for the late train, and father and daughter returned home alone. Neither of them spoke.

Georgina went to her room, put on a pretty muslin, made her whole aspect as meek and as charming as she could, and then came down and waited on her father. Indeed, seeing he was unhappy, she gave him a tender kiss, which revived his affection. 'Poor, poor child !' he thought. 'No, I won't scold her. She was so unprepared, and is such an innocent victim !' Georgina brought him a dainty supper of all the things he liked best. Mr. Bryant had no appetite, but the attention pleased him. Her time had come; the opportunity was golden, not to be missed.

'Poor, dear papa ! What a comfort that we have each other !' she sighed; 'how I suffered during those few minutes I doubted you, papa !'

'Georgie, I cannot conceive how, on the authority of that outrageous woman——'

'Oh, papa, no. *Not* on her authority. It is your own conduct that has been so strange.'

'What do you mean, Georgie ? '

'Papa, you will be frank with me, won't you? You will let me for once be frank with you? You must remember I have no one to look to but you. No one to whom I can reasonably go for advice, or for sympathy. Friends, yes; but few here; no brother, or sister, or near relative.'

'Well, well, well?'

'I am dependent on you, papa. I trust you. You will not fail me? Oh, papa, be frank with me. Tell me all.'

'What do you want to know?'

'I want your bearing explained. How long have you known this ghastly secret of your wife's?' He was silent. 'Surely, surely, papa, you have not let me live here with that—with her, knowing the sort of woman she had been?'

'Georgina, I will not endure a word against her.'

'I will be careful, papa. But *did* you deceive me in that way?'

Alas! he had told the falsehoods already, and for consistency's sake had to repeat them.

'Papa, how incomprehensible! Why, you have been just the same to her! A woman who had deceived you, and in the cruellest way possible?— and you treat her exactly as you did while you trusted her!'

'It is not for you to censure her, Georgina.'

'No. It is for *you*. If what you tell me is true,' said the daughter.

'Very well. Consider I have done it. There is an end of the matter.'

'I am afraid not, papa. Papa, *is* it true?'

'Why do you ask?' Georgina rose and stood before her father.

'*Because no one will believe it, if you go on as before,*' she said, after a pause.

Mr. Bryant looked at his daughter searchingly. He was proud of the girl; affectionate too. But he was afraid of her. 'It would have been so easy to have shielded Mrs. Bryant, if you had wished,' said Georgina, relentlessly. 'I must be open with you, papa, and you must forgive me—our position is so serious. Papa, as things are now, no one will believe what you say. I shall not believe it myself. Remember I heard Mrs. Leach, and *so did others*. No one is likely to forget. If you keep this un-happy wife of yours living with you; if you expect me to associate with her; if you pass her off on other people as a virtuous woman fit for the society of ladies; I shall never believe you have spoken the truth! I shall not believe that she deceived you.'

'Think what you choose, Georgina.'

'I shall consider, and so will every one, *that you have been a deceiver yourself.* And I shall not stay in your house, papa.'

'Where will you go, Georgina?'

'For to-night I shall go to Lady Katharine Leicester. *I shall tell her all*, and ask her assistance.' Mr. Bryant started to his feet. All colour had left his cheek and lips.

'You shall not,' he said. 'You seem to forget that Sir Vincent——'

'I have forgotten nothing, papa. Sir Vincent's mother is a most unsuitable person for me to go to, but I have no one else.'

'Sit down, my dear; Emma will be here in a few minutes. We must have this over before she comes.'

'Papa, I am very sorry, but if she returns, I shall leave you.'

'She is my wife.'

'Oh, dearest papa, forgive me! She is your wife. But unworthy, as you admit—as you *must* admit. I am your daughter. *I* have never been undutiful. Are you going to drive me away, when I have not a soul belonging to me but yourself?'

'I cannot drive my wife away.'

'She has forfeited her rights; surely.'

'She has not.'

'I am not unreasonable in asking to be considered. I am too young to be thrown upon the world alone. I am not so young that I do not know what opinion will be formed by the world of this unfortunate wife of yours ; and, papa, of *you.* I tell you candidly I do not love her enough to endure her tacked on to me in the character of a penitent.   Come, papa, I have lived in the house with you.   I know that whatever was the case once, you and Mrs. Bryant are no longer very fond of each other.   And she has relations ; she has a *daughter.'*   Georgina sat down and waited ; Mr. Bryant also reseated himself, his head on his hand. He could not get rid of the feeling that Georgina knew more than she said.   And her tone was hard and resolute, while conscience made him a coward.   Ten minutes passed.   'Well, papa ? '   He rose.

'I have no more to say, except that I forbid you to go to Lady Katharine.'

'But I shall do it,' said Georgina, calmly.   'I cannot meet Mrs. Bryant again ; if you bring her back here, I will go straight to Lady Katharine.' It was her ultimatum.   Mr. Bryant, remembering what he chose to call Vincent's 'insolent' expression, felt her resolution intolerable.

He met his wife—the poor Emma whom he had wronged, whom he loved, to whom he desired to make restitution, *who was a clog*—at Tanswick station.   'Now, my love, do pray attend to me for a moment.   Whatever were you about,' he said, taking her aside, 'letting Georgina go to X—— ?   It has brought on a catastrophe. The shock of learning things in that manner has entirely upset the child. I have had a most painful scene with her. She is furious with us. She declares she will leave the house.'

'Georgie and me never got on together,' said the injured woman, feebly. 'I can't think how ever we'll do with each other now.'

'Oil and vinegar!' ejaculated Mr. Bryant. 'I am afraid, Emma, judging by her behaviour to me, she will be excessively rude. I dread exposing you to her while she is in this passion. Is there any place we can send her? Our neighbours are all so far off, and we are so little intimate with them. Who is there we could possibly take into our confidence?'

'Would it do, Edward,' said Mrs. Bryant, 'if I stayed with Nannie for the night? She has been so upset. I cannot bear to leave her.'

'Oh, Nannie, Nannie eternally! Have you no thought for any one but Nannie?' cried Mr. Bryant, all the more irritated that the suggestion furnished him with a resource.

'I don't like the idea of seeming to turn you out, Emma; that's the fact,' he said presently, in a low voice.

'Dear heart! I shall be happy enough with Nannie,' said Mrs. Bryant, eagerly. Mr. Bryant promptly offered the pony carriage. It seemed to him a sort of saving clause. No one could imagine he was slighting his wife when he put her ceremoniously himself into her carriage.

'There, my love! Take the child to the Farm and stay with her, or come on home, just as you think best.' And he helped Nannie in quite effusively. 'I will come for you early to-morrow, Emma,' said Mr. Bryant, putting the reins into his wife's hand, 'and we will talk matters over. Georgie will be better tempered and more reasonable by that time, I hope. You are sure the plan is agreeable to every one? What do you say, Nannie?'

'I will take care of Aunt Emma,' said the girl, looking at him steadily. He had overdone the unusual civility to herself, and Nannie perceived that this sudden unlading upon her of his unworthy wife was his refuge from a difficulty. Her quick mind understood the position from what she supposed Mr. Bryant's point of view, and she was not unwilling to come to his assistance.

But Mrs. Bryant had no overwhelming sense of her unfortunate position. She felt so innocent that she could not believe herself blamed, and she had not Nannie's talent for looking through other people's spectacles. Her husband had no sooner abandoned her than she remembered that her nieces were disagreeable, and that John was blunt and contemptuous and rough, as his father had been before him. 'I'd a great deal rather have brought you home with me, Nannie,' she murmured.

'No,' said the girl, vigorously, 'Miss Bryant never would have allowed that. I wonder you don't see how it is, aunt. All this seems very dreadful to Miss Bryant; it *is* very dreadful. You and me had much better keep out of her way for a day or so.' And Nannie looked at the uncomprehending, helpless woman with some indignation.

'Nannie,' said Mrs. Bryant, 'you'll just let me sit in your room, won't you, love? I have a sort of dread of the others—your sisters, as you call them.'

'Oh,' said Nannie, 'but, Aunt Emma, I thought you knew! I am not going home. I am staying with Aunt Ann. I shall have to take you to her house.'

'Oh dear!' said Emma, anxiously. 'Mr. Bryant would never have let me stay if he had known I was to go there!'

'Aunt Emma,' said Nannie, seriously, 'you can go home to the vicarage if you like, but I am *quite* sure Mr. Bryant didn't want it, just for to-night; only he was too kind to say so.'

'It's a queer thing,' whimpered the poor stupid thing again, 'if my own husband would rather I stayed away from him!'

They were waiting all this time for the walkers, for Nannie had already resumed charge of the distracted Mrs. Leach, and begged now to be allowed to take her in the carriage. Ann's entry was presently effected, and Nannie suggested that she had better herself be the driver, for Mrs. Bryant, not too skilful at any time, was blinded now by tears. 'Oh, I understand all about ponies, don't I, John?' said the girl, with a liveliness she was far from feeling.

Mrs. Leach gave a new turn to the conversation. 'Ain't you maybe feeling faint, my precious?' she said to Nannie; 'Mrs. Maria, give me the smelling bottle before we go. She'll let the horses run, if she goes faint. But I can hold the smell to your face, my deary, if you feel it coming on. Whatever will Sally think, to see me riding in a carriage, and bringing Emma home with me! Eh dear! it has been a sad and a dignified day for us all.'

CHAPTER V

BUT in the morning Mr. Bryant was no nearer the problem's solution than he had been the evening before. Georgina was patient and affectionate, and as charming as possible, but there was no sign of relenting about her. She referred to Lady Katharine once or twice in a pointed manner, which he understood well enough.

However, he was resolved to dare the worst, and to fetch his wife home from the Farm ; nor was he without remorse for having let her go there. But he postponed the expedition half-hour after half-hour, dreading the crisis and feeling as if in a bad dream his will were paralysed. And to-morrow was Sunday, and the helpful curate having failed, he would himself be obliged to preach : and the events of yesterday and their train of causes would certainly require some allusion, for Everwell was a very small place, and Alick had been too notable to be passed over in silence, now that justice had exonerated him. This pointing of a moral upon the man who was holier than he, seemed to fill Mr. Bryant's mouth with gravel. He opened his books and tried to write something, resolving not to go for Emma till the afternoon, when he would have leisure to attend to her affectionately. Still the sermon did not progress. An interruption was welcome. It came in the person of young Sir Vincent, who was attended by his noble grandfather. Mr. Bryant received them most graciously. It was some consolation that distinguished people were still glad to shake hands with him.

The clergyman looked ten years older than when he had come to Everwell. His hair had turned white, his eyes were sunken, and he was thin. Within the last ·fortnight lines had appeared about his mouth and eyes that betrayed deep grief and carking anxiety. Vincent Leicester also looked older; his lips were less apt to smile; he had lost the mentally lazy, self-occupied air which belongs to ease and irresponsibility and the flattered importance of youth. This very morning he had had a passage of arms with his grandfather, who wished of course to give an opinion about Nannie. Vincent listened with a respectful patience, and replied with a quiet gravity, which convinced the old man that the affair was serious, and that nothing he could say or do would alter the lover's intentions.

'Well,' had said Lord Henslow, at last, 'I beg you clearly to understand that if ever you make such a marriage as that, we decline your acquaintance for the future.'

' I hope you will see grounds for reconsidering that hasty decision,' Vincent had replied; 'if not, I can only say I am sorry you should think it necessary.'

' You are your own master,' said the old man; ' only remember the warning I have given you.' He was seriously disturbed about his grandson, but he rather liked him. 'He is deeper than Charles,' he reflected; ' and what does Katharine mean by saying he is impatient ? '

' Oh yes ; ' aloud, ' I will go with you to Mr.

Bryant. What are you going to say to him?'
Vincent made no explanation; and they went together to the vicarage.

Lord Henslow talked to Mr. Bryant for some time with much cordiality, and Vincent stood gloomily by the window, rubbing his dog with his foot, and listening. At last there came a pause, both Mr. Bryant and Lord Henslow feeling it was desired; and the clergyman could no longer refuse to meet his patron's eye.

'You have some business with me, Sir Vincent?' His manner was a little stiff, and he was always imposing. Vincent flushed up to the roots of his hair, for his errand was disagreeable.

'No, only a suggestion; perhaps I may say a request.'

'Name it. I am always happy to oblige you.' He spoke easily, but he did not like Sir Vincent's expression. Lord Henslow could not conceive what was coming.

'Our relations are not likely in future to be satisfactory, Mr. Bryant,' said Vincent, with a gravity which took off the bluntness of his words. 'I am a fixture here. My suggestion is that you should consider the advisability of leaving Everwell.' He made no sort of apology, but looked straight at the clergyman, and the wretched man was convinced that he was detected.

Lord Henslow, who had submitted to ejection himself a week or two ago, was astonished and annoyed now beyond the power of expressing so much as an interjection. He turned sharply on his grandson; but something in Vincent's air checked his remonstrance.

'You have forestalled me, Sir Vincent,' said Mr. Bryant, calmly, 'and, allow me to say, not very gracefully.'

But then the grocer's son tried a little bluster, and damaged himself irretrievably in the nobleman's opinion, who had at first been inclined to mediate.

'Oh, my dear sir,' said the old Earl finally, 'I am quite sufficiently bothered by my grandson's *amourettes* to wish to hear any more of them. They are his own affair. Miss Bryant can have nothing more than a flirtation to accuse him of, I think? If there had been any serious engagement, you would have remembered it before this morning; is it not so? No, no; we won't drag your charming daughter into this question. I think not. I think not.' Mr. Bryant was vanquished.

'You are a cool hand, Vincent,' said Lord Henslow, as they drove away. 'What did you take me there for?'

'Because I wanted a witness. It is a pity I hadn't a witness in all my conversations with Georgina,' he said, hotly.

'And may I ask further, what you believe this man to have done?'

' As I did not tell him, is it not a little unfair to tell you ? '

' In confidence, boy, in confidence.'

' Well, in confidence then, and merely as a matter of unproved personal opinion, I think he's a snob, a humbug, a coward, and a liar. I believe his wife is an inoffensive, weak woman, of whom he has taken the meanest advantage. I believe he has lied right and left, and has bought lies from other people. And what is more, he knows I think all that, and he didn't dare to deny it. No, he dropped the subject, pocketed the affront, and will simply make off. He daren't bring his story to the proof, for he knows it would fall to pieces. Do you know he has turned his wife out ? The brute. She is down in the village at the Leaches, crying, poor fool, and wondering who will make his chocolate, as Georgie lies in bed till eleven. Mrs. Bryant is a fool, and he has made use of her folly to save his own skin.'

' Well, if you think all that, you are right to try and get rid of him. We must all do our best to keep the Church pure. But I expect you are mistaken, and in any case you should have spared the scene. Scenes are youthful. I'd have let him resign and have smiled on him to the last.'

' But I wanted him to be under no delusion as to my opinion ; besides, I don't believe in that letter of resignation lying already written in his desk !'

cried Vincent, scornfully; 'if it was coming, depend upon it, I should have had it a fortnight ago.'

'Certainly you have a poor opinion of him. It is a pity you were so headstrong about bringing him here.'

'It is,' said Vincent; 'I will seek advice in choosing his successor.'

'Your cousin Augustine.'

'Perhaps so; perhaps not. I will seek advice. I perceive that I know very little of parsons.'

'You are cutting your wisdom teeth, my boy. And now I suppose you will be informing me 'again that Everwell is asthmatic?'

'It is true I have an appointment for this evening which may prevent my paying you the attention I should wish,' said Vincent, smiling sadly.

'Indeed? If you had hinted at it yesterday, I could have stayed away; but your invitation seemed hearty.'

'Yes; for I knew you would attack me about Nannie, and I wished it over as quickly as possible. My appointment this evening is with *her*,' he confessed, gravely.

Lord Henslow turned round and stared in unfeigned astonishment, and a little involuntary admiration.

Meanwhile Mr. Bryant had sat down again to his sermon. He was feeling very angry and sore, and the sermon was a refuge from thought; his mind was in a state of white heat, and he turned it all on to the intellectual labour of the moment. Sentence after sentence of eloquent discourse fell from his pen without the smallest trouble. At the end of four pages he read it over. 'Very good; couldn't be better; absolutely satisfactory.'

He was alarmed to find how well he had done it, without one atom of interest, while his mind was really fixed on Vincent Leicester's scandalous rudeness. Certainly Mr. Bryant's temptations to charlatanism were very great. He had had a hatred of deliberately lifeless sermons; but he found out now that he could compose one perfectly well. The lifelessness would never be detected. He felt a movement of horror. Lifeless sermons were perhaps to be his work for the future. Lifeless prayers would follow. In fact, he was reaching Alick's point of despair, and was beginning to believe himself God-forsaken. But Mr. Bryant was perfectly sane; it was not to be expected that he would care so much as Alick. He began to cast about as to how he could best get on without God; if he were never again to be an earnest and sanctified minister of the Gospel, he felt attention necessary to make him an efficacious and admirable praying-machine. Just then Georgina put her dainty head in. 'What did they want, papa? I saw Vincent looking very consequential.'

. 'I am going to resign, Georgie,' he replied, evasively.

'Vincent ordered you to resign, papa? Why?' asked the relentless Georgina. 'Shall I answer the question for you?'

Mr. Bryant perfectly understood her meaning; Vincent Leicester was just a specimen of the world; the world at large would credit his story no more than did Vincent Leicester, if he persevered in his present ambiguous attitude. He took a sheet of paper and wrote a letter, which he dated some days back.

'DEAR SIR VINCENT—The unhappy events of the last few weeks will have prepared you for the communication I now place in your hands,' etc. etc. etc.; with platitudes of apology and regret. 'My successor will, I trust, be one to continue with happier fortune than mine the work which has been to me so congenial and so hopeful. You will understand me when I say I must leave Everwell as soon as will be convenient. Its associations are too painful for us all, and my beloved wife feels that among strangers she will most easily secure that retirement which is now our best hope and our only desire.' And then came an affectionate ending.

The epistle, misdated and sealed, he enclosed in another.

'DEAR SIR—I send the letter which I mentioned

to you this morning as lying directed to you in
my desk. Had it been written subsequently to
this day's conversation, it would have been differently worded. However, I will let it pass.—
Your obedient servant,   E. BRYANT.'

These despatches he sent up at once to the
Heights, and in the course of the afternoon received
the following reply :—

'DEAR SIR—Your resignation is in my hands,
and in accepting it I desire to express my regret
that it is inevitable. You will allow me to say
that if I have wronged either you or Mrs. Bryant,
in thought or word, it has been unintentionally, and
with the very greatest pain to myself.—Your
obedient servant,   V. LEICESTER.'

CHAPTER VI

MR. BRYANT felt less depressed after sending his
letter, and wrote away diligently. The afternoon
wore on and he had not yet gone to fetch his disastrous wife home; nor did he feel any more inclined
to do it. And now there came more visitors.

Distinguished visitors again; old friends too,
admiring and sympathetic ;—Mr. Myers, the London
clergyman who had visited Mr. Bryant in the first

days of his affliction, and with Mr. Myers his
brother, the Bishop.   As we know, the Bishop had
long had his eye on Mr. Bryant, and had welcomed
him to his diocese, though he had not, for some
occult reason, seen fit himself to give him a living in it.

Mr. Myers had explained to his brother many
particulars about his old friend, and asserted that
his career had been spoiled by that wretched wife.

'When he married her,' said the good man,
unconsciously exaggerating the part he had himself
played, 'I warned him that she was not his equal.
I distrusted her from the first.   But no ; her beauty
infatuated him.   He would listen to nothing.   We
see the result.'

' Quite so, quite so,' said the Bishop.   It happened
that his own wife was a singularly disagreeable and
deceitful person, whom he had married in a moment
of infatuation, and who had more than once almost
succeeded in ruining his own career.   Naturally his
sympathy went out to the vicar of Everwell.

These visitors were most cheering to Mr. Bryant.
Finding the detrimental wife away from home, they
accepted his invitation to remain for a few hours,
and Georgina took them out to walk, and showed
them (tearfully) the precipice, scene of tragedy ; the
fishing village with its overhanging houses and red
roofs, the beck, and the wooden bridge where the
russet nets hung over the motionless water.

'And we must leave it all!' said Georgina, transfixing his lordship with eloquent eyes; 'my poor father is heart-broken. He was so much beloved—so successful here. Oh, is it not sad how suffering falls on innocent people?'

'My dear young lady,' corrected Mr. Myers, 'the sinner is the worst sufferer.'

'Not in our case,' said Georgina, impulsively, and with a sob of deep feeling; 'my poor noble father is suffering a thousand times more than—than the person who has ruined him!'

Very delicately the Bishop tried to find out from Miss Bryant what was going to be done with that wretched woman. 'She is not at home at present?'

'Oh no. She is with her own relations. Poor papa—it is miserable work for him. He would sacrifice everything for her; but there is always the question, isn't there? "Would it be right?" And there are other claims, are there not? especially on a clergyman. And I do think,' said the young lady, looking eloquently at the Bishop, 'papa feels very much that there is a point where forbearance becomes weakness. He will always be very kind to her; but I know he is terribly perplexed. She is away at present. I hardly think he will see his way to——'

The brothers thought Georgina unutterably charming; and Mr. Myers invited her to pay his

daughters a long visit in the spring. He stayed in
the drawing-room with Miss Bryant, and the Bishop
sat in the study with her father. It was suitable
that the perplexed and sorely tried minister should
take counsel from his spiritual superior. Somehow
throughout the conversation the Bishop seemed to
take for granted that Mr. Bryant had no course
open to him but a separation from his unworthy
wife; and before his lordship left, the clergyman was made aware that the fat living, which
had long ago been nearly his, was not yet per-
manently bestowed, and the *locum tenens* was anxious
to get away to the south of England.

'Which means, papa—' said Georgina, playfully,
when she heard this piece of information.

And at last, when it was getting late, Mr. Bryant
walked up to the Home Farm to seek his wife
and bring her home. He had risen in his own
estimation since the morning. The sermon was
excellent; every one except Vincent was civil
to him. He had talked matters over with the
Bishop, and it is a fact that the Bishop's credulity
and sympathy and kindliness had made him feel
comfortable, and as if he had spoken the truth.
Just such a feeling of satisfaction had Jacob
at the moment when he had stolen the blessing
from Esau; he had acted basely, and remorse was
certain to come; but for the moment, well—he

had got the blessing. And, as Georgie said, the Bishop had evidently a plan for him; he had not come all that way merely to offer sympathy. 'After all,' Mr. Bryant reflected, 'I am thrown away upon these barbarous fishing folk. I am really better suited to preach to persons of education and of culture.' And then he recalled his thoughts in the usual way. 'No. I have forgotten. Emma is unsuited to the society we should encounter at X——. No; I must refuse and seek some humbler sphere.' He hurried along, remembering angrily various things. 'I can't help it!' he said between his teeth, 'Georgie shall do what she pleases, but my one duty is to shelter—to make restitution to Emma. Even if Georgie finds out——'

By this time he had reached the Farm, and was being informed that both Nannie and her aunt, Mrs. Bryant, were entertained by Ann Leach and her noisy progeny.

He turned and walked off to the village, with his heart swelling. It had been displeasing to the clergyman to seek his wife at the Farm—a farm is a vulgar sort of place, and he disliked John Randle; nevertheless John and his belongings were respectability personified, and Mr. Bryant could survive some contact with them. But Ann Leach! A woman who drank, and whose talk about her two husbands reminded him of the Wif of Bathe;

whose children were scarcely superior to the bare-legged fishing imps; whose son was a sort of dissenter and had been charged with crime! To a fastidious gentleman like Mr. Bryant the bare idea of taking a wife out of such a house as Ann's caught his breath. Surely Emma must know that for her to associate with Ann Leach *and* with her husband and his lady daughter was impossible! However, he walked on resolutely, aware that this instinctive feeling was unseasonable. It was more his own fault than Emma's that Ann had given her hospitality for a night and a day; and the world's view of Emma's conduct was of more consequence than its view of her relations. Only, of course, it was the two combined that made the difficulty! He had felt that long ago, and he felt it more strongly now than ever. If she had been refined and well connected (like himself) people would have made excuses for her wretched early misfortunes; they had tolerated her odious relations on the ground that she was herself an excellent woman. But a woman who had got into trouble *and* who associated with her sister-in-law Ann Leach, was, there could be little doubt, an inconvenient wife for Mr. Bryant.

Once walking to church through the London streets, Mr. Bryant had dropped his Bible into some peculiarly unsavoury mud. He had felt it a duty, for the sake of reverence, in the presence of spectators, to fish it out and carry it home, and had done it with concealed disgust and steady resolution, knowing all the time that, though the dropping had been his own fault, the book would never be of the smallest use to him again, and that to cleanse it would be impossible. As he stepped along resolutely to-day to Mrs. Leach's house in the village street, he somehow found himself living over again that un-pleasing moment of plunging his white gentlemanly hands into the black pool wherein he had lost his sacred treasure.

CHAPTER VII

NANNIE was out, Sally sat on the steps with the baby, and Jimmy, Lizzie, and Polly were with their mother in the little shop, which had been closed since Alick had left them. The girls were crying, and Ann as usual was talking.

'We shall all be in the Union a month after your brother's in the 'sylum,' she said; 'there is rent owing now to Sir Vincent and wages to Alick's lads, and all our savings are gone. I can't carpenter like Jim Leach your father gone to glory, nor paint nor do up oak like your brother gone mad. Alick's gift of fasting come from Jim Randle, and don't agree with me, nor with none of you Jim

Leach's children, saving though it would be. It ain't comely to go naked, and the shops won't provide us clothes for gratitude. Lizzie Leach, and you there, Mary Ann, who's a big lass now, answer me. What are you going to do for a living? Who's going to feed you and clothe you and keep you 'spectable now your stepbrother's put away? I am glad to see you sob, Lizzie, for it shows a feeling heart and a sense of your circumstances. Cry away, my dear; tears was the meat and drink of David, but Lord! it's a footy sort of nourishment! To-morrow, my dears, I'll take your little hands, and we'll go to the workhouse.'

Lizzie knew that her mother did not mean it, and she had boundless faith in her cousin Nannie; but she was a nervous child, and could no more help crying when her mother lamented, than she could help screaming when Alick preached about the devil; and naturally little Polly cried for sympathy. But Mr. Bryant, who seldom passed a weeping child without a kind word, pushed to-day past the sobbing creatures impatiently, and made his way into the little parlour, where, according to Sally, he would find his wife.

Yes, she was there—pale and miserable herself, with tear-stained eyelids and red patches on her cheeks; untidy too—not more untidy than often at home, yet still, to Mr. Bryant's eye, infected by her surroundings

It seemed by mutual consent that any kiss or ceremonious greeting between them was omitted. 'Come now, Emma. I have arranged matters. Come home at once,' said the husband. Mrs. Bryant stood, with her hands nervously clasped together, but she did not speak. 'Georgina is in a better temper,' he continued, gloomily ; 'at least I hope so. We must put up with her at any rate. You cannot remain here. You shouldn't have come.'

'Shall you let me bring my child home with me, Ned ? '

'No ! not now !' he cried, exasperated. 'You are unreasonable, Emma, to make such a request at this moment ! Our difficulties are overwhelming already. I cannot burden myself with that girl at present.'

'She is my child, and I love her better than any-thing in the world, though you have turned her against me, and she thinks me the wickedest of wicked women, because I have let her and other folk believe what is not true.'

'What is the use of reproaches, Emma ? All I did or suggested was in your interest,' he said, in a tone sulky from despair; 'my ruin would involve yours, wouldn't it ? We are not ruined now, if you will only be reasonable and come away quietly, from this house first, and then from Everwell.'

'You have been very selfish to me, Edward !' said Mrs. Bryant, without moving.

'Oh, my God! this is intolerable! Well, well, have it so. I *have* been abominably selfish. We can't mend it now, so do, for God's sake, let it be.'

'I'm not speaking of that, Edward. I was willing to bear reproach for you, because I thought you had always been kind. But it seems I was born to be deceived by men who speak to me fair and seem fond of me,' said Mrs. Bryant, raising her voice tremulously.

'What on earth do you mean, Emma?'

'If you'll let me have her now to be with me —to love and to comfort me—maybe I'll never say much. But I cannot love you like I did.'

'What do you mean?'

'Edward, you knew she was alive all along! You let me mourn for her death and cry at her grave—me who was acting a mother's part to your child—and you knew she was alive and growing up motherless and to despise me. It was *you* who did it. You hated my darling, and wanted to be rid of her. It is all one as if you had murdered her!'

Mr. Bryant let her say all this without interruption. For a minute or two he had foreseen what was coming; his heart was beating violently, his soul torn as if dragged by his good and bad angel at once. When she paused with an angry sob, he only shrugged his shoulders sneeringly and asked if she had got this wonderful story from Ann; and Emma replied—

'Of course I got it from Ann. It was she who helped you to do it. Is it not true, Ned?' cried Mrs. Bryant. But he turned from her sharply and stood at the window, looking out. A strong breeze was blowing from the shore, and making white curls on the edges of the black waves; already evening was appearing in the gray sky, and the fishermen were preparing for the night's work. The aspect of the street and the tossing ocean graved itself in Mr. Bryant's mind, though he had no consciousness of looking at anything. After all, the man loved his wife, and his long treachery to her had been an intolerable burden. There would be luxury in confession to this woman whom he at once loved and despised. She, if none other, would surely forgive when he told her the agony his sin had been to him. It was with something of enthusiasm that he turned and faced her, for his good angel had triumphed.

'Emma,' he began almost eagerly, 'be merciful to me! I protest I loved you then and I love you now. I have never loved any woman but yourself, and from first to last the thought that I was causing you distress has been acute suffering. Emma, my dearest, my wife——'

Alas! she was not magnanimous. She interrupted him.

'Then you have deceived me as bad as ever *he* did, and I don't see no more reason why I should forgive you than forgive him.' Mr. Bryant's confession got no further. He turned away, his arms folded, and kept silence.

'It's what Frederick would never have done!' she cried, 'to steal my child, and then to make me say I had deceived him when I hadn't! And you pretending to be a better man than he! I wish I had never seen you! I wish he was alive now that I might go to him, and tell him, and tell everybody, how you have served me!' There was a pause; then Mr. Bryant forced himself to speak, hoping thus to stem the torrent of evil thoughts bursting over him and overwhelming his soul.

'Very well, Emma, go and speak now. By Heaven, I believe it would be the best thing could happen to me!'

'Will any one believe me now, Edward?' He shrugged his shoulders. 'Will you confess the truth?' There was a silence. Then he stepped to her side and held her arm with the grip of a vice, and his voice was loud and hissing.

'Emma, say no more—now—to me nor to any one. There are dangers—temptations possible to me which you do not foresee. Come away; let us begin a new life.'

'No, I won't come,' said Mrs. Bryant, bitterly.

I can't forgive you. I will go away and live with my daughter ! '

Mr. Bryant dropped her arm and stood back with clenched hands, his white face seamed and shrunken.

' For God's sake, Emma ! ' he cried, ' make to me no such horrible suggestion ! '

CHAPTER VIII

ON the shore, Nannie had said, and her lover was there an hour before the sundown. At last Nannie was seen picking her way swiftly and unerringly over the slippery sea-weeds and the pools and channels left between the rocks by the retreating tide. There were children about, fishing for crabs and mussels ; the lovers could not well talk together here, though less careful of spectators now that their secret was out. They moved on silently, Nannie with her eyes down and her head bent, till they had turned the great cliff which bounded the southern side of Everwell Bay, and they were half way, by the low-water path, to Tanswick. Here they stopped at the edge of the retiring waves, which were restless and mournful to-night, plashing angrily at their feet, the foam ghastly under the faint gray

clouds, and unillumined by the yellow streak of the
sun's descent.   It was here they had once met each
other before, at the edge of the deep tideless basin
with the forest of coloured sea-weeds.   In it Vincent
had seen the fair girl mirrored under the rosy sunset light, long ago when he had come and had thrown
himself at her feet ; and now she paused by its
quiet depths and looked down sorrowfully as she
saw her companion's chastened face in the mirror
beside her own ; and a sob arose in her throat, and
a tear fell from her tender eyes into its translucent
calm.

I suppose to a casual observer Nannie was far
less fair than she had been that long past evening
in the sunset glow.   Now her soft bloom had faded,
her cheek was wan and thin, her eyes were heavy
with watching and with tears, the pleased, playful
smile which had lurked in her dimples was lost.
Then she had been a vision of youth and joy—a sea-
nymph, a grace, a dream of nature and delight, of
fancy and of hope made perfect.   To-night, in her
girlish form, she was a suffering woman, worn with
care and tried by pain ; thinking that mirth and
gladness and play were over for ever for her now,
like the dolls and the sweetmeats of her childhood.
But her lover looked into the soft depths of her
saddened eyes, and did not question if they sparkled
less ; for him they were starlike still.   He did not

think her less beautiful. It no longer mattered to him if she were beautiful or not. She was Nannie, and he loved her.

At last the girl met his look. She held out his ring. 'Take it,' she said, 'and forgive me that I did not give it back before. I wanted to say good-bye in giving it.'

'Why have you done this, Nannie?' he asked, quietly.

Nannie pressed her hands to her breast as she answered, 'There were many reasons; only one I need tell you now. You know it—Alick.'

'But you cannot marry Alick,' he said slowly, in a low voice.

'Can I not? Will he never be well enough for that?'

'I don't suppose so. I don't know that he will ever be free again. If he were, still you could not do it. He has no right to marry.'

'Why? If he were cured—' said Nannie, trembling.

'I do not know that they are ever thoroughly cured. It is a curse. It breaks hearts; it leaves homes bare; it plunges into crime. It brings end-less desolation, and sometimes remorse. You have seen all that, Nannie? Marriage for a man or a woman with that disease means spreading it. Listen, Nannie; if it were *you* who had lost your reason, not Alick, though you were to be cured within a month, I would not have you for my wife.'

There was a pause. 'I wonder if you could be right!' said Nannie; 'no one else has spoken so to me. Every one does not think so?'

'Yes, Nannie, I believe I am right. People owe a duty to their race—to their children. If he recover, he is just the man to understand your reason and to acquiesce. Whether he understands or not, you must not marry Alick.'

'And then——'

'Then you will marry me,' he said very gently, coming a step nearer and holding out his hands.

'No,' said Nannie, steadily. There was a long silence.

'Have you given up loving me, my very dearest?' he said at last.

'Not quite. I wish I had. I am trying every day—every hour. I have succeeded so far that I can talk quietly, you see, to you about it, and can tell you that—that—I don't any longer *want* to do it,' said Nannie, with an agitation which belied her words.

'What have I done, my Nannie?'

'You? Nothing.'

'Some one has been talking to you? My mother——'

'Yes. She, and my brother, and my own sense. I should be unsuitable to you. I had it all ready to explain before ever I was carried away to Faverton. But I don't want to explain it now. There is a bigger barrier between us, and we cannot climb over it, and we must not try. It is Alick.'

'But—' he hesitated, afraid to press the question of her love for the unhappy Alick.

'What you have said,' continued Nannie, 'even if it is true—ah, please, sir, forgive me! I know you wouldn't say what you didn't think, and hadn't good reasons for thinking; only—it doesn't seem so to me. And it makes no difference.'

'No difference, Nannie?' The girl did not answer at once; at last she spoke slowly, looking far away at the horizon and the out-faring fishing sails.

'Do you remember, sir, how we agreed, when you had asked me to marry you, and I had said, No, there were too many difficulties, how we agreed to wait, you and I? To wait for ever perhaps, but to be sweethearts still?'

'Of course I remember. It was fantastic. It would not have been serious with any one but you and me. It was not very serious with us, Nannie; you knew that when you yielded to Alick. I regret very much, Nannie, that you and I ever

declined into anything not entirely serious. I ought
not to have suggested it ; I ought not to have
allowed you to do it. It would not have been
understood ; and as it was, it brought difficulty.
I ask you to-day, Nannie, for forgiveness.'

She raised her eyes to his, surprised by his
self-reproach. 'I do not regret anything,' said
Nannie, gently ; 'for that which you call fanciful,
but which made us happy, has taught me, now that
everything is very difficult and very sad, what to
do about Alick.'

'What are you going to do about Alick, my
dearest ? '

'I have been to see him,' said Nannie, in a low
dreary voice, looking at the sand below her feet ;
'he has broken down ; the long strain, and the
trouble, and hearing all that about himself, has
been too much. He is very ill. He cannot think
or speak like other people. There can no longer
be any doubt— And what has made him so is
sorrow—sorrow in his soul. But he knew *me*. He
was glad to see *me*—oh so glad ! He called me
his sweetheart, and his own, and he said if I would
be true to him he could endure all the horrible
misery ; I was the one bit of joy he had left. And
I told him, Yes, I would be true. I told him I had
not spoken lightly when I had given him my
promise, but I had thought it well over, and was

prepared to hold to what I had said. I told him he might love me, and I—' Nannie paused, 'I would love him as I had promised before this terrible trouble came upon us. I told Alick all that this morning. I mean it. I shall not go back from it. My promise is the only bit of comfort he has in a world that has all turned to ashes. And I will never take it back from him.'

'Even if you know he can never marry you, Nannie ? '

'I do not know that yet. But yes, I will be his sweetheart. His wife who is parted from him, for ever perhaps ; but his faithful wife still.'

'Do you think an unrealisable hope, a barren fancy, will be a comfort to Alick ? '

'I know it will. An unrealisable, barren fancy was a comfort to me.'

Vincent shook his head. 'You and I were not hopeless, Nannie ; and it seems we were not serious.' He spoke a little bitterly and paused ; then resumed gently, 'I think you will only make him restless ; keep up in his mind a vain fire that will consume him and lead in the end—to nothing.'

'No. It is not so with Alick now. If ever I see it is bad for him, I will end it somehow. But only for his sake. At present it is good, and I am ready for it to be good to the end. And,' added Nannie in a low, firm voice, 'if ever he claims the fulfilment of my promise, I will be his wife.' Again Vincent shook his head gravely.

'You don't think of yourself at all, Nannie?'

'Oh no,' said the girl, simply.

'Nor of me?' She coloured, and held out her hand impulsively.

'I couldn't be yours anyway!' she cried; 'if I could, I might be puzzled. But even then—yes, I am sure, even *then*, I should ask you to give me up! Though I would cut off my hand to please you, I should give you up and hold on to my poor Alick! He has nothing else; and he is weak and broken, and unable to suffer. And you, oh yes! you have many other hopes and joys; and you are so strong, so strong! You can bear it, and he cannot.' Vincent was too much moved to speak. He had taken her outstretched hands in his and was pressing them to his lips. For a moment she leaned her head against his arm and sobbed a little. 'I want you to help me!' she murmured, raising her tear-dimmed eyes to his again. 'It feels very hard sometimes. It wasn't that sort of love I ever wanted to give Alick. Is it wrong to feel that?'

'Wrong? Oh, my sweet little Nannie!' His lips touched her hair. Then he released her hands and reseated her, taking up his own position again at a little distance.

'Nannie, may I speak very plainly? Once and for all?'

'Yes, if it is to help me.'

'I suppose men are selfish brutes,' said Vincent, slowly; 'they don't easily mount to the peaks of self-sacrifice, upon which women stand quite naturally in idea, and some women—like you—in practice.' He could not keep up the cynical tone. 'Very likely you are miles nearer the right than I; but I question, and very seriously, if that sort of selfabnegation is justifiable—if it *is* right, in fact. It may be; but oh, my darling, my darling, be very sure, before you do it; before you spoil your own life, and the life of the man you love —' he paused, giving her an opportunity to correct that expression if she wished.

'No, your life is not to be spoiled,' interrupted Nannie, earnestly; 'you have many, many things left—you know it!'

'True; never mind me. But before you spoil your own life, for the sake of a distraught mind which does not know the sacrifice you are making; for the sake of a poor fellow to whom, after all, you can give no solid boon; and who in the end may sink into mere oblivion, and reward you for your life's sacrifice by ingratitude and even by dislike.

If you loved him, then indeed— Ah, my darling, consider if it be not overstrained, unreal; a
mistaking of the relative value of things, that is *not*
pleasing to the gods, Nannie, and that will bring
disaster upon us all. I am supposing that Alick
will never be well enough for the question of
marriage practically to arise. But if he should be
again given his liberty, your position will become
still more difficult. I have given you *my* decided
opinion that marriage in such a case is a distinct
social wrong. Supposing you had come to think so
too, would you not find it more difficult and more unkind to draw back then than now? There, dearest,
I had to say it. I daresay I am wrong, and what
you want to do is really magnanimous. But I don't
see it altogether so—the deed I mean, not you; and
I prefer that you should know my opinion.' Nannie
was long silent.

'Perhaps you are right,' she said at last; 'you
are much wiser than I. But I do not feel as you
do, and I must go by what seems right to *me*,
mustn't I? One can't go by any one else's
feeling, even if it is a very dear friend. Merely to
suggest deserting Alick would break his heart.
There is very little I can do for him, but it seems
right to do that little. I am sure I should not
have a moment's happiness if I didn't do it. Don't
you see?'

'I see that you are a darling,' said Vincent.

'Oh!' cried Nannie, bursting into tears, 'I do feel that so much of it was my own fault. I hindered you, sir, when you wanted to help him; and I didn't speak plain enough to him about you and me; and I helped to set the people against him; and that day—that dreadful day—just when he needed me most, I had run away and left him.'

'I am beyond words thankful that you had run away, Nannie,' said Vincent.

'I thought he was wanting to hurt *you*,' murmured Nannie.

'Darling, you must not fancy any of it was your fault,' said Vincent, his arm round her, for her sobs pierced his heart. Yet he remembered how at one time he had himself felt, and almost indignantly, that she was deceiving the unhappy Alick.

'Don't you see,' whispered Nannie, her hand in his, 'I *know* I should have repentance and remorse to my life's end, if I did not try to restore him out of his great misery. No one can do it but I, and there is only the one way I can do it. Please, please don't say any more against it. I should like to say good-bye now,' said Nannie, with trembling lips.

The sad waves were rolling shorewards again, and the sun had long vanished. A gray, rainboding twilight was enwrapping everything. There was no boat at hand to-day, and they rose slowly and moved homewards, chased by the steadily encroaching tide. His arm was still round her, and Nannie was still now and then shaken by her subsiding sobs. Before they had rounded the point into Everwell Bay, Vincent stopped her.

'Nannie, if ever you should change your mind about Alick——'

'I should be so grateful if you would not say that kind of thing,' she murmured.

'I must say it this once. If you should change your mind about Alick; if you should want me for your lover again, Nannie, dearest, dearest Nannie! you will tell me.' She shook her head sorrowfully without answering. 'And before we part, for it is parting—I am going to ask you very humbly, and, Nannie, gratefully oh, my darling, for one dear, last kiss.' He spoke very quietly, standing before her with his hands pressing hers, but making no advance till he had permission. The girl's face became white as ashes as she gazed at him. She seemed to realise for the first time what she was requiring of him.

'Oh,' she cried, vehemently, 'yes! we have kissed each other! I shall never forget it. But since then Alick has kissed me, and it is his right to do it again. I cannot, cannot go from one to the other like that. Do not ask it!'

'I can never tell you, Nannie,' said Vincent, gravely, 'how I love you; what it costs me to give you up like this.'

PART XI

SOME ARE MARRIED, SOME ARE DEAD

CHAPTER I

GRASS grows green upon every grave, and long before three years were out, the Randles and the Bryants, mere meteors at Everwell, had disappeared; Alick and Nannie were seldom mentioned; and the whole nine days' wonder had, to all appearance, vanished from every one's memory. Of the actors in it, none remained at Everwell except Sir Vincent Leicester, who still lived at the Heights with his mother.

Changes were in progress under his *régime.* Tanswick was not yet a fashionable watering-place, but the hotel on the plateau was actually in operation, and that barbarian, the speculative builder, had arrived, leased a plot of ground, and begun to run up two pretty little red houses in the modern style, designed to be Let in Apartments. The hotel was a plaything for Vincent, and he kept it under his own thumb, delighted when he encountered the ladies in poke bonnets and the artists with velvet coats and large leisure, who were as yet the most numerous visitors.

Vincent had sold the Faverton estate to the Manchester manufacturer, who had first taken the house upon lease. Lord Henslow protested, but had no arguments ready when his grandson explained that he wanted money; and no one suggested that Vincent was not laying out his money reasonably at Everwell. He had arrested the old house in its march to decay; was restoring the church and pulling down the worst of the fishing huts, which clustered round the mouth of the beck. And there was a new landing-place for the fish and a pulley for the boats; a commodious establishment too for the endless herring-curing, of which the old appointments had been enough to reduce salt herrings to the catalogue of unclean meats till the end of time. Everwell was less picturesque, but it was more wholesome. There had been even some exercise of despotism on the matter of beach proprieties, mounds of decaying fish-heads and other unseemlinesses being rigorously prohibited. Dr. Verrill had fewer fevers to study and if there was still drinking there was less brawling, and if there had been no revival of hymn-singing much of the obscene and blasphemous ribaldry had somehow gone with the fish-heads. Dr. Verrill, that minute philosopher, perceived a difference, and had to confess that some of it was the result of a stern policy of eviction which Sir Vincent was pursuing with the ruthlessness of an

Irish exterminator. 'You are ruining your own soul by it,' he said to his landlord; 'already, Sir Vincent, I observe in you physiognomical signs of deterioration towards cruelty ; but I admit you are acting in accordance with nature, which is immoral from first to last.'

Vincent, however, was very fond of the man of science, and showed so much interest in the vegetables that Dr. Verrill was never without hope of improving his character, when (as he expressed it) some of the fires of youth had burned down in his stomach. 'Wait till that day, my dear sister,' said the little man, ' to bid him to dinner with us. At present he is a glutton. I tell him so daily, but I don't expect him to *listen* till his morbid appetite begins to fail. You never saw a *hungry* man dine on Brussels sprouts, did you ?' concluded the doctor, triumphantly.

Friends with Dr. Verrill, Vincent was also at peace with his grandfather. Old Lord Henslow, in warm weather, was often at Everwell, and Vincent and his mother were much at Henslow, for the Countess had died; and the Ladies Jane and Elinor were somewhat grim companions for the old man, who was not on the best of terms with his sons. He had taken a liking for Vincent; had even got into a senile way of asking his grandson's opinion, to Lady Katharine's delight and to Vincent's amusement; for the ideas of the latter were not cast in the same mould as those of the Kane family, and he had sometimes a difficulty in getting them even comprehended. At the present moment Lord Henslow was much exercised by two projects for his grandson: one was to get him into Parliament; the other, to marry him to Victoria Leslie, a Scotch heiress, who with her parents was on a visit to Henslow at the same time as Vincent and Lady Katharine.

'A magnificent girl!' said the old man, daily; 'as handsome as young Astley's bride elect, the beautiful Miss Bryant. Eh, sir?'

'No,' replied Vincent; 'Georgina takes the apple. But I daresay Miss Leslie is better tempered.' He smiled, for the breadth of his grandfather's hints was amusing; but he was not annoyed, for he had no hankerings after Miss Bryant and Victoria was charming.

'If I had seen her long ago!' he said to himself sometimes. 'She would have worn very much better than Georgina.'

Victoria was an active, lively girl, with a kind word for everybody, especially, perhaps, for the old and dull, by whom she was idolised in consequence. All her short life she had passed in a blaze of sunshine, and it had not scorched her; on the contrary, she had blossomed gratefully in it, like a flower.

Vincent, who for three winters had been thinking all women uninteresting and all amusement forced, was surprised by his own liking for this pretty lady; the onlookers saw sometimes a kindling of enthusiasm in his eyes as he watched her—eyes grown, as Lady Katharine had feared, inveterately reserved and grave. She smiled on the girl as, after a long day in the saddle with Vincent at her side, Victoria, scarcely more fatigued than he, chatted to him familiarly over her music books in the evening; and Mrs. Leslie indeed smiled too, for she thought Vincent would be a very suitable husband, and did not feel herself able to cope with the fortune hunters in the great world, whither she was even now bearing her richly dowered and trustful and beloved only child to be exhibited and bargained for. But neither mother could hear the conversation between the two young people who were standing together at the piano, looking over some new music. Victoria now and then played a few notes or hummed a few bars in a rich contralto voice; but Vincent was no great musician, and though he liked Miss Leslie's singing, was at the present moment becoming a little bored, and trying to hear what Victoria's father was saying at the far end of the room about a new Conservative paper. He opened one of the songs at random.

'Why, how grave you are!' exclaimed Miss

Leslie presently ; 'have you found something nice ?
Do let me see.' She jumped up impulsively and
looked over the page with him. Vincent left the
sheets in her hand. 'What pretty words !' said
the girl, and read aloud in a sweet, measured voice,
of no emotion—

'Alas, that Spring should vanish with the Rose !
  That Youth's sweet-scented Manuscript should close !
    The Nightingale that in the Branches sang,
  Ah, whence, and whither flown again, who knows !

Ah, Love ! could thou and I with Fate conspire
To grasp this sorry Scheme of Things entire,
    Would not we shatter it to bits—and then
Remould it nearer to the Heart's Desire ?

Ah, Moon of my Delight, who know'st no wane,
The Moon of Heav'n is rising once again :
    How oft hereafter rising shall she look
Through this same Garden after me—in vain !

And when Thyself with shining Foot shall pass
Among the Guests, Star-scatter'd on the Grass,
    And in thy joyous Errand reach the Spot
Where I made one —— turn down an empty Glass.'

'Don't you think that is pretty ?' cried the girl.
But he made no reply, and looking up she perceived
that his thoughts were far away and sadder than
her own. 'What is the matter ?' she asked, impulsively, and Vincent saw a glowing, sympathetic
face close to his ; she was looking at him, quite
forgetful of herself. He laughed a little hollowly.

'I believe I was turning down an empty glass, he said; 'never mind. No, don't sing those sugary lines. Let us find something else.'

'I wish you would tell me what they made you think of!' said Victoria, out of sheer kindness of heart; 'you looked so sad!'

'Did I? What manners!' Then, as she seemed distressed and rebuffed, he added, looking at her, 'You would not see the connection if I told you. But I have sometimes raged at the moon for rising and looking down as usual on the garden from which the nightingale has flown. Haven't you? Hasn't every one?'

No, Victoria had no sad memories of any sort as yet. She coloured deeply with a sort of awe at her intrusion into the young man's secrets, and of delight that he should talk to her of them.

'Was it — is she dead?' whispered Victoria, with dewy eyes and a sense of great compassion for the comrade who had laughed and played with her, as if his heart had been ever as untouched as her own.

'No,' said Vincent, retiring into his shell again, and thinking her very young, unable to imagine any bereavement but by death.

'Then I do hope you will meet her again some day,' she said, earnestly; and Vincent only smiled, repeating to himself that she would have worn very much better than Georgina.

But his thoughts had flown to the suffering Nannie, to whom he had said farewell in the gray light of the autumn sunset, while the ruffled waves plashed dolefully at their feet.

'Oh, my darling! Two whole years and a great deal more, and I have never seen her. I wonder if Nannie thinks I have forgotten!'

CHAPTER II

THE unhappy Alick was still in confinement, but surrounded by every comfort possible to his condition. His calm was untrustworthy, and he had never recovered from the melancholy into which he had sunk; still he was for the most part quiet and rational enough. He found occupation in his painting; he had Nannie for a hope, and at least one friend whose frequent visits were a pleasure. For Vincent Leicester, with persevering kindliness, had at last succeeded in thawing the icy reserve in which Alick had enshrouded himself; *he* was the friend, and always welcomed now with brightening eyes, a wan smile, and at least a few sentences of unconstrained and sometimes eager talk. Alick had seemed to Vincent a bequest from the parting Nannie, and even if he had had no personal affection for the sufferer, he would have tended him to the extent of his power for her dear sake. And Alick often seemed to forget that his friend had been his rival; seemed to see in him now the one only person who understood the ins and outs of his relation to his sweetheart, and felt for him in the mingled joy and sorrow of his accepted love, followed by bitter and almost instantaneous separation from his betrothed.

'She is waiting for me,' the captive would say; 'she is ready to wait a long time. Maybe it won't be very long now. I'd be sorry to keep her waiting much longer now.' Vincent did not answer, for these hopeful moods of Alick's touched him more than his far more usual gloom. 'You see a change in me, sir, don't you? You think I'm better? The doctor says so.'

'You look first-rate, Alick,' said Vincent; and it was true, for the moment. Alick laughed, and stretched his arms before him, with the air of a strong man preparing for some hard work which he enjoyed.

'When I get thinking of my Nannie,' he said, 'and how she loves me and is waiting for me, I almost forget that I've had any troubles. She's like the shining sun to me. It would be a poor sort of world, sir, wouldn't it? if every day was like yesterday with a murk over the sea from rise to set. Oh! I mind me how the sun used to shine over the morning sea at Everwell, and how the

sparkles come in my Nannie's eye to see it. Will
you tell her, sir, when you speak with her next, that
she's the sun to me, breaking through the murk and
shining out over the sea.'

'But you forget Nannie is not at Everwell now,'
said Vincent.

'Ay, I forgot that,' returned Alick, as if disappointed. 'It's hard to think of her anywhere
else. Is mother a sober woman nowadays, sir,' he
asked presently, 'as she's got my Nannie living with
her?'

'I expect she is, but I only hear of them through
you, so I cannot inform you,' said Vincent. Alick
found Nannie's last letter and studied the address,
smiling as he read a word or two.

'Charles Street, she says. Do you know where
that is, sir?'

'I could find it if you wished, Alick,' said
Vincent, looking at his watch; 'I am going to
London before long.'

Alick flashed a doubtful look at him, and was
silent for a time.

'London's a big place, they say. The Babylon
it talks of in the Revelation, with the merchandise
of gold and cinnamon and horses, and souls of men.
It's to be thrown down by an angel some day, like
a millstone, till there's no more at all the voice of
harpers and musicians, nor of bridegroom and bride,

nor no craftsman any more, nor light of a candle. I do not so greatly like my Nannie being there. But our minister here says I was mistaken in thinking it meant London. He says it's Rome and the pope. What do you think, sir?'

'I think it might have been old Rome,' said Vincent, 'before the pope was invented. Shall I bring you a book about it?'

'Ay,' said Alick, listlessly, evidently thinking of something else. Presently he resumed in the same inattentive voice, 'I like the way the words go in that Revelation chapter. I was making views from it. I've took to charcoal lately, sir; it goes quicker than the chalk. There's one of the merchants standing afar off from the smoke of her burning. And another of them with dust on their heads, weeping and wailing— Maybe my Nannie would like to see the sketches if you'd take 'em to her,' he ended suddenly.

'I'm to go then, Alick?'

'Ay,' said Alick, in a very low voice. He looked up beseechingly at his friend, who was bending towards him a little, meeting his gaze. A flush rose and faded on Alick's worn face, and there was silence. Presently he looked away again, and said in a broken voice, 'I'd like some one to see her and tell me if she's looking well—my lassie.' Vincent's time was up, and he rose, taking the man's hand and pressing it with more meaning than usual.

'I'll think it over, Alick,' he said, slowly.

CHAPTER III

MR. BRYANT, in coming to the final arrangement with his wife, had expressed his desire that she should 'live like a lady.' He had himself selected a nice little house for her in a quiet part of London, and had put her in possession of an income; no very large one, for the fortune inherited from the worthy grocer had not gone so far as had originally been intended, and Mr. Bryant had an expensive daughter and an expensive sphere of labour in the Cathedral city, where he speedily became the bosom friend of the Bishop. Still he was as liberal to his wife as he could afford to be, and the house he chose was very nice, and he furnished it himself very nicely and comfortably indeed.

But there were more people in that house than just Mrs. Bryant and Nannie. John Randle had given his sister a little fixed allowance, quite a fortune for a working girl, as he supposed her to be; but Ann Leach and her children had no source of revenue at all; and greatly to the clergyman's annoyance, all these persons belonged to Mrs. Bryant's establishment. For Nannie had altogether refused to abandon Alick's mother; and it would not have suited Mr. Bryant that his wife should not have the company of her so-called niece. He perpetually soothed his conscience with the reflection that he had—at great sacrifice to himself—given Emma the great wish of her heart—her daughter. So Mrs. Leach and her progeny, from Lizzie down, lived in the kitchen, and Mrs. Bryant sat upstairs in the drawing-room. It was not at first very clear to which floor Nannie Randle belonged.

After a month or so, however, Nannie awoke to the fact that these arrangements were unsatisfactory. Mrs. Bryant was lonely, unhappy, and uncomfortable; and Mr. Bryant wrote a severe letter, saying that if all these people lived in his wife's house, they must pay for board and lodging, like any other honest lodgers. Nannie, with a tear of remorse, set to work again and reorganised the establishment. 'A proper servant' seemed to be Aunt Emma's great wish, so her niece smoothed the way for one; and she told Mrs. Leach she must get some employment so as to pay for the children's clothes, food, and schooling. No one ever thought of resisting Nannie; but on this occasion Mrs. Leach sat down and cried, and wondered why she had ever come away from Everwell.

'It minds me of the days of my first widowhood, Nan,' she said, 'and when I was just wondering how ever I should do, Jim Leach come along. I was young and 'andsome then, Nan, and my poor boy was a taking little chap. Jim Leach noticed him. I doubt if Polly and Jimmy and my posthumous darling hadn't been his own children, he'd never have noticed *them.*' Nannie smiled.

'Come now, Aunt Ann; what work will you do?'

'I suppose I could go charing or keep a grocery,' answered Mrs. Leach without hesitation, and Nannie laughed again.

The girl put on her hat and walked down two streets to a house with a brass plate : 'Dr. Stilford ;' she had seen the gentleman in church, and had studied his countenance, and she felt he was the man to help her now. No one ever saw Nannie without taking a fancy to her, and the old doctor was no exception to the rule. He spoke to her with the utmost kindness. Nannie gave a slight sketch of the family history, enough to awaken his interest ; and then said her aunt wanted work ; she was for the moment entertained by a kind relative, but she wanted to support herself. She was handy and clever. Could not Dr. Stilford get her some jobs of nursing ?

'Send her to see me,' said he ; 'but, my dear girl, all the ladies and gentlemen want hospital-trained nurses now.' Nannie smiled a little and replied—

'Aunt is rather a funny-spoken person, sir. I don't think she would suit ladies and gentlemen.'

Who could refuse Nannie? Dr. Stilford inspected Mrs. Leach, wrote to Dr. Verrill for 'references,' and finally sent his new lieutenant to see after the family of his greengrocer, in trouble with a new-born baby, a boy in the croup, and a consumptive sister-in-law. And a highly successful nurse Mrs. Leach proved.

'My precious,' she said to Nannie, having returned after her night's watch, 'take the key and open my desk Jim Randle gave me, and take out my pledge card signed by that wicked man, Ned Bryant, and bring it to me.'

'Yes, auntie. Did you cure all the sick folk?'

'Ay, their bodies is better; it was a deal of it dirt as ailed them. And there was that poor man and his brother (who's his partner and a widowman, and civil to me, and is good-looking, with a blue suit) thinking kidneys a right thing for breakfast! I made them some turnip porridge, for they had over many roots in their shop. And didn't they relish it! Run, my dear, and get me my pledge card.'

'Yes, auntie, but why?'

'I want to see how soon it will be out, Nan,' said poor thirsty Mrs. Leach.

'Nonsense, aunt!' responded Nannie, cheerfully, as often before.

And so Mrs. Leach got into work; and if she broke her pledge once or twice it was never disgracefully, and she always came much ashamed with a confession to Nannie, and many marvellous excuses. Nannie watched her with great satisfaction, and wrote happily of her to the poor fallen prophet.

But it was never easy to comfort Alick. 'Lassie, lassie,' he wrote, 'for mercy's sake, do not leave thy poor lad's mother, nor think she has no more need of thy help and of thy prayers.'

Ah! those despairing letters from Alick! Nannie always read them alone, and with scalding tears, and sometimes a supplication that he might die and end his hopeless grief in the quiet oblivion of the grave. But as the months rolled on, his letters did become a little brighter. He seemed to have partially forgotten what the sins were for which he was punished, and to dwell more on his thoughts of her, and the hope of some day possessing her at last. 'I hope it too,' Nannie would say to herself, pressing her hand to her aching heart; 'oh, I do—surely I do hope it may end so.'

By degrees Nannie learned the whole of Mrs.

Bryant's history, and grew tender in her thoughts of the deserted woman.   But they had found each other far too late ; and, aunt or mother, Mrs. Bryant's nature was unsympathetic to the girl's.   Nannie in her youthful inexperience did not perceive that just as surely as Alick's reason had been overthrown by disappointment, so also was this weak woman's house left unto her desolate.   The great crises in her life were past; all or one of the storms she had weathered would have shipwrecked many a heart of sterner stuff; but to her they were simply un-comprehended and desolating.   Hers was a simple, guileless, loving nature, which could smile at a pleasure or weep at a harsh word, adequate for the little joys, the little griefs, the little cares of an ordinary happy woman's career.   She had never been meant for a heroine or a tragedy queen.   When she had recovered her daughter—the girl for whom she had mourned and agonised—she could only give her childish caresses and exigent complaints.   'I have wanted you all these years, Mary,' she would say, ' and now you will not even dine with me !'   Nannie, in whose imagination was a widely different ideal of a mother, did not at once see the pathos of it.

But after a time she did consent to sit at table with the poor lonely lady, and to be waited on by Emily the maid ; and in the afternoons she came into the drawing-room and helped Mrs. Bryant with her

fancy work.   One day Mrs. Browne, the vicar's wife,
and her sister, Miss Heath, came to call, and they
found Nannie sitting thus with her aunt.

'What a pretty creature!' said the two ladies
to each other as they came away; 'and with such
a nice modest manner.   We will ask that girl to
tea some day when we are alone.   And there is
nothing visibly scandalous about Mrs. Bryant.   We
feel sure she does not drink.   She seems a very
quiet person; not quite a lady probably.   We may
safely invite both her and her niece to our missionary meeting.'   And then, like every one else,
they added, 'Poor Mr. Bryant!   What a sad
business this must have been for him!'

Emma never got on with Mrs. Browne, the
model, bustling vicar's wife, such as she ought to
have been herself.   But the two ladies took a great
interest in Nannie, and the girl responded to their
kindness with gratitude and friendliness.   Mrs.
Browne asked her a great many questions, and
Nannie answered them simply enough, and with a
feeling of pleasure in having a counsellor.   'When
we came to London,' said Nannie, 'I thought we
were all going to live as working people.   Aunt
Leach never could possibly be anything else.   'Aunt
Emma and she are fond of each other, but they have
a few words now and then.   I don't think it would
do for them to be too much mixed up.   I hope I

am not wrong in being so much with Aunt Emma?
I don't want to pretend I am a lady; but she is so
lonely all by herself!'

'You are quite right, my dear,' said Mrs. Browne;
'and you are quite fit for poor Mrs. Bryant's drawing-
room; and for mine. Don't be shy. You have a
better manner than Miss Mustard, my governess,
who goes everywhere. When you are in doubt
about some little question of etiquette don't be
ashamed to ask me or my sister. Now, you will
come to my little girl's birthday party, won't you?
You will enjoy it. There will be games, and a little
dancing, and a number of our young friends, some
about your own age.'

'Oh no, no!' cried Nannie, 'I could not go to a
party!'

Nevertheless every one seemed to wish it; and
Nannie eventually submitted, partly out of curiosity.
Mrs. Bryant bought her a grand evening dress,
copied from one of Georgina's fascinating frocks,
and Nannie, terrified by the first view of her own
splendour, was by far the prettiest girl in Mrs.
Browne's drawing-room. Even the chaperons admired her, and young Mr. Braithwaite, the *jeune
premier* of the occasion, asked her to dance. But
Nannie, who had played at all the childish games,
was not for dancing. She sat aloof with the question-
able governess's dowdy sister, whose mother kept a

Finishing School; became friendly with the young lady, and learnt the names of those sciences in which her education had been deficient. 'Perhaps you would like to join some of the girls' classes?' said Miss Mustard, eagerly, on the watch for new pupils.

When Nannie returned late that night, having walked home, the pretty dress bundled up under a cloak, Mrs. Bryant met her anxiously in the hall. 'My dear, my dear,' said Emma, 'why ever didn't you have a.cab? Were not you frightened in the streets at this hour and in that dress?'

'Oh no!' said Nannie; 'I am not easily frightened. Do ladies never walk away from parties, Aunt Emma?'

'No, love, *never*. Did you enjoy it, my darling? Were they all polite to you?'

Nannie rested her chin on her hand, and looked abstractedly into the fireplace.

'I was glad to go for once,' she said, 'and everybody was very kind; and there were such lovely little children. But no, I shan't go no more to anything of the sort. Parties are for rich people who are young and have no sorrows. I am not very old, but still it was quite unsuitable to me.'

'Why, Nannie,' said Mrs. Bryant, 'I daresay many of the smart people you saw to-night have tears in their eyes often.'

'Then why were they there?' cried Nannie.

' It is like the Arab women we heard about at the missionary meeting, who make feasts on the tombs in the graveyard! There are graves in my life, aunt; they don't show much, but ah! I will not dance and feast on them. Thank you for the lovely gown. I look nice in it, don't I ? I heard some one call me pretty—me, little Nan, with the red hair! But I shall not dress up so again. I went once to look on. I shall not go again.'

In her room Nannie did not, however, immediately tear off the pretty dress. She looked at herself in the glass, and she thought of the compliments, the admiring eyes, the young man's wish to dance with her. Nannie was not elated; but she had appreciated it all, and was pleased. ' I wish *he* had been there to see me,' she thought; ' it is nice to think there are little ways in which I was not altogether unworthy. I should soon learn what they call the etiquette; and if it is only a matter of French and piano playing— Ah, how silly I am ! I know quite well those are not the things which make a lady ! And why on earth should I want to be a lady? I have thrown in my lot with Aunt Emma and with my poor suffering Alick. To be a lady would bring me no nearer to *them.*'

Nevertheless Nannie, having a good deal of time on her hands, made Mrs. Mustard's acquaintance.

CHAPTER IV

CHARLES STREET,' said Vincent to himself; 'they
have moved then. Where, I wonder, is Charles
Street ?' It was a fortnight since Alick had given
him the message for Nannie. Vincent had taken a
fortnight to consider if he would do well in under-
taking the commission, in breaking the long years'
silence. A few communications had passed between
him and Nannie during the first month or so of her
life in London. He had insisted, because John was
away and the girl had no protectors except the two
silly women to whom she was guardian angel. But
as soon as everything was arranged, and she had
dropped into her place, Nannie had written no
more, nor had Vincent pressed her to continue the
correspondence against her will. Now, however, after
two years and nearly a half, at Alick's wish, and
with a really friendly, though at times a consuming,
anxiety to know how the strange household was
getting on, Vincent decided that he did well to go.

'Perhaps,' he said cynically to himself, 'I shall
find upon seeing her that I have got over it. Two
years is a very long time, and Victoria is beautiful ;
and would, I feel no doubt, make a very nice
and a very trustworthy wife, and my mother would

be pleased. I will go and see if Nannie is, of a truth, all that my memory represents her; if she is not—come, I will do my very best to fall in love with Victoria! *Quand on n'a pas ce qu'on aime, il faut aimer ce qu'on a,*' he said, still cynical, and weary of long restlessness and discontent.

He found Charles Street—respectable but dingy, and on the north side of the Marylebone Lane. It was not the sort of house he had expected, and he was surprised too by the aspect of the woman who opened the door, and who, when asked for Miss Randle, murmured something about the second storey, and called some one else. But Nannie had 'gone to business,' and there was none of her family at 'ome except the youngest, which was being minded till his mother's return. Vincent was surprised again; he had surely understood that Mrs. Bryant had allowed her niece no business! But he had made up his mind to seeing dear Nannie to-day, and to be baulked was entirely out of the question. He got the address and then drove away in a hansom, travelling a long distance in the direction of civilisation and fashion, till he had reached a shop—small, elegant, probably very expensive—a gentleman's shop for gloves, ties, and such like. 'What, I wonder, does Nannie do here?' thought Vincent, and entered, feeling like one walking in a dream.

And the cynical mood fell off from his spirit

like any other artificiality in the presence of truth. It is a kind of defensive armour we put on to baffle certain spiritual adversaries, which are only half visible to ourselves and generally wholly unperceived by the wondering crowd. 'I must have forgotten Nannie after two years,' Vincent had said to himself, 'and it were convenient that I should marry Victoria Leslie. And is not Nannie a woman? After two years she will no doubt have forgotten me; and very probably she has, after two years, forgotten Alick as well.' He shrugged his shoulders and spoke bitterly, but he did not believe one word he was saying. It was defensive armour against thoughts which he feared. For Nannie's action with regard to her hapless cousin, Vincent had never approved, and he had to-day no doubt that, if she loved Alick no more, she would do well in cutting her trammels. Nannie was of worth far greater than Alick; sacrificed to him she must not be; unless in the one case of her own imperative desire. And there was a contingency which Vincent allowed no voice at present, but knew as possible,—that Nannie, weary indeed of Alick, and longing to escape from her self-imposed fetters, should be crying out for the love of her old lover, whom she had loved first, whose side she should never have quitted. Ah! he would take her then, and with unspeakable joy; take her too without tormentings of self-blame, or hesitation and questionings of right and wrong. But disloyalty of no sort came natural to Vincent; and to take Nannie thus, with the haunting recollection of those suffering, trusting eyes of the man whom after all she had deceived, nay, of the man whom he had deceived himself, in accepting the commission without warning or protest—would it not be disloyalty? justifiable indeed, but disloyalty still? He strengthened himself in the cynical mood.

But in Nannie's dear presence no unreality had power over her lover's spirit; the cynical armour dropped off of itself as he crossed the threshold within which she was, and heard already the soft, familiar tones of Nannie's beloved voice. All sense of strangeness in place or time of meeting, all memory of the two years' severance, all recollection that she had cut herself off from him, all distrust of her, or belief in his own fickleness, vanished like a dream. He was back at Everwell, on the wild shore where the sunlit waves plashed quiet music; in the glen with the moonlight changing familiar boulder-stones and moss-grown tree stumps into friendly goblins of the uncouth solitude. He was back to the freedom and the delight and the poetry of their early love. He was in her presence; a moment more and her sweet eyes would have gladdened at his coming; her arms would be round his neck; she would be pressed to his heart, and he would hear the tender sigh of her great happiness.

Two customers were in the shop, and behind the counter was a single young lady serving them. She was very beautiful; that could be plainly seen in the eyes of the gentlemen, whose purchases were not, perhaps, very necessary ones. Could it possibly be Nannie? Could the long-legged little girl of the blue petticoat and the sun-bonnet have expanded into this magnificent young queen, rustling about in black silk, with a spray of flowers at her throat, and piles of elaborate hair crowning her shapely head according to the latest fashion? It was undoubtedly Nannie; under the glove-like bodice was the graceful form which had adorned the simple frocks of her early girlhood; and the face was the same fair, sunny face, with its purity of line and faultless proportion, lighted by thoughtful eyes and softened by the smiling of tender lips, which latter had now, however, a well-marked pinch of sadness.

'Not now.' Her soundless whisper to him was imperious, and she did not raise her eyes. She went on attending to her customers without change of manner, and presently she asked aloud in her usual tone, 'What can I show you, sir?' Yet Vincent knew that no lightning flash could have

been swifter than her recognition. Perhaps ever
since she had sold gloves and neckties for Mr.
Egerton she had been daily expecting that her lover
might chance some day to come!

It seemed to him that his agitation must betray
him, and, what were worse, betray Nannie also to
the strangers. He selected a pair of gloves at
random and began putting them on, as if to account
for his presence. He heard as in a dream a few
questions and answers around him, a chink of
money, the departure of the two customers, ob-
viously gentlemen; the entry of three more, flown
with good spirits and self-satisfaction and youthful
insolence. She served these also, undisturbed, it
seemed, by their stare.

It was Nannie in a quite new light; a shop-girl
and a recognised beauty; yet, for all this, still the
same unspeakably sweet Nannie, of the soft voice,
and the starry eyes, and the delicate, not-to-be-
forgotten smile. And Vincent knew that she was
the one woman in the world for him.

The moment they were alone she turned to
him, wan and anxious now under her finery.
'There—there is nothing wrong, is there?' questioned Nannie. 'You have not come to tell me
anything bad about Alick?' That was it! every
day, every hour, she lived in a state of apprehension, a dread of hearing of some new tragedy!

Once reassured on this point, Nannie sent her visitor away, bidding him to come and see her at her home, where they could speak to each other undisturbed. So that evening Vincent rang again at the door of the shabby house in Charles Street, and Nannie opened it herself and brought him in. Mrs. Leach was out; Polly and Jimmy were washing the tea-cups in an inner room, and Nannie hushed the four-year-old youngest child on her knee as she talked. Her hair was twisted now in its old simple knot, she wore a rough linen apron, and her sleeves were pushed half way up her arm.

'I understand you better now, Nannie,' said Vincent, aimlessly enough; 'this morning I felt quite afraid of you.'

She coloured and answered bitterly, feeling as if the gulf between them had somehow widened, 'I am obliged to dress like that! I have to call every morning at a hairdresser and have my hair done. If I am pale, they touch me up with rouge.'

'I see. You are a decoy duck,' said Vincent, bitterly, in his turn.

'Yes. The advertisement said "a young lady of good appearance."' Nannie spoke defiantly, with tears not far from her voice.

'And why did you take that situation, Nannie?

'Because it is an honest one,' she flashed out, 'with kind people. It is supposed I can sell gloves better than an ugly woman, and so I am better paid. That is why I took the situation!' Vincent was silent; he did not like it.

'Oh, do you think it is wrong?' cried Nannie, piteously. 'I know Alick would think it wrong. He would say my looks were not given me to sell! I have not dared to tell him quite all—about the rouge and all! But it was so hard to get on for a while; and it seems that most of the things a girl can do are so badly paid and take so long to learn. We have put Lizzie to a dressmaker, but you know she earns nothing yet. And so many of the people didn't seem to like my appearance,' ended Nannie, cheering as she detected forgiveness, and looking down with a half smile. Then she blushed very deeply, and fixed her eyes on his with a dumb request that he would not notice her momentary relapse into the old playful way of leading for a compliment. Vincent understood her; and he never again betrayed his repugnance to the necessary evil of her presence in Mr. Egerton's shop.

'But, Nannie, I do not understand,' he said; 'I thought Mrs. Bryant——'

'Yes, I will tell you all about Mrs. Bryant,' interrupted the girl, 'only I must hear about my poor Alick first. Oh, tell me,' she cried; 'you said you had a message from him for me! You said there was nothing the matter. He is not worse! You are sure?' Vincent was silent. He felt a great unwillingness to speak of her disastrous lover. A bright spot grew on Nannie's cheek as she watched him, and observed the dogged, reluctant air unusual on his face. She handed him some of Alick's letters.

'I want you to read these,' she said, gently. He glanced at a few lines and put them down.

'I know all this. He has showed me some of your letters to him,' said Vincent, turning from her and leaning his head on his hand.

'I am so glad. You see,' said Nannie, with quivering lips, 'it is the greatest pleasure he has— these letters; to know he may say what he likes to me—' she paused, 'to think that I love him.'

'But—if it is not true,' began Vincent, trying to speak coldly ; but his voice shook.

'It is not for you to say that to me, sir,' said Nannie, very gently. There was a tenderness in her tone which made him look up. She was standing by him, the child in her arms, and she met his eye with the fearless, grieving, loving look of a saint. 'Yes, it is true,' said Nannie. 'I have chosen him for my love.' Yet she was too much in sympathy with her old lover not to show the compassion which she felt. She laid her touch softly on his shoulder, and Vincent turned away again, covering his face with his hand. He had under stood her. The thing he had half dreaded, wholly desired, was not to be. She was true to Alick. There was a silence. Then Vincent roused himself.

'I saw him a fortnight ago, Nannie. Yes, he seemed to me well then; cheerful, and interested in his painting. He sent some sketches to you, and showed me others—larger things which appeared to give him occupation and genuine pleasure.'

'Were they good?' asked Nannie, with a touch of her old pride in Alick's paint-brush.

'Well, they were too allegorical. There was one quite terrible picture of a drowned girl on the sea-shore in an atmosphere of horrors. It was gruesome, but strikingly and cleverly done. In that and in all he had put in familiar faces, his own again and again, and always maligned. And yours generally the central object. He gave me a very beautiful little sketch, Nannie, of you and your colts at Faverton.'

'Ah, my poor Alick!' sighed Nannie.

'In most of the pictures, you were the guardian angel, the saviour—a hope and a helper and a blessing.'

'Thank you for telling me that,' said Nannie. Vincent had approached Alick's message, but could

not yet bring himself to give it.   They talked on of
his painting, interested in what they were saying,
yet each with a background of deeper interest to
their words and thoughts.

'Might he have been a great painter?   Would
that have saved him, sir?'

'I don't know, Nannie.   He might have played
for too high stakes at that.'

'And it would not have been so much use as
the preaching.'

'Do you think not?'

'He thought the preaching the highest work.
I could not bear to doubt it.   I like to think his
sorrow is only for this world; that when he wakes
in the next he will find his first thought was the
right one; that he was a true worker for God, and
that his work was blessed.'

'Ah!   A great deal of our work will look rather
scamped on that occasion, I suspect.   But I daresay
it has had its use all the same.   It doesn't do to
be always looking back and wishing we had done
something different.   There was too much repentance in Alick's scheme of religion.   We want now
to get him to look forward; to work or to anything
else.'

She was long silent, Vincent watching her with
solicitude.   Then Nannie spoke abruptly.   'There
never was any one who remembered every little

thing like Alick! Only it has all turned dark for him! Sometimes I wish he would get a great deal worse; and forget, forget, forget—till he was like a little child again!'

'Those cases are very painful, Nannie. I prefer to think my poor friend is still a human being. I don't fancy he would purchase relief from his suffering by degradation to the level of a brute.' Nannie made no answer. And then somehow their eyes met.

'Would you be mine, Nannie, if it came to that?' cried Vincent, suddenly, with the bitterness of suppressed passion. The girl looked at him for a moment, then she dropped her head on her hands and wept bitterly.

'Nannie! Nannie! Forgive me!' said Vincent.

'*You* would not wish to purchase relief from *our* suffering,' she sobbed, ' by *his* degradation to the level of a brute.'

'No,' said Vincent, quietly. He held her hands for a few minutes in silence. Then in a low voice he gave Alick's message. 'He told me to tell you, Nannie, that you are as the sun to him; breaking through the murk and shining across the sea.'

CHAPTER VI

I<small>T</small> was not till the next day, when Vincent and Nannie had recovered their calm, that Mrs. Bryant's history was told.

For more than a year and a half the clergyman's wife, her sister-in-law, and the young people had lived together quietly and not too uncomfortably in the manner already described, no cause of anxiety coming to the surface. Mr. Bryant appeared now and then, but increasing intervals elapsed between his visits, and it was evident to Nannie that his wife and he were drifting farther and farther apart. Each time he came he seemed more embarrassed by Nannie and Mrs. Leach, and each time he had less to say to Emma. And Mrs. Bryant, without meaning to be resentful, had a way of brooding over her wrongs, and referring reproachfully to them in a way exquisitely painful to her husband.

'I could see,' said Nannie, 'it was torture to him to think how he had served her; and I believe if she had been thoughtful for him, and had forgiven him and said no more, he would have been thankful to take her back, and to be oh! so kind to her.'

'Now, Nannie,' said Vincent, 'I must interrupt. You have come round to my view of Bryant ? '

' Yes,' said Nannie, slowly, ' I think I have.'

' Then don't talk to me of Mrs. Bryant forgiving him.'

' But she is his wife ! ' said simple Nannie.

' Nonsense. She couldn't forgive it. A saint like you, Nannie, might ; though I doubt it. But never a flesh - and - blood mortal like Mrs. Bryant or me.'

' Oh, I don't know ! When she thought how good he had been to her in other ways ; and how much of it was unintentional. And then, how wretched he is for having done it ! '

' Bryant ? He is most extraordinarily happy and prosperous.'

' No, he is unhappy. I am sure of it. He hates his prosperity. I can't explain what I mean, but I have a feeling that·so much of what happened was her fault. She might have helped him when the temptation came, and she didn't. She failed him when he wanted her most, and so he sank.'

' A man shouldn't want holding up by his wife.'

' I know *you* never would. But I have seen some men who weren't so very strong. Perhaps she chose her husband badly ; but having got him, oh ! she ought not to have failed him ! ' Vincent smiled, for Nannie's remarks were characteristic.

It seemed that the first decided anxiety had been caused by the boy, Tom Leach, a clever, unsteady lad, left at Everwell in the employ of Mr. Soanes, the Tanswick fish-dealer. He had written in great alarm to Nannie, imploring her at once to send him money to replace certain peculations of which he had been guilty, before they should be discovered.

' We were terribly frightened,' said Nannie, ' but we sent the money. I had just got my three months' allowance from John, and Aunt Emma helped.'

' You were a goose, Nannie,' said Vincent, re-solving to see after Tom when he returned home.

Mrs. Leach, continued the girl, had been troubled by this anxiety concerning her son. She said dole-fully that all her children got possessed as they grew up. Evidently it preyed upon her mind; and one day, her pledge's term having run out, she felt a necessity for something cheering. Nannie couldn't help smiling at this part of the tale, but indeed it was very sad. After drinking more or less for a week, and becoming daily more terrifying to Lizzie and to Mrs. Bryant, Ann Leach had one night gone, rather muddled, to a patient in a critical condition; had set the bed-curtains on fire, and frightened the invalid into fits. This catastrophe caused Mrs. Leach to re-sign the pledge on the following day, and for the rest of her life; but it had a bad effect

on her prestige as a nurse. Dr. Stilford was tired
of his *protégée*, for she had carried out to the full
a grateful intention she had formed of teaching him,
and Nannie's pleading had this time no effect, since
(dreading the effect of her sweet eyes on his judg-
ment) he had refused to see her. 'But almost all
Aunt Ann's work had come through Dr. Stilford,
and after that she got hardly any more, till we came
here; and now she doesn't go to such nice families,'
sighed Nannie; 'and he had seemed such a kind
old gentleman!'

'Does she keep her pledge now?' asked Vincent.
'Alick is anxious on that point.'

'Very well indeed,' said Nannie, 'but you
know, she is not a person who would *ever* do
without some one to look after her! And then,'
the girl went on, 'Mr. Bryant had come. The very
day Aunt Ann was like that. And he was so angry.
He seemed to think she was *always* tipsy. And
she would talk to him. And you can fancy the
extraordinary things she said, and the names she
called him! And how she went on about the
things he had done! But Lizzie and I and the
maid were all listening, and no one could stop her.
He said it was all a great pack of lies, and she
should not stay another day in Mrs. Bryant's house.
And Aunt Emma got into a nervous state, and
sided one minute with one and the next minute

with the other, and stirred them both up. Mr.
Bryant was quite quiet, but he was *very* angry. ' I
felt sorry for him, among so many women, who all
seemed very ill bred to him! Ladies and gentlemen never quarrel, do they? I mean, not out
loud. And Mrs. Bryant had gone back from being
a lady since she had left him.'

'Since she had been with you, I suppose,' said
Vincent, in parenthesis.

'He sent for me,' continued Nannie, 'and made
me show him all the bills and tell him how Aunt
Emma's money was going. He wasn't at all pleased,
and called the Leaches, and me too, dishonest and
paupers, and impostors and everything; and the
end of it was, that he turned them all out! And
he stayed three whole days, till Aunt Ann had gone
and all the children. But the thing was, *I* had to
go too; for I knew she never would keep her pledge,
and the children would run wild and perhaps starve,
unless I was there to help. Of course I had to stay
with Aunt Ann!' ended Nannie, thinking Vincent
looked rather doubtful. 'She is Alick's mother!
She belongs to me!'

But the worst of this upheaval was that it had
occasioned a more serious quarrel between the
husband and wife than had yet occurred. They
parted in anger, after cruel words on both sides,
and with a half-meant resolution to meet no more.

And so poor Emma, whose life had been one long failure, was left alone ; every day to realise more fully her husband's great sin against her—the sin that no one else appreciated, the sin which to her was worse than the mere lying and treachery called by Vincent unpardonable. Edward had robbed her of her child ! For Nannie had been restored too late, at a time when she had entered into other relations and admitted other claims, not to be put aside by one of her faithful nature. 'She did her best for me,' said the disappointed woman, 'and never was anything but gentle and kind. But she didn't love me in her heart. She always thought of Sarah as her mother, and made believe still that my Mary was dead in Faverton churchyard. She wouldn't ask me a thing about her poor father, nor care to learn the truth of it all. She just set her face dead against it the moment she knew he was Sir Vincent's uncle, and when she saw what that dreadful man, Alick, had done. She said it would drive her wild unless she might believe she was Nannie Randle still, and when I called her " Mary " it made her angry. I have never had my child from beginning to end. And I have been a very unhappy woman. And it is Edward's fault.'

How much Mrs. Bryant suffered in those lonely days must for ever remain untold. She was one of the weak of this world whom none pity, and who are crushed out ruthlessly by the survival of the fittest. Day after day she sat alone and un-occupied. She was no reader. Needlework she had none, for her house and her dresses, which no one saw but herself, had no interest for her. She embroidered a laborious antimacassar sometimes, and had no satisfaction in it when it was done; or she made a flannel petticoat very slowly, and asked her servant to find some poor person to give it to. She would sit quite still with her hands in her lap and remember the pleasant mornings she had spent in her London vicarage, making blinds or curtains, and listening for her husband's cheerful voice when he came in from his parish. One day she even took a cab and went to look at the outside of that house, which would know her again no more for ever. 'Oh, if I might sleep, and wake up there, and find it all a dream; and that I had never been to that terrible place by the sea; and *he* had died long ago, as I thought; and Mary was dead, and Edward was kind to me!' Vain fancies. She returned to her solitary dwelling, bereaved of husband and child and every good.

Mrs. Browne and her sister Miss Heath would come in and talk to her, and try to interest her in something, or to make her visit the poor. 'Oh no!' she said, 'I—I could not undertake it. I never was fond of parish work.' Nannie's friend, poor ugly Miss Mustard, would come and play on the hired piano, which still stood in the drawing-room, and wonder why the woman said nothing and had tears in her eyes. Emma was not specially fond of music; but she missed, oh, how she missed, the scales and exercises and little easy tunes that had fallen from Nannie's unpractised fingers, interrupted sometimes by a girlish laugh at their incompetence. She did not visit the child after the first time—one Sunday, when her visit had not been satisfactory; for Nannie had seemed somehow usurped by Ann Leach's children, and had quite a common dress on and a rough apron, and did not look like a lady one bit; which was disappointing after all the trouble Mrs. Bryant had taken with her manners, and the money she had spent in educating her a little! Things were better when Nannie came to see her, especially after she had got the situation at Egerton's, and wore a stylish hat and her hair in the hair-dresser's splendid coils and plaits. She looked quite as well as Georgina when she was dressed so! But Emma was always grumbling at the idea of Nannie's having any business at all; and the girl wearied of the endless protests, and did not realise, perhaps because she did not sufficiently care, alas! how the lonely woman wanted her. Later, when Vincent Leicester had heard the whole story, a bit

from one person and a bit from another, more than
Nannie had ever known, he discerned that the
daughter's presence had been needed.   But he
never told Nannie.   She had not understood, and
besides, what could she have done ?   As far as she
knew she did her best ; spent little hours with Mrs.
Bryant on Sundays and other days when her heart
was elsewhere, and literally never gave twenty
minutes to idling or amusing herself without a
care for the many depending on her.   She sat up
late writing to Alick ; and she was awake half the
night with the delicate baby; and she arranged
clothes for Polly, and coaxed Aunt Ann, and comforted Lizzie, and played with Jimmy.   And always
there was the long day at Egerton's, a good situation
with kind and careful people, but which meant
forced cheerfulness and a constant attention to
propriety not natural to the lively girl.   Nannie's
day was laborious ; there was not much time in it
for Mrs. Bryant.

So Emma sat alone, deserted now by her child,
as she had been deserted by her husband ; not
noticing that the winter was over, and that the sun
was shining, and that spring flowers were selling in
the streets.   Her servant, a lazy, contemptuous girl,
did not observe that day by day her mistress sent
her dinner away scarcely tasted, nor that she spoke
less and less.   Was the woman ill ?   What matter ?

She was of no use to anybody; it couldn't matter if she even died. If she were ill, Emily would give notice. If she were very ill, Emily would abandon her month's wages and go off at once. She could get a place any day in five minutes, for she was a G.F.S. girl, and her Associate was bound to get her one. But for the present the woman was all right and the place was an easy one, which exactly suited Emily.

There came a day when Mrs. Bryant, after a restless night and a short doze troubled by dreams towards morning, awoke with a pain in her back and a cough which frightened her. She consulted Emily about it, but the girl only laughed. A great longing for her husband seized poor Emma. He had always been so kind when she was ill! *He* never said it was fancy. Oh, if only he were with her now! It was at this moment that Emily flourished open the door with more ceremony than she accorded to Miss Mustard, or even to Mrs. Browne, and announced 'Sir Vincent Leicester.'

Poor Emma, unhappy, unstrung, and ill, was quite overcome at the sight of a friend. She had often recalled Vincent's kindness in the early days of her trouble, when all the rest of the world had turned against her; he seemed a positive messenger from heaven now. Shocked by the change in the unhappy woman, the visitor did not speak at once, but held her hand forgetfully; and poor Mrs. Bryant, after a moment's ineffectual struggle, lost all self-control under the influence of sympathy and the sense that some one had come to her rescue. She burst into tears.

Presently Vincent said earnestly, leaning towards her a little with his hand still on hers, 'Mrs. Bryant, don't you know that I love Nannie better than anything else in the world? All her friends are my friends, and all her concerns are my concerns. And because I think you are her mother, if for no other reason, I hope you will let me be at your service now, in any way I can possibly be of use to you.' The eagerness with which the poor woman turned to him in response to this invitation was almost startling. Vincent stayed with her for a long time, and as she talked, her words often interrupted by her cough and by her tears, his indignation against Mr. Bryant reached boiling point.

That evening the young man was engaged to dinner; but early on the morrow he met Nannie and walked with her to her place of business.

'I want you to do something for me,' he said. 'Mrs. Leach is all right for a day or two, isn't she? Leave her to her own devices and go and look after Mrs. Bryant.' Nannie did not answer, and he continued, 'I went to see her, as you wished. She was glad of an old friend, and I got her to tell me a good deal. She is sick and lonely and horribly dull. Perhaps you are right, Nannie, and she would do better to shut her eyes to her husband's transgressions. I have a scheme in my head which may come to nothing, but which may as well be tried. I propose to go and see Bryant to-morrow and sound him. Till you hear from me in a day or two, will you take care of her? She wants her daughter, Nannie,' said Vincent, gently.

'Yes, I'll go,' said Nannie, and walked on with her head down for a minute or two. 'It isn't certain, is it?' she asked, abruptly. He guessed her meaning.

'No, there is no certainty,' replied Vincent. 'You are Nannie to me and to everybody, and always will be. Nevertheless——'

'Wouldn't it make you hate me?' said the girl again, still without raising her eyes.

'Nannie,' said Vincent, gravely and quietly, 'nothing could make the smallest change in my feeling for you.' They walked on silently.

'I will go for a day or two,' said Nannie, at last, 'but I am quite sure I couldn't leave Aunt Ann for long, because she wants some one to take care of her, and I promised Alick, years ago,' she cried; 'you don't know how many years ago. Before ever I saw you,' said Nannie, the thread of her thoughts not very apparent.

'I see,' said Vincent, quietly. And then they parted for an indefinite time, without even saying good-bye.

CHAPTER VII

MRS. BRYANT sat all the evening after Sir Vincent's visit, coughing and brooding over the things he had said to her. Emily was not attentive, but certainly more propitious than usual. The grandeur of the visitor had impressed her; and he had, on going out, slipped a coin into her hand and had said, 'Fetch the doctor for your mistress.' It was a wet evening, and Emily thought it needless to obey immediately, but she quite meant to do so in the morning. She spent hours in thinking of the tall young gentleman. 'He's a Sir,' she said; 'that's something awful swell; and rich, or he'd never have tipped me for nothing. And my! ain't he good looking! Who'd ever have thought Mrs. Bryant, stupid, ugly, old thing, would have such a grand un to visit her?' But in the morning it was raining still, and Emily did not fancy spoiling her new boots to find Dr. Stilford. And Mrs. Bryant had come down early to breakfast, and declared she was quite well, and was going a little trip by train.

Emma had made up her mind. For some time now

the idea had been floating in her brain; Vincent
had precipitated it; feverishness determined her to
act upon it at once. She would return to her
husband. ' I can't bear it any longer,' she said;
' I'll go and ask him to forgive me, and I'll tell
him I'll forgive him everything, and I'll give up
my poor Mary and go back and live with him like
I used.'

She wished the very train bearing her to him
would hasten, no doubt of her welcome crossing her
mind as she journeyed along.

' You have a bad cold, madam,' said a sympathising lady in the compartment with her.

' Only fit for a hospital, I should say,' added
another, who was irritated by her suffering air, and
who had a child in charge. ' I hope it is nothing
infectious.'

Mrs. Bryant made answer to neither. Her
eyes were glazed and wandering, and the ladies
began to wonder if she were not half delirious; but
in point of fact she was merely absorbed in her
own thoughts. She was counting the hours till she
could reach her home—to be with dear Ned, like she
used. She scarcely remembered Georgina; that it
were a new house and a new place she did not care.
It was not Everwell; at least that was a comfort.
Yet she thought of Everwell not without tenderness.
Sir Vincent lived there ; Sir Vincent was always

kind.   Sir Vincent had advised her to be reconciled
to her husband.

Late in the afternoon a fly drove up to Canon
Bryant's house in the Cathedral city, and a weary
woman, with flushed cheek and trembling hand, and
a bright light of hope in her eye, got down, and
gave a handful of uncounted silver to the driver,
and toiled up the steps, and knocked at the
door.

'It's a comfort to have got away from low people
at last,' she thought, remembering with a vividness
not indicative of health Ann Leach's two bare
rooms and Nannie's simple country ways. '

A very smart buttons opened the door and sur-
veyed the visitor with surprise.   But for once Mrs.
Bryant was authoritative.   The little boy was not
clever, and had only been a week in the place.   The
lady's name suggested a relative of his master's,
and he took her to the drawing-room.

There was an air of comfort, luxury, and fashion
about the house, which somehow puzzled Mrs.
Bryant, and gave her for a moment the feeling that
she had come to the wrong place.   On the stair
was a pile carpet ; choice ferns in pottery vases
adorned the lobby window-seats ; ebony brackets
with china, the walls ; Emma's solid old-fashioned
furniture had disappeared.   The house was pretty ;
but Mrs. Bryant was not the person to notice that.

She felt it warm and comfortable, but strange. Where was her husband?

At the piano Georgina was singing to her lover. 'I say, look here,' said Captain Astley, interrupting, and calling her attention to the curious-looking woman advancing with a manner at once hesitating and excited. Georgina was handsome as ever, in her dark, close-fitting morning-dress with a bright coloured waistcoat. She looked round and grasped the situation; then rose, without any appearance of hurry, making a little grimace of half-amused vexation.

'Would you step this way?' said the stepdaughter, with very commendable civility; 'my father is away with the Bishop.' She got the woman safe out of the drawing-room, but paused to say distinctly, 'Don't go, please, Fred, till I return. I may want you.'

'Georgie,' said Mrs. Bryant, trembling, 'you don't mean to tell me your pa is not at home?' They were in the dining-room by this time, and Georgina had been civil long enough.

'He is from home for several days, I am thankful to say. He will be spared this intolerable annoyance. How dare you come here?'

For a moment Emma thought herself fainting. 'Oh, my dear,' she replied, tremulously, 'don't speak to me so. I'm not very well and I can't stand it.

You aren't going to keep me from my husband, Georgie, are you? My dear, do please go and tell him I want him.'

'Do you suppose *I* tell lies?' sneered Georgina; 'my father is not in the town at all, and will not be home for several days. You need not attempt to wait here. You must go away at once.'

'Oh, my dear—my dear——'

'I must request, Mrs. Bryant, you will not make a scene. If you don't go away quietly at once, I shall ask Captain Astley to show you the door. It is against my father's wish that you intrude here, and you know it. I won't have you in my house,' said the young lady.

'It ain't your house!' cried Mrs. Bryant, starting up with sudden passion.

'Shall I call Captain Astley?' asked the girl, calmly. She was a little frightened, however, by the pallor which overspread the unfortunate Emma's countenance, as her sudden anger faded. 'You must go back to London,' or you can stay in a hotel, if you choose; you shall not stay here, Mrs. Bryant. You can't see papa to-night, no matter how important your business is; not even if Nannie has run off again with Sir Vincent,' said the young lady.

Mrs. Bryant sank back in her chair quite cowed,

and scarcely conscious; while Georgina stood over her like a young Minerva.

'My father will not receive you into his house again,' asserted the girl presently.

'Oh, Lord! Georgie, did he say that?' moaned Emma.

'Again and again. To every one. You know it as well as I do. Now you must start for the station at once, or you will be late for the train.'

'I gave all my money to the cabman,' faltered Mrs. Bryant.

'Oh, you have come to papa for money, have you? When he has impoverished himself for you and your relatives! Well, I can lend you enough for the journey.'

'My dear, it's pouring with rain. And I have a terrible cold,' said Emma, feeling unable so much as to cross the room.

'You shouldn't have come,' said the step-daughter.

Georgina reflected that it would not do to have the woman at an inn, telling every one she was Canon Bryant's deserted wife. Of course most people knew that he had a wife, but the less allusion made to her the better. 'I must see her out of the town,' thought the girl, and told Emma she would walk with her to the station. Georgina went up-stairs and dismissed her betrothed; then put on strong boots and a thick, fashionable, waterproof coat. Mrs. Bryant's clothes were light and unsuitable to rain; she wore thin shoes, having anticipated no walking. It did not occur to Georgina to lend the woman a wrap. She did think of some tea, but by this time it was too late to set about getting it. When Mrs. Bryant made the request, the stepdaughter bestowed just the proverbial cup of cold water. Then they started through the drenching drizzle, and Georgina hurried, because she disliked the damp, and dreaded encounters with acquaintances. Mrs. Bryant only spoke once, for her breath was short and she had enough to do to keep up at all.

'That is not true what you said of Nannie, my dear,' she gasped, tremulously.

Georgina laughed. 'I suppose then Sir Vincent is tired of his toy?' she said, with her sneer. Miss Bryant paid for a second-class ticket, and put her stepmother into a carriage by herself, and waited till the train had fairly started. Then she called a fly and drove home.

'Papa ought to be satisfied when he hears I walked with her in the rain. I can say she insisted upon returning. What a blessing he was out. The woman simply *must* keep away till my wedding is over. After that I care for nothing. I hope Fred didn't make out who she was.'

CHAPTER VIII

GEORGINA had said her father would be absent for several days. That, as she knew, meant till to-morrow. He returned about luncheon time; tired, in arrears with his work, and rather bored by the Bishop. Georgina thought the moment inopportune for mentioning Mrs. Bryant's visit.

Since her engagement, Georgina had been out of favour. The Canon sighed often over his magnificent daughter. She was prodigiously admired, what is commonly called 'a great favourite.' Did any one love her? He had no idea that she could be brutal; but was she amiable? upright? good, and unselfish, and faithful? He dared not answer these questions. He told himself she had turned out as he had wished, a thorough lady. Was she not a lady? Georgina had a style and manner she could never have acquired in the homely parsonage; yet often her father bitterly regretted that he had sent his daughter long ago to live with the Baroness. 'It was the beginning of it all,' he said; 'it left Emma alone, and it spoiled the child.'

But it was only in good spirits that Mr. Bryant blamed circumstances for his fall; and good spirits were now the rarest of his visitants. As his prosperity increased—and he was wonderfully pros-perous and popular, his own church and the cathedral crowded when he preached, his house thronged from morning till night, his clerical brethren reverential and affectionate—it was noticed that he grew personally sadder and sadder. '*Il y a un page effrayant dans le livre des destinées humaines; on y lit en titre, les désirs accomplis.*'

'It is his wife,' so the whisper ran; 'poor man, he made an unfortunate marriage, and has been obliged to separate from his wife. It weighs upon him. The Bishop knows all about it. Mr. Bryant was not to blame in the smallest degree. One can see on his beautiful, refined face the marks of great suffering.' Of course the speaker was a lady. Among his female flock, Mr. Bryant had almost the prestige of a widower; was believed to be such by a good many, and wished unwedded by many more.

'Georgie,' said her father, calling her to him, 'my dear child, let me have a few grave words with you. You are still resolved to marry this man?'

'Yes, papa.'

'Break it off, Georgina. Break it off while there is still time. You do not love him; you do not respect him. You will not be happy as his wife.'

'I intend to marry him, papa.'

'My dearest child, listen to me. I have heard

more about him since I have been away. He is
unworthy of you. Merely from a worldly point of
view——'

'From a worldly point of view,' interrupted
Georgina, 'he is all right, and I don't intend to
look farther. I never met the man yet whose
merit would bear scrutiny. Some people,' said
Georgina, looking at her father, 'profess a great
deal, but, to quote the lesson you read in church
last Sunday, "in time of temptation they fall
away." To put it plainly, they are hypocrites.
Have not you known some people like that ?' Mr.
Bryant's look of sadness deepened. Presently he
returned to the charge.

'There is danger to yourself, Georgina, in
marrying a man like Astley.'

'When I am in danger, papa, I will come to
you for advice. At any rate there has never been
any hypocrisy about *you*. *You* are eminently
fitted to teach by precept and by example.'

'God forbid, Georgina, that you should imitate
me. But I know a right-fearing man when I see
him. I repeat, Astley is one to whom I cannot
give you without the keenest regret. My demands
of moral excellence are not exorbitant, my child.
Take an instance. I would have given you to Vincent Leicester ; he professes little, but he has pro-
gressed on the upward path since I knew him first,

five or seven years ago. Can Captain Astley's
friends say that of him? There is no standing still
in the journey of life, Georgina. It is upwards or
downwards with all of us. Are you going to link
yourself irrevocably to a man travelling down?'

'Five or seven years,' said Georgina, reflecting;
'it is a long time. Have you gone up or down
yourself, papa, in five years?'

'It is a question for us each to ask ourselves,
Georgina, and the answer may be known to none
of our fellow-men. My dear,' he said, rising, and
looking at her steadily, 'there may be in my silent
answer to that searching question, that which
deprives me of my full right to command or to
reprove you. Take the more heed to yourself,
Georgina, and believe me when I say I have no
stronger wish than that my child may be spared
the intolerable regrets which I have had to feel.'

'In consequence of a foolish marriage, papa?'
But she desired no unseemly disclosures, and hastily
changed her tone, putting her siren face up for a
kiss. · 'Papa dear, you see I know Fred better than
you do, and indeed he is not what he is painted.
And how could I have Vincent Leicester when
he wouldn't have me? But, papa, look out of
the window and see who is coming up the steps?
Vincent Leicester himself! Must we suppose he
has come to interfere between me and Fred!' said

Georgina, gaily; and away she ran to change her dress for a still prettier one, saying to herself, ' I have lost my opportunity for telling papa that the woman was here.'

But Vincent, when he had knocked at the door, did not ask for the fascinating Miss Bryant at all. He was shown into the Canon's library and received with great stiffness, for Mr. Bryant remembered that their parting had not been exactly pleasant; and Vincent was embarrassed by his reception no less than by his errand. Canon Bryant, for over two years the Bishop's intimate friend and constant companion, was an influential personage here in the Cathedral city; the whole room somehow bespoke his importance, and the young man from the wild coast of a less civilised county, who made no pretension to be spiritual, and had blundered in some of his social experiments, would have seemed to the Bishop, for instance, totally insignificant in comparison.

' May I ask your business, Sir Vincent ? ' said Canon Bryant, calmly, after reasonable patience; ' we expect friends to dinner, and my time, I regret to say, is much occupied.'

' I wished to tell you,' said Vincent, abruptly, ' that I have been in town this week; and I saw Nannie Randle and Mrs. Bryant.'

' Indeed ? ' Mr. Bryant raised his eyebrows without striking sign of emotion. Still Vincent fancied a little tightening of the pale lips; and he was silent for a space, looking at the handsome careworn face, old now for its years, and remembering Nannie's words, 'He is unhappy; he hates his prosperity.'

'Nannie is not living with Mrs. Bryant now,' continued Vincent, awkwardly; 'I suppose it was unavoidable, but your wife misses her.'

The clergyman gave a slight shrug to his shoulders. 'Well, you know,' he said, with a trifle greater warmth, 'I was excessively sorry to deprive Mrs. Bryant of her niece's company; I did my best to retain Miss Randle. But it was impossible to allow Ann Leach to remain in the house. She was not merely living on my wife in an altogether un-justifiable way, but was reducing her to positive terror.'

'Certainly.' Vincent was a bad hand at beating about the bush. Moreover, he had little tenderness for Mr. Bryant's feelings. He resolved to speak out and submit to the consequences. 'Mrs. Bryant is left alone,' he said, with unintentional sternness, 'to brood over the past and to dread the solitary future. She appeared to me to be ill, and she is certainly—' he could think of no other word, and after a short hesitation said, 'neglected.' The colour faded slowly from the clergyman's worn face, leaving it gray and ashen; his air of resentment failed; he had apparently ceased to care if his mask dropped a little. A struggle was going on in Mr. Bryant's mind, and he was on the verge of capitulation. For in Vincent's already strong suspicions of his honesty he saw chance of an alliance potent to force him out of the dishonourable and detested position in which the confidence of all his remaining friends conspired to entrench him. A very small amount of confession would be enough for Vincent. Mr. Bryant felt instinctively that a cry for help would meet with response.

'Did you come here to reproach me, Sir Vincent?' asked the Canon at last, in melancholy accents of profound dejection.

'I came to tell you,' said Vincent, 'that Mrs. Bryant spoke frankly to me. She explained the circumstances which had induced her to leave you; by her own wish, she asserted; and evidently by yours.' He paused, as if expecting contradiction; then went on quietly, 'I may be wrong; it may be impertinent in me to interfere; but I believe Mrs. Bryant·is ready to forget the entire past if you will give her a single call.'

The blood rushed over the clergyman's face. 'Ah, my God!' he exclaimed, in a low voice.

It was done now. There was no more to be said. Vincent bowed and was withdrawing, feeling somehow more kindly to his old friend than when he had entered.

He was detained by the entry of the smart little buttons with a telegram. Canon Bryant opened it listlessly, with a mute request to his visitor to delay his departure for a moment.

The pink paper fell from the clergyman's hand, and a cry of horror broke from his lips. 'What does it mean?' he asked, hoarsely. Vincent picked up the telegram and read it. It was from the station-master of Mallton, a small town half way between X—— and the metropolis.

'Emma Bryant from London is here dangerously ill. If a relation, come at once, or wire reply.' The two men stared at each other inquiringly.

'Where did you see her?' gasped Mr. Bryant.

'In her own house. In London.'

'What does this mean then?'

'I have no idea. Unless,' said Vincent, 'she was on her way to you.'

'Ah, my God! Let us go at once!' said the Canon, rising; and putting his arm through Vincent's, he leaned upon him heavily. 'You said she was ill?'

'She had a cold. She was not so ill as this seems to imply. It must be some one else.'

'Perhaps so. But we will go at once.'

'Upon reflection I am convinced it cannot be Mrs. Bryant. Nannie went to her yesterday,' said

Vincent, with serene confidence that Nannie was a perfect guardian.

'I must go at once. There is time to catch this train if we hurry.' He did not invite Vincent to accompany him, but the arrangement was gainsaid by neither. Mr. Bryant recovered his authoritative air of an important church dignitary; but he did not lose the pallor and rigidity betokening a weakness to which the support of a friend's stout arm was welcome. Georgina had to entertain the guests alone; her father merely told her that he was summoned away, without saying by whom or whither.

CHAPTER IX

THEY reached Mallton after a silent journey. Mr. Bryant was cold and unapproachable; yet, it seemed, glad of Vincent's company. Of what was passing in his mind the latter had no idea, but the young man was hopeful on poor Emma's behalf. Whether the sick traveller at Mallton were she or not, the adventure would surely lead to reconciliation.

It was Vincent who addressed the station-master when Canon Bryant and he alighted.

The lady had been travelling by herself in a second-class carriage of the up-train last night, so the man explained, but she had been discovered and taken out at this station, apparently dying. She was in his house and had every attention. An address in London had been found on her, and a telegram sent to it. Canon Bryant had not been alluded to till this afternoon. A young lady had come from London, and was with her now.

'You are sure it was the up-train?' said Vincent, puzzled.

'Yes, sir.' Then in a low voice, 'The young lady, sir, says that she's the Canon's wife.'

'Oh!' Vincent turned to Mr. Bryant, who had stood silent all this time as if turned to stone. 'I fear your surmises were correct. Will you go up?'

They moved on; the station-master talking of course about a doctor, lungs, and the heart, drenched clothes and fever.

'Yes, yes, we'll hear all that another time,' said Vincent. Then the station-master's wife appeared and wanted to talk too.

'Poor dear, she's been very bad all this afternoon, light-headed, and since five o'clock——'

'Let her husband go to her,' said Vincent, pushing the strangers aside. Then they mounted a narrow stair to a dark passage; and a train at this moment rattled through the station and shook the house like an earthquake.

'Yes,' said the woman, 'the noise is very bad; shocking on the nerves.'

And now a door opened and Nannie came out. Vincent had guessed her to be the young lady.

'Wait a moment,' she said, closing the door after her and holding the handle. She fixed her eyes on Mr. Bryant. 'You are too late,' she said, gravely. Still not a word from the clergyman. He stared at the girl, as if unable to think or to frame a word.

'She is not *dead*, Nannie?' said Vincent, inexpressibly shocked.

'She died five minutes ago. She has been dying since six o'clock.'

Mr. Bryant opened the door silently and groped his way forward, as if blind. The others watched him with their hands clasped. Vincent got a glimpse of a white, peaceful face on a child's bed. Then Mr. Bryant shut the door and locked it.

'Heaven help him!' exclaimed Vincent, under his breath.

CHAPTER X

'HADN'T we better send for the doctor, sir?' asked the station-master's wife, frightened. Then she turned angrily to Nannie. 'Miss, you should have called me if she was took worse. When I went up

last you said she was just the same. I am sure,
sir, I'd never have left the young lady alone to see
her die if I had known; but I'd gone to lie down
for a bit——'

'Have you some one you can send for a doctor?'
said Vincent.

He and Nannie sat together on the stair, not
knowing where to go in this strange house.

'Were you frightened, Nannie?' he asked, tenderly.

'No; she died very quietly. Death is not
terrible, I think.'

'The struggle to live is terrible sometimes.'

'Not in her case. I did not call the woman.
I thought a stranger would be no use and might
worry her.'

'Was she conscious?'

'No. She kept on asking for Mr. Bryant, but
I don't think she would have known him if he had
been there.'

'Did she know you?'

'When I came. Not lately.'

'But, Nannie, what does it all mean? Tell me
all you know.'

They spoke in whispers, fearing Mr. Bryant
might hear their voices. Nannie had gone, according
to her promise, to Mrs. Bryant's house on Tuesday
evening—yesterday—but had found her aunt was

out. Emily admitted that she had a cold. She did not know where her mistress had gone, but had understood she would not return for a day or two. Nannie had thought it 'queer,' and had even been to Mrs. Browne for advice. That lady suggested that Mrs. Bryant might have gone to her husband.

'And after what you had told me,' said Nannie, 'I saw at once it must be so.'

'But it was not,' interrupted Vincent. 'I have been at X——, at Bryant's house, and he said nothing about it. You don't mean to suggest, Nannie, that he had seen her!' exclaimed Vincent, out of his profound distrust of the clergyman.

'She had been there, I think, but I don't know if she had seen him. You see, she couldn't answer questions. But she said several times, " Georgie made me walk so fast, it set my heart beating," " Georgie shouldn't have taken me in the rain when I had such a cold." Georgie means Miss Bryant, doesn't it? She had seen Miss Bryant, I am sure.' They were both silent, thinking of Georgina. 'I fear she must have been rather unthinking,' said Nannie, apologetically.

'Heartless, you mean,' replied Vincent. Nannie glanced at him. No, he could never have loved Georgina very much, to speak of her quite in that tone. Nannie went on to tell how in the morning, no tidings having come, she had gone to business as

usual, leaving directions that any news was to be
sent to her at once.   Emily, however, had not
brought the telegram as soon as it had arrived.   'I
did not get here till five,' said Nannie, 'though I
was as quick as I could be.   She just knew me, I
think, and smiled, and she talked for some time.
But I couldn't make out what she said much.   She
said how kind you had been to her, sir.   And she
asked again and again for her husband, and seemed
troubled at not seeing him.   But there was nothing
connected, and after about eight or so, she scarcely
spoke at all.   I saw she was dying.   And I was
so thankful to be with her!'

'You are very brave, Nannie,' said Vincent.

'I didn't expect *you* to come with Mr. Bryant,'
whispered the girl; 'I was oh so glad to see you!'

It was a strange, dreary episode altogether: the
little dark house with the trains rattling above it,
all so unfamiliar and unsuitable; the strange people
fairly sympathising, but evidently oppressed and
worried; the deserted, lonely woman, dying without
knowing where she was or what had happened,
expecting her husband, and not understanding his
absence in this supreme moment, barely recognising
the child for whom she had agonised; her sorrowful
life extinguished suddenly, and almost by accident,
without one touch of happy fortune.   And she had
been a beautiful girl once, joyous and promising as

the morning! Betrayed now and deserted; weakened in mind and body, till even she herself was unable to estimate her suffering; after she had borne with the dumb anguish of a stricken animal, the loss of her reputation, her home, her husband, and her child—all the grievous blows of Fate which she had deserved and understood so little—it had literally been the petty persecution of a thoughtless girl that had killed her. She had tried to explain her life's tragedy to the watchers by her bed, but all she could say was, 'Georgie dragged me so fast to the station, it made my heart beat. Georgie shouldn't have made me walk in the rain when I had such a heavy cold.' Vincent and Nannie had some dim comprehension of the poor thing's long sufferings; yet by degrees their talk strayed away from her, as they spoke together in low tones, their hands clasped half unconsciously.

'Is it wrong,' said Nannie, softly, 'to be glad and thankful that her poor eyes have closed? She was so uncomfortable in this world!'

'I had hoped,' said Vincent, 'that things were looking up for her; and that she was to have her home and her husband again. I regret this meaningless end before the experiment was even tried.'

'Was he going to take her home? That was your doing!'

'No, only in so far that he let me see he *wished*

it.' Vincent meditated, the apparent impotence of some people's wishes being very surprising to him. 'Well, it might have been a failure,' he resumed presently, 'whatever is, is best, I suppose. Do you believe in that comfortable doctrine, Nannie ?'

'Yes,' replied Nannie, gravely, 'because I believe in God.'

They were on the platform now, waiting for the train, and having preferred the open air to the strange house. Nannie had elected to return at once to her home in London. Here her work was done, and she felt her presence would now be only embarrassing.

'Don't go setting up an ideal of Christian resignation,' said Vincent ; 'there's a sort of " giving in " about that talk of submission to the will of Heaven that I cannot away with. In nine cases out of ten, the "will of Heaven" is simply the laziness or the weakness of man. There—Alick taught me that much, years ago.'

'But if it is really the will of God ? ' suggested Nannie.

'The tenth case? Well, I suppose one can't vanquish that. But not even in that case, Nannie, shall you hear me say a manifest evil is a good. I shouldn't believe it if I did, and you'd never persuade me such a belief was acceptable to the gods.' Nannie stood looking up at him gravely, like a child learning a lesson, and trying very hard to take it all in. Her meek, serious face amused him in a fashion.

'You say Alick taught you!' exclaimed Nannie; 'I begin to see how little Alick and I know about things—even the things we know best.'

'Not so very little, Nannie. And what you describe is every one's experience.'

'But you used to say Alick was wrong in his "passion for reforming the world." Weren't those your very words once to me?'

'It is flattering to have one's very words remembered, Nannie, but don't poison the flattery by a demand for consistency! Reforming the world seems a presumptuous sort of task, like doctoring without a diploma or a knowledge of your patient's diseases. I have no responsibility for another man's conscience. If he gets in my way, or hinders me from keeping my own doorstep clean, I kick him off it, that is all. Were those my very words on the occasion you allude to?'

'I think one may be responsible for other people sometimes,' said Nannie; 'I think one might have to keep them on the doorstep; I think one might even *wish* to do it. Were you laughing at me in talking like that?' she asked suddenly, looking up with her sunny smile. And Vincent smiled too as they waited and talked on.

But after she was gone, Vincent stood long in the cold night air looking down the dim path of her departure. It had been a strange meeting. He had spoken cheerfully, but Nannie would have been surprised by the dejection which overtook him now in his solitude. 'She loves me still,' he said to himself, 'but not as I love her. It is not wonderful. But I wish she did. My God! I wish she did.'

CHAPTER XI

VINCENT had shrugged his shoulders and said bitter things to Nannie of Canon Bryant, declaring that he had no further responsibility for another man's soiled conscience than to remove it and its owner from his doorstep. Nevertheless, when the girl had asked if he were going home at once, he had answered, 'I shall see the fellow through, I suppose,' not unkindly. Nannie, who was rather fond of Mr. Bryant, was glad to think he had a guardian in his grief. By this time she knew that her lover's action was generally pitched in a higher key than his words.

While the young man and the girl were walking up and down the station platform at four in the morning, yawning and shivering, and heartily glad of each other's company, Mr. and Mrs. Bryant only vaguely remembered as the cause of their presence in this strange place at this strange hour—the clergyman himself was alone with his dead, no longer acting or posing at all, but abandoned to the stab of bereavement and the stings of self-reproach. There was no one to see the white haggard face, the despairing eye fixed hopelessly on the dead woman who had called to him in her last agony, and had called in vain. He understood it all now. She had come to him with an instinctive cry for help in her fast oncoming weakness; and his daughter, the beautiful Georgina for whom he had sacrificed his wife, had chased her away, cold, hungry, and wretched, with her mortal sickness already clutching at her life. His daughter had given the finishing blow; yet he was not thinking so very much of Georgina. He was thinking far more of all he had done himself—was recalling with exquisite suffering the romance of his early love for this unhappy woman, his own faithlessness to it; the miserable compromises he had made between his love and his ambition; the long serving of two masters; the crooked ways into which he had forced her, wounding her spirit; the cowardice, treachery, and desertion by which he had broken her heart. And yet he had loved her all along; he had loved no other woman. So that he had committed the very worst of sins; he had sacrificed, he had been false and cruel to one he *loved*. And for what? For a mean and a selfish lust for praise and reputation, and a seeming of something other than he was. He saw it all now; he realised what he had done, and he knew that his hour of retribution had come.

Vincent Leicester was still lingering on the platform, watching the eastern windows of the dawn and thinking of Nannie, when the signals moved for the passage through the station of the Scotch express. He felt a languid interest in seeing the quick train go by, and remained where he was, half hidden in the gloom, and leaning against the wall of advertisements. Presently he saw Canon Bryant walk quickly from the station-master's private door on to the platform, almost to its edge, where he stood looking at the coming express. Then with an uncertain, hesitating step he moved back a little, his hands pressed to his brow and his head bent. 'What is he about, I wonder?' thought Vincent; and joined him, putting his arm through the clergyman's and holding him like a vice till the train had clattered past them and had disappeared into the still unconquered darkness.

Mr. Bryant had started at this unexpected appearance, but offered no resistance to Vincent's intrusion and support. When the train had passed, Vincent dropped his arm and looked at him questioningly ; Mr. Bryant smiled bitterly.

' It would soon crush one,' he said.

' May I ask if you were thinking of trying it ? '

' I hardly know.' Mr. Bryant spoke in a slow, cutting, yet far-away voice, as of one finding pleasure in self-torture ; ' the final leap requires courage. Once,' he continued, ' I saw a woman and a girl almost run over by a train. I was near enough to rescue them. But I came away? '

' Did you ? What became of them ? '

' They were saved somehow. I never cared to inquire how. I had no hand in it. I was afraid of danger to myself, moral and physical.' Vincent wondered how much of this was acting. He left the subject.

' Stay out here awhile,' he said, ' the cool air is pleasant.'

Mr. Bryant seated himself on the platform bench and buried his face in his hands, and Vincent stood near him and waited. It seemed a long time before Mr. Bryant raised his head and said in a low, broken voice—

' Will you stay with me, Vincent, for a day or two ? '

' Certainly, if you wish it. Would you like me

to send for Georgina?' he asked presently.   Mr. Bryant shuddered.

'My God!' he said, 'I feel as if I could never see Georgina again!'   He was silent for a time; then said, still in the broken voice which seemed at last to come from his heart, 'Can you conceive what it must be to have two selves; and one a false self?   If I go back to Georgina and to X——, it is to return to the false self.'   Vincent reflected, and remembered Nannie's words about enduring the undesired upon one's doorstep.

'Come to Everwell,' he said, 'and we will lay her in the churchyard beside her brothers.'   There was a pause.

'I shall never return to X——,' said Canon Bryant, 'never.'

'Don't make plans now,' said Vincent; 'come home with me.'   He was thinking that his mother would know how to deal with this lost soul.

'It is intolerable,' groaned the clergyman, 'to think she was dying among strangers, while I—— Oh, my God!'   Canon Bryant had spent that morning in the company of his Bishop and many distinguished people, all hanging upon his lips.

'But it was by her own wish that she was not with you,' said Vincent.

'Do you suppose I could not have prevented that wish?'

'You were going to put an end to it. You would have recovered yourself—made her some sort of restitution.'

'You see I am not permitted to attempt it.'

'But if you had a genuinely willing mind, I suppose it is not impossible that she is now able to read it? and that for the world below, thoughts have more value than deeds?'

'A genuinely willing mind? How dare I say I had it? I have succumbed too often before paltry difficulties to be certain I should have vanquished new ones. I had long desired to make restitution —your words—but should I have done it? God knows. I do not. I have no confidence in myself. Georgina is leaving me; yet remembering my position at X——, and the network with which I have surrounded myself, I scarcely dare to believe I should not have become entangled in some new compromise, some new deceit, a mere continuation of the old. I might have been able to comfort her a bit—my poor Emma—she was not very exigent; but you see God will not have us think to put things right by a plastering up of a whited sepulchre full still of dead men's bones and of all unclean-ness. I don't know why I trouble you with all this,' ended the clergyman, abruptly.

'I wish I knew how to reply,' said Vincent, and was long silent. Mr. Bryant forgot that he had expected an answer, and became absorbed in his own torturing thoughts.   It surprised him when at last Vincent spoke, taking up the conversation where it had been left, as if he had been thinking seriously. 'If you feel all that,' he said, slowly, 'I think you should be glad the possibility of building up a whited sepulchre of compromise is out of your way. If shipwrecked, one would have more chance of get- ting to land when dropped into the water, than while still dangling in the air by one of the ship's ropes.'

Vincent's unquestioning belief in Mr. Bryant's self-accusation was unpalatable to the latter.   He discerned in it a distant gleam of hope ; yet he was already half regretting that he had spoken so freely.

'I am not sure there is another man,' he said, with the bitterness of conflicting emotions, including much remorse and some resentment, 'who would refuse me credence if I chose to return to-morrow to X—— and to lie about this too,—to say Emma had been false to me—anything ; to keep my own place and position, and let her reputation go.'

Vincent stared at him in disgusted astonishment. 'You shall not do that,' he said, shortly, too much shocked to continue the conversation ; and he turned and walked away to the end of the platform.   He was not a priest accustomed to confessions, nor even a curate with a yearning after souls ; he had no wish to be Mr. Bryant's confidant and the guardian of his conscience,—felt no special interest in his reformation, and had of late, indeed, gone near to hating the clergyman, the more because once he had been rather fond of him.

But then Vincent Leicester belonged, on the whole, to that man's family who said, ' I will not,' but afterwards repented. He had no idea of shirking anything he was fairly in for. And here was this wretched man depending on him to cut the ropes by which he was still, it seemed, clinging to the sinking ship !

' You shall not do that,' Vincent had said shortly, and walked away ; yet presently he returned, involuntarily moved by the attitude and expression of despair, and by what seemed the appealing look of the hollow eyes fastened on him as he stood at a distance. But Canon Bryant's soul was still fluctuating between remorse and resentment. As Vincent left him, he had feared desertion by a helper ; when he returned, the priest writhed under a sense of humiliation.

' What do you expect of me ?' asked the Canon, rising and recovering with ease that dignity of manner which was part of his acting character. But the day was past in which it could impose upon Vincent.

' Mr. Bryant,' he said, gravely, ' you know what I, what any honest man, must expect of you.

Any one who has put himself into a false position is bound to get out of it as soon as he can.' He paused. 'If you want an immediate prescription,' he added presently, 'I should say, don't return at once to X———. Come to Everwell, and consult my mother.'

CHAPTER XII

So Mr. Bryant brought his dead to Everwell, and poor Emma was laid beside her brothers in the windy churchyard of the sea-battered cliff. Vincent Leicester and his mother were very good to Mr. Bryant, and had little doubt that his remorse was genuine. He remained at Everwell for some time. Lady Katharine insisted upon Georgina coming to her father, and Vincent, after some demur, consented; and even went himself to fetch her, and explained to her what had occurred. 'It will be a very painful meeting for them both,' Lady Katharine had said, 'but an estrangement between parent and child is not to be thought of.' Georgina behaved very nicely to everybody; was kind to her father, modesty itself to Vincent, and to Lady Katharine told sobbingly such a plausible story about poor, dear, *unfortunate* Mrs. Bryant's visit to X——— that the gentle lady (always fond of Georgina, and not at all fond of Emma) was quite taken in, and gave Vincent a good scolding for insisting that the girl had proved herself heartless. Captain Astley joined them also several times, and Vincent submitted upon his mother's recommendation, and abused the guardsman only very privately to herself.

'Vincent, dear,' said Lady Katharine, taking alarm, 'if you know anything really to that young man's discredit you ought to come forward and prevent dear Georgie——'

'He and Georgina are most admirably matched,' interrupted Vincent; 'pray don't let us interfere with them.'

It ended in Miss Bryant's wedding taking place on the day long arranged, but very quietly, and in Everwell Church. Georgina, who was greatly afraid of losing her husband altogether if she did not secure him, had, with Lady Katharine's help, carried her point as to the date. Vincent put the pair into their going-away carriage with much decorum of manner and relief of feeling.

'And I fancied myself in love with her once!' he exclaimed; then meeting his mother's solicitous eye, he added in pure exuberance of relief, regardless of what interpretation she might put on his words, 'Confess now, mother, is not Victoria superior in every respect?' It was too much to expect of Georgina's faithful advocate.

'Indeed, Vincent, it is most fortunate that you think so, dear,' replied the widow, marvelling at his simple taste. But Vincent said no more of Miss Leslie, and his mother was half sorry, half relieved, and very greatly surprised.

About a week after his wife's funeral, Canon Bryant, who spent most of the day in his own room, wrote a very long and very full letter to his friend the Bishop, explaining his humiliating reasons for returning to X—— no more. It was a disagreeable thing to write, and as he did so, it seemed to Mr. Bryant utterly impossible that he should ever make up his mind to post the letter. However, he struggled on to the end; read it over and thought it would do, and then put it aside to sleep upon it. In the morning he was much struck with what a horrible thing it was, and what an upset it would cause in his life. He devised another plan. He would go home to X—— after a week or two, and explain no more than that his dear wife had died suddenly under exceptionally painful circumstances. Neither Vincent nor his mother had any connection with X——, nor would be likely to add audible commentary to this statement. In fact, Vincent had said pretty plainly that he was not going to soil his own fingers by throwing mud at Mr. Bryant.

'If ever I were questioned,' thought the Canon,

'God knows I would try to speak the truth, but why should I volunteer this? I will go on with my work. My punishment is surely great enough without outward degradation; remorse is a daily and an unspeakable torture, and that I shall never lose.' He walked up and down, the letter in his hand, in a painful state of indecision, feeling his moral courage momently ebbing away, as his physical courage would have ebbed away had he attempted to leap under the Scotch express.

At the moment, Vincent and his mother were talking of Mr. Bryant in the library.

'What is he going to do, dear? do you know?'

'No. He told me he would not return to X——, but I am sure I don't know if he meant it. He only made the remark once. I have not dived into his confidence since.'

'Poor man!'

'Poor man indeed! Well, I don't know, or care to know, the details of what he has done; but he shouldn't be a canon, making eyes at fat deaneries.'

'Perhaps,' said Lady Katharine, meditatively, 'he will do the same as the priest I once heard of, who assembled his congregation as usual, and in the course of the sermon confessed, with terrible anguish, that he had been guilty of an atrocious crime which his conscience would no longer permit him to conceal. I believe the effort and the agony killed him

on the spot.' Vincent shut the book he was reading with a bang.

'Good heavens!' he exclaimed, 'we aren't in a
theatre!'

Then a message came to Vincent. 'Canon
Bryant, sir, would be greatly obliged if you would
speak to him for a moment.' Vincent went upstairs.

Without a word the clergyman handed him the
open letter; then stood very pale and almost giddy
by the window, looking out at the sea. Vincent
glanced at him over the top of the paper for an
instant, and read the document in silence.

'Thank you,' he said, drily, returning it. And
he went away, leaving Mr. Bryant directing the
letter. 'I suppose I ought to be gratified by acting
as fulcrum,' said Vincent to himself, perceiving his
friend's motive in exhibiting the document.

The young man was no sooner gone than Mr.
Bryant took the letter out of the cover and read it
over again to see how it must have appeared to
Vincent. And he had a return of all his old indecision.

After a long time he wrote again, to the effect
that his lordship would have heard of the circumstances under which he had been obliged to absent
himself last Sunday from his pulpit. For the same
reasons he must crave to be excused from attending
his lordship's valuable clerical meeting on Thursday,

and from accepting his invitation for two days to the palace. Upon his return to X——, in a few weeks, he would probably feel it necessary to trouble his lordship with a short personal explanation. Till then his recent bereavement would be accepted as an excuse for temporary neglect of his clerical duties.

That evening at the hour when the post-bag was locked, generally by Sir Vincent himself, to be despatched to Tanswick by a groom, the young man came upstairs to his visitor's room, entered without knocking, and shut the door.

'Your letter is to go, Mr. Bryant?'

'Certainly.' Vincent handed him the missive directed to the Bishop, and Canon Bryant turned it over once or twice with trembling fingers.

'Why not?' he said, returning it.

'You have by accident,' said Vincent, 'used a very transparent envelope. This is a short letter, not covering one side of note-paper. It is all right, no doubt; only it is not the letter you showed me.'

They stood and looked at each other for some moments. Then the clergyman, pallid before, became ghastly. He unlocked the desk, took out the original letter ready directed but unsealed, and held it, almost stupidly, it seemed. Vincent waited a moment.

'Give it to me,' he said; then lighted a candle

and sealed it himself, looking from time to time at the Canon, who was watching him intently. 'Shall I burn this other?' asked the young man, drily. Mr. Bryant bowed his head. Vincent destroyed the substituted letter in his presence, and then went away with the original document ready for the post. It reached its destination in due course, and Vincent never mentioned that little incident to any one.

Mr. Bryant never returned to X———, and he never attained to any high position in society or in the Church. He dropped his title of Canon. After being abroad for some months he took a curacy in Stepney, where he laboured indefatigably, and where he was much beloved. He published anonymously two volumes of sermons, which attracted notice. He was considered quite old, and he was always alone, living very simply—a poor man among the poor, giving most of his money away. His vicar knew all about him, but to most persons he was an enigma. He seemed to have very few friends, but apparently this was from choice, for many knew his name and spoke of him with affection and esteem. The only person with whom he appeared intimate was a young baronet from the north, who sometimes spent a few days with him, going about at his side in the parish like a son, and talking pleasantly to the poor people. The clergyman had been to visit this young man ; Everwell was the name of his property. Mr. Bryant had a picture of the churchyard at that place, strikingly painted. He kept it locked up ; but once some one coming in unexpectedly had found him looking at it with sorrowful eyes. There was another picture beside it—a portrait of a middle-aged woman, with faded cheeks, and brown hair turning thin and gray. Mr. Bryant permitted the intruder to look at the pictures, and explained that they had been executed from memory by a very clever artist who had lost his reason, and who devoted most of his time to painting scenes and people he had known in happier days. Then Mr. Bryant locked the pictures up, and no one saw them again.

He had a portrait, too, of a very handsome young lady, understood to be his daughter—married, and very fashionable. No one had ever seen her in Stepney, but her name appeared sometimes in the newspapers among lists of grand people who went to drawing-rooms and balls.

Once a woman, who had a baby to be baptized, asked the old curate what name he would recommend for her.

'Well,' he said, in his kind way, 'this is my daughter's birthday. Suppose you name the little woman after her—Georgina.'

CHAPTER XIII

NOT quite yet had Vincent and Nannie parted. He had not been more than a day or two at home, when he had received a despairing letter from the girl.

'I am really in great trouble now, and you told me to tell you if I was in trouble. Aunt Ann has disappeared. She went away the day I came to poor Aunt Emma, and she has taken baby with her. She told the children I would take care of them, and she would come back soon. But she has not come back, and I am dreadfully frightened, and I can't get news of her, and I don't know what to do. And it seems just like Aunt Emma going away, and we know how that ended. And I have been to every one I know, but no one seems able to help me; and Mrs. Browne and Miss Heath are away. Oh, please do write and tell me what to do, for I am frightened out of my senses, and I think it will kill Alick, if he hears I have let her come to harm and dear little Boy too.'

Of course Vincent darted off to London at once. Mrs. Leach had no doubt taken a drop too much and got into some scrape. Poor, little, hapless Nannie!

He made a few hasty inquiries at police-offices before going to Charles Street, but learned nothing. However, that was not wonderful; the matter would have to be gone into more systematically. As to a few stray persons fished out of the Thames and awaiting identification, none of their descriptions seemed to fit Mrs. Leach. Vincent might have to inspect their corpses to-morrow, but he would see Nannie first. She might by this time have a clue. Somehow, in spite of his gloomy conjectures, Vincent did not expect anything very tragic. There was always a sort of method in Mrs. Leach's madness, and the young man smiled to himself, as he ascended the creaky stairs to her two rooms in the mean house of the plebeian quarter. 'But how am I to comfort my sweet Nannie?' he asked himself as he rapped at the door. Oh, joy! he heard not only Jimmy's chatter, but Nannie's own soft laugh, quickly hushed indeed, as if she remembered recent grief; but would she laugh at all if she were supposing poor Aunt Ann and the posthumous darling lying cold and hungry and uncomfortable at the miry bottom of the Thames?

Oh, how pretty Nannie was as she came forward in her dark dress, tired and fragile-looking, but with her soft eyes bright and her cheeks still dimpled from that recent laugh. She flushed deeply, however, when she saw who her visitor was, and Nannie's flush was always the prettiest tender pink in the world. Most refreshing she was to the eyes of Vincent Leicester, after that be-tailored and be-dancing-mastered Georgina.

Nannie looked very demure as she replied to his opening questions, her eyes cast down and her smile resolutely banished.

'I am sure I don't know what you will think of me, sir. You will forgive me the liberty, I hope——'

'Don't, Nannie, talk in that—that *stupid* way,' said Vincent; and she couldn't help looking up for one moment, and for the life of her she couldn't help a little smile.

'It was very good of you to come,' she said, demure again, 'but I do wish I hadn't been in such a hurry to write and to give you so much trouble for nothing.'

'Trouble, Nannie? But come, I see you have had news of your aunt.'

'Yes.'

'Well, where is she? What has happened to her?'

'She has gone and got married,' said Nannie.

'*What?*' Vincent was not sure he had heard

aright. It would not do. They both went into fits of unseemly laughter, though Nannie made quite desperate efforts to stifle hers and be dignified.

'She has just been here and told us,' said the girl at last. 'Oh, please, don't laugh any more. The children will think us so queer, and, indeed, it seems to me there is something rather dreadful about it.'

'An elopement! You were a bad duenna, Nannie. What sort of a man has she married?'

'He is a very respectable man. We have known him a long time—ever since we came to London. And all his family. He and his brother have a large green-grocer's shop, near where we lived first. Mrs. Browne deals there and thinks a great deal of them. He is younger than Aunt Ann, and he was a widower, and,' said Nannie, drily, 'I believe one of his names is Jim.' And then they laughed again, till the tears ran down Nannie's cheeks.

'Well; it is not so disastrous then? But why did she run away for the wedding, Nannie? Had you refused your consent?'

'I? I never dreamed of it as even possible! An old woman like Aunt Ann!' cried Sweet-and-twenty, indignantly. 'I am sure I don't know why she kept it a secret. She likes to be wonderful. She said she wanted to surprise us all; and never thought of the fearful, fearful fright I was in. I can't help laughing now ; but the children can tell you how I cried yesterday, and walked about all day looking for her. You *know* I must have been terrified, or I should *never* have written to you. And she all the time gone down to Margate with her new husband, quite happy, as if she had never had any troubles at all! And she took baby, thinking sea air would do him good, as he was born by the sea! And she has brought me such a great big, huge bag of prawns, for a wedding present she said. I can't think whatever I shall do with them all. Oh, please sir, could *you* eat some of them ? I don't know how I can laugh like this,' said Nannie, rubbing her merry eyes, ' when I remember how wretched I have been, and where it was I saw you last. It is very heartless of me, and indeed I don't feel amused, except just on the top as it were. Do *you* think it very amusing ?'

'Yes, I do,' said Vincent ; ' why shouldn't we laugh ? You really think well of the man ? I may report favourably of him to Alick ?'

'Oh dear! What will Alick say? Yes, Mr. Fisher is all right. But I do *not* think one woman ought to have three husbands, and I am sure you don't.'

'The sentimental objection,' said Vincent, ' may apply to a second marriage. But I can't see how it applies to a third! This is likely to be a great relief for you, Nannie.'

'Oh,' cried the girl, 'if only it had happened before, if only I had known it was going to happen —then I could have gone back to poor Aunt Emma! It seems now as if it was all Aunt Ann's fault; and yet yesterday I was thinking I ought not to have left her for one moment, and that Alick would never forgive me for my neglect of his mother!'

'Nannie, you had too much to do,' said Vincent; and she replied—

'Yes, sometimes it seemed as if I was too little and too stupid! I must have managed badly for both of them. And now there is very little I can do for either.'

'Is there anything? Your work is done.'

'No. I have not quite done with Aunt Ann. Mr. Fisher can't know yet what a *funny* woman she is, and may want a little advice from me.'

'Nannie, Nannie!' said Vincent, laughing.

'And I am so afraid she will starve him. She is determined to make him a vegetarian, because he's a greengrocer. Do please remember to tell Dr. Verrill. He may be pleased. I am not sure any one else will!'

'Now, Nannie, if she has married this man,

you must leave her to him. You had better come home to Everwell. I am quite serious, Nannie.'

She started and looked down. 'I think the same reason that made me go away from Everwell will keep me away,' she said, in a low voice.

'You mean—— Nannie, I will promise never to give you five minutes' annoyance.' Nannie clasped her hands, much distressed, and kept silence for a few minutes.

'No,' she said suddenly, with decision, 'there is not a person belonging to me in the place except Tom! And I should not like living with Tom *at all!*' Vincent smiled.

'Perhaps you had better go to Sydney to your brothers.'

'Caroline says so,' said Nannie; 'she says she got a husband at once, and even Patty is like to have one, and maybe I might have a chance. Oh dear, I wish I didn't want to laugh so much to-day! No, I will not go to Australia. I told you why long ago!' said Nannie, fiercely. Vincent was silent. She stood before him defiantly, with her arms crossed on her breast, and her head thrown back to meet his look of disapproval. But she had lost all mistrust of him, and even dared to sail a little near the wind.

'And you?' said Nannie presently, turning

away. 'When some people can love even three husbands, very soon after one another too——'

'Well, what about me?'

'I was only thinking, among so many different kinds of love—I mean it would make me really glad, and happy, to hear that you—that there was some lady——'

'My grandfather has found one for me,' replied Vincent, easily; 'very eligible and nice.'

'Not Miss Bryant?'

'Oh no. Miss Bryant was not considered eligible. Moreover, she is engaged to a fellow with spurs, and two inches taller than I am.'

'But—the other lady?'

'She is called after the Queen. She is very pretty, and very good, and very rich. I don't think she is very clever, but if she were she would only find me stupid.'

'Oh, do think of her!' cried Nannie, so earnestly that he had difficulty in keeping up the bantering tone.

'I am sorry to say we bore each other sometimes already. Nannie, sometimes when I look at her, I think Mrs. Bryant may have been like her; a pretty, tender, climbing plant, which could only perish miserably, if thrust out into the rough world without a prop to sustain it.'

'Ah, do think of the lady!' repeated Nannie,

discerning some little tenderness for Victoria. 'She has a pretty name. I shall like to think of her!' Vincent smiled.

'It must be very pleasant,' he replied, 'to be so easily suited as Mrs. Leach.' And Nannie laughed again, this time a little hysterically.

PART XII

CONCLUSION

CHAPTER I

ONE evening in the early autumn, some two or three years later, a young lady, carrying a few books and a brown paper parcel, came out of Mrs. Mustard's Finishing School, and walked away slowly towards the Regent's Park, with her head bent, and evidence of some anxiety sitting on her fair, sweet face. Before she had gone very far, she was joined by another girl, who, if not quite so tall, was the more solidly built and robust looking of the two. She was dressed with a trifle more pretence and less taste; however, there was nothing in the costume of either to attract the smallest notice. It was dark coloured, plain, and neat, of the ordinary fashionable cut; just the everyday garb of two very respectable, middle-class women, who might have been impecunious ladies, their own dressmakers, or what the wearers actually were, working girls of good position. They were both pretty, and the elder seemed the younger and the more fragile. A stranger might not have guessed that she was the leading spirit; nor would he have suspected that the blooming Lizzie had once passed through a somewhat severe nervous crisis, the result of actual trouble and not unreasonable panic. Nannie's discipline had answered; work, companions, affection, and general success had made the hysterical child into a strong young woman, quite on her own feet now, and likely to prosper and be in health, even as her soul prospered.

'Lizzie, dear,' said Nannie, as they sat together on a bench in the Park, 'has Madame said any more about taking you into her house ?'

'Why, yes. She says she must have me or Miss Heap, now Miss Smithson's going away. It would be like training to be forewoman. But I do think it'll be hard if Susan Heap gets ahead of me after all, when I began first !'

'Lizzie, why haven't you closed with Madame's offer ?'

'Well now, Nan! if you aren't a queer girl! You'd be jolly lonely if I left you by yourself with those two children.'

'Listen, Liz. The children are going away. Mr. Fisher has bought a business at Beckenham, ten miles out, and they are all to move in a fortnight; and Aunt Ann wishes to take Polly and Jimmy too.'

'To the country !' said Lizzie, with contempt.

'Well, I ain't sorry. I don't pretend I shall miss mother much. The way she do talk! It sets folk laughing at me.'

'I suppose the children must go. But what are we to do without them?'

'I like the girls in the workroom better,' said the young dressmaker.

'Lizzie, you had better go and board with Madame. It's a pity to refuse a rise like that, and I want you to stay on with her.'

'But, Nannie, you can't be left alone.'

'Oh, I don't know,' said Nannie, restlessly, rising and shading her eyes from the sun, and looking at some pigeons wheeling round a dovecot beyond the trees. 'I think I may try something new altogether. I am not so fond of London as you are—and I get very, very tired of all the streets, and the noise, and the pale, sad people, who work so hard and earn so little, and have so few pleasures, and some such ugly ones.'

'That's the same everywhere,' said Lizzie; 'and there's plenty of fun to be had even while you sew your fingers to the bone. I wish you'd gone in for the dressmaking too, Nannie.'

'There's more pleasure in other places,' continued her cousin; 'I don't care for the trees in the park so much; they are planted and railed in, and you mayn't pick the flowers. And there are wild beasts shut up in prisons over there, to be looked at as a show. And if you stand up to see a bird fly, as I did then, there are men passing who stop, and stare, and wonder what you are at. I think of my old home in the country, where it was all grand and solemn, and there were great trees come up of themselves, and little wild creatures in the fields; and there were no strangers, and people cared for you. And if you had some day been dead and buried, there'd have been some one to be sorry!' cried Nannie, vehemently.

'Why, lass!' expostulated her cousin.

'I've had a deal of suffering and sorrow, Lizzie, since I came to London; a deal more than ever I told you. And sometimes it seems the loneliness will kill me. Look, Liz; here we are, you and me, not old, nor ugly, nor disagreeable; and we sit here on the bench and nobody cares. And if we neither of us came no more, there is not a person would wonder, or ask what had happened to us.' Lizzie was not used to this wild strain. She looked at her cousin half frightened.

'Why, yes; Madame would; and Mother Mustard. Besides, any one so pretty as you——'

'Oh, that is not what I mean!' cried Nannie, impatiently; 'I wonder you don't understand. I feel *lost* in London, and lonely, and sometimes scared. If I am pretty, I'd like to be with them who would love me for being pretty, and in a place where I had friends, and wasn't frightened at my own face, and trying to hide it up and keep people from finding out about it!'

'But, Nannie——'

'Sometimes I think I'll go to X—— to be near Alick. He seems a bit better lately, and maybe I could see him often. But X—— is a big town too, full of strangers. Oh, Lizzie, I wish I might go home to Everwell! I wish there was a corner at Everwell for me to fit into!'

'I cannot think what makes you so fond of Everwell.'

'Cannot think? Lizzie, you are a woman now, and I thought you'd understand. Have you forgotten the sea rolling in over the rocks, with the wild-birds screaming and the white spray, Lizzie, and the children climbing over the Scar—so happy! —not like the pale children here! Oh, Lizzie, I was fond of that place! And the valley with the moss and the boulder-stones, and the sheep straying about; and always a glimpse of the sea beyond. And the strand where Alick and I stood together, and the people listened to him, and sang with us of the heavenly country. Oh, how happy I was then! A little lass, younger than you, Lizzie, and so pleased to be loved, and when folk told me I was pretty! I remember one day at the Farm, when the roses were out, and I sat on the ground making wreaths; and Joe, my brother—Lizzie, I had brothers and sisters then!—was helping me, and looking at me as if he was proud of his sister; and I threw roses at him and was happy. And the sun shone over us all; and Alick came too; and—and—' She paused.

'But you'd find it lonesome now, Nan,' pleaded Lizzie; 'those people are all gone away.'

'No, no, not gone—not those whom I love best!' cried the girl, passionately; and then she burst into tears. 'I wish I was a little lass again,' she sobbed, 'whom folk played with and took care of and loved. I wish I was on the Scar by the pool, with the seaweeds and the white foam flushing it; or in the valley near my home at evening time. I was seventeen then, Lizzie; and I was thoughtless and happy. I did not know what a sad, lonely life I was going to have. I wish I had died then! I wish I had died then!'

'Poor lass,' said Lizzie, kissing her hand lovingly. 'Alick was an unlucky sweetheart for thee.' There was a long silence, broken only by Nannie's sobs and little loving words from her cousin. Then the latter whispered doubtfully, 'Maybe thou shouldn't think of him so much, Nannie. Maybe it were better if you could get Alick to give it up. I think, perhaps, dear lassie, thy mind is running on Mr. Filby.'

Nannie started up and dashed her tears away. 'I am not a faithless woman, Liz,' she said, indignantly; 'and no, it is not of Mr. Filby I am thinking. Don't mind me, lass,' Nannie went on, forcing a smile. 'I'm just a bit low to-night with losing the children. Long ago I remember Miss Verrill telling me that all old maids, and particularly women who had loved a man well enough to want to mate with him, had a deal of heartache to bear before they got to their lives' end. She said it was worst between thirty and forty,' said Nannie, with a little laugh, 'but maybe it comes to some folk earlier.'

Lizzie was relieved by this change of tone.

'Well,' she said, 'I'll never believe Miss Verrill had much chance of a husband that she need fret. But you now, Nan, you were a likely looking girl, It's a pity about you.' Presently they rose and began strolling home slowly through the emptying streets. Now and then an involuntary sigh escaped from Nannie; but Lizzie was self-absorbed, like most young things, and her mind, at any rate. was running on Mr. Filby; who was a highly respectable bagman, almost the only bachelor of their acquaintance, and long a rapt worshipper of the beautiful Nannie, and a warm friend of the blooming Lizzie.

'Do you think, dear,' said Lizzie, at last, '*I* shall ever have a chance of a good offer?'

'Oh, I hope so!' replied Nannie, 'for your mother always told me, and I think she was most likely right, that there was something disgraceful in a woman without a husband.' Lizzie glanced at her cousin, feeling again the pathos of such a dismal prospect for one so likely looking.

'Nannie, lass,' she said, stopping on their door-step and putting her arm round the slight frame of the elder girl, 'Nannie, you gave up all your chances in life for my brother, and it's little for me to give up a rise at Madame Vera's for thee. Let us live together a bit longer, Nannie, like we have done so long.'

'Dear, dear Lizzie,' said Nannie, clinging to her affectionately.

Then they entered, and Nannie found a letter, and carried it into the inner room while Lizzie prepared the supper.

The girls still lived in Charles Street, but their rooms were less bare and dreary than of old. They were not poor, for Mr. Fisher paid liberally for the keep of the two children; Lizzie had good wages, and Nannie her little income and her earnings. There were pretty curtains in the windows, books and photographs on the tables; geraniums and creeping jennies on the sills. But they lived very quietly, Miss Mustard or Miss Smithson almost their only visitors. 'We are regular old maids,' grumbled Lizzie sometimes; and verily Nannie had of late been feeling the cares of a chaperon. It was one reason why she welcomed Madame Vera's proposal to take Lizzie to live in her own house; for the girl refused to frequent her mother's establishment, and had no proper courtship facilities. Even Mr. Filby was never able to see her apart from the involuntary rivalry of her lovely cousin. So Nannie, who always in the end got her own way, was quite sure that her work for Lizzie was done, and that she had no right to retain the girl longer, whatever Lizzie's protestations, or whatever the cost to herself. But she had not calculated upon losing Polly and Jimmy as well as their sister. A sense of desolation overwhelmed her at the prospect.

That evening Nannie was so long in coming to supper that at last Lizzie went to look for her. She was kneeling by the darkened window, her eyes fixed on the evening clouds above the chimney tops, and her lips moving as if in prayer. Lizzie took the open letter from her trembling hands and began to read it aloud, frightened by Nannie's pale looks and dry, sorrow-filled eyes, which told of freshly fallen trouble.

This is what Lizzie read—

'DEAR NANNIE—Have you courage yet once more to watch by a sick, it may be by a dying, bed?

Alick is ill, and he has asked for you. That is enough, I know, to bring you at once. But do not think there is any immediate danger.—Yours very truly,   'V. LEICESTER.'

'Lass,' said the younger girl, as Nannie jealously took back her letter, 'I cannot help thinking it would be a mercy if he was taken.'

'How simple, Lizzie, it all appears to thee!' said Nannie, bitterly.

Lizzie put her arms round her; 'Nan, it seems to me just common sense. You won't never give him up, and yet it's spoiling your life; and considering as his is no sort of pleasure to him—' Lizzie stopped short, thinking, 'Yes, she will marry Mr. Filby,' and believing herself very generous for being able to contemplate this probability with resignation.

'Don't, please, say no more, Liz,' said Nannie. 'You don't understand. It's easy to you to talk of my giving Alick up, or of his dying and everything coming right! There's a deal more in it. Don't, please, say no more. Oh, lass, lass!' she cried, falling on her cousin's neck, 'if thou knewest how I wish I might have died when I was seventeen. When I was seventeen, Lizzie! Oh, I wish I might have died then!'

Nannie did not sleep that night; she seemed

to have gone back to that terrible time in her life when she had said, 'I won't think.' The long dull season of despair and apathy which had intervened between then and now seemed like a dream. Instinctively she felt it was ended. Her work for all the persons to whom she had given herself in their need was done.

'When I get there,' she said, 'I know I shall find him dead, and without one parting word. And then—oh, God, what next? what next? I cannot, I will not think.'

'I shall go to Australia,' she told Lizzie, 'if my Alick dies. I will go right away and keep house for Joe. Poor Joe! he was always fond of me. He minds me of summer time and roses. I will go to Joe, and work, and work, and work, and never think. I am a working girl,' cried Nannie; 'I won't be a nursery governess, whatever Mrs. Mustard says, nor never again a dressed-up doll in a shop for people to stare at. I will go far away, and work, work, till I die of it, like a cab horse.'

But somehow she could not see herself landing in Australia—a working girl in a cotton frock. She could not see herself anywhere.

'My life seems come to an end,' groaned Nannie within herself. 'I cannot guess another step. Perhaps I am going to die in X—— with Alick, and be buried with him. At Everwell—at

Everwell! We both had our hearts there, within sound of the sea. Sir Vincent will do that much for us, I know. And he will bring the lady Victoria, or whoever it is, to look at our graves, and I think he will tell her a little about me. That will be the best end, I think. I would rather sleep there at Everwell among the folk who loved me, than be a toiling, sad woman, whom no one wants very much, far away in Australia, and always crying for the past.'

CHAPTER II

ANXIETY, a sleepless night, and a hurried breakfast, no less than long suffering and gradual invasion of loneliness, idleness, needlessness to others and indifference about herself, had made Nannie into a wan, faded woman, with sad eyes, worn and sunken, and sweet lips compressed and pale. Vincent met her at the station, and his manner was perfectly restrained and quiet; but the change in her shook him terribly. This, his radiant Nannie?

'Is my Alick dead?' she cried out, clenching her hands and turning from him.

'Hush, Nannie,'—so Vincent spoke gently; 'be brave, as you always are. Alick is expecting you.

They do not say that he is dying; only it looks a little like it.'

'Let me go to him,' said Nannie; and presently she added with a sob, 'Thank you so much, sir, for coming to my poor Alick.'

After that they were silent till they had reached the door of Alick's dreary home, and then Vincent said—

'I should tell you, Nannie, that he is quite himself. There is nothing to be afraid of.'

The doctor and the attendants looked a little curiously at Miss Randle, as the gentleman, who was well known to them all, led her to her sweetheart. She had not been there many times before, and she had always come with Mrs. Leach, whose plebeian aspect was unmistakable. No one had thought much about Nannie, except that she was a pretty creature. Perhaps they were impressed by Sir Vincent's having gone to-day to meet her. At any rate one of the nurses said, half aloud, 'She looks too good for Randle.'

Nannie noticed nothing till they reached the private ward where Alick lay—a clergyman sitting beside him friendlily, and looking at his drawings. The immediate cause of the man's illness was rheumatism. However, he was rid of the pains, and now fairly at ease. Only he seemed to have no rallying power, and to be trembling on the verge

of a general break-up. But the eyes he turned
towards the opening door had all their old intelligence and their own brilliance. He smiled as
Nannie entered, and held out his hands to her. It
was no longer the gloomy maniac, the victim of
remorse, disappointment, and despair; it was the
Alick of her girlhood and her pride and her boundless hope.

'Oh, dear, dear lad!' she murmured, folding her
arms round him; 'thy Nannie has come.'

'Lassie, lassie!' said Alick, and lay back and
looked and smiled at her with happy, loving eyes,
such as she had not seen for long, long years—
never during the days of their ill-starred betrothal.

'You are thin, Nannie,' said Alick; 'thin and
very white, more like a lily now than a rosebud.
It has been too much for thee, lassie.'

'Oh no—no, Alick.'

'It's nigh ended now, Nannie,' he said, gently.

'No, no,' she repeated, with the vehemence of
self-reproach; 'you are better, lad. I have often
made you well before. You shall get well now for
your Nannie again.' She had forgotten the two or
three other persons in the room, and Alick, accustomed to being watched, had not noticed them.
Now his eyes travelled slowly round his companions till they rested on Vincent. He summoned
him with a glance.

'Tell her,' said Alick, in a low voice, slowly, and touching her head with loving fingers, 'all you said to me last night.'

Vincent looked down silently at the shaken girl. 'Not now,' he said, presently. Nannie raised her head half defiantly, but Alick was smiling still, with loving eyes meeting hers.

'He will tell you some day, Nannie. I thank my God that He has given me this little minute of quiet at the last, and that I was able to talk to yon man and to know that he spoke to me well. Thou hast done for me, lassie, what no woman ever did for her lad before; but now thou must wish for nothing better but that I may go down to the tomb in peace, and sleep there till the Resurrection morning. I would not murmur against God's will,' said Alick, 'if it pleases Him to raise me up in a measure, so as to go on living here, and aye trying to find Him in the dark. I have been a grievous sinner, and it's fitting I should be punished. But if my strength returns and my chastisement goes on, I will not have everything just the same, lassie. I have been given my senses to-night to settle that. I will not blight thy life, Nannie. I will give thee up. And if I say different another time, thou must not hearken to me, for it will not be I that say it, but the minister of Satan sent to buffet me.'

'Alick, Alick!' said Nannie, reproachfully, 'I

did not come hither to hear such things from
thee.'

'No, lassie,' he answered, quietly, 'nor I will not
say them again, for I think there is no need. I lie
here and I look out of the window on the great bright
clouds and on the garden tree-tops, and see the sun-
light on 'em, and the little wind ruffling them, so
they shimmer with silver and gold, till I think I
have come within sight of the throne set up like an
emerald, and the Tree of Life for the healing of the
nations. And I hear a voice, like the good voices
I heard long ago, telling me as the punishment is
over, and He is calling me to Him; to lead me,
after all, through the pearly gates into the, golden
city where their sins are not remembered any more.
I cannot tell—it may not be His will, or it may still
be long to wait; but a flood of glory has been
poured into my soul, and it is aye waxing brighter
and brighter, and I cannot tell what it can be, if it
is not a drawing near to the city, which has no need
of the sun, for the Lamb is the light thereof, and it
shines for ever and ever.'

'Dearest Alick!' said Nannie, 'oh, it is good to
see you so happy!'

'Ay, lassie,' answered Alick, in the same measured voice, not wholly without the richness of its
past, 'when He giveth peace, who then can make
trouble? It seems a dream now, the evil I did and

the evil I suffered. I cannot mind it exactly. Maybe the Lord thinks I have mourned for it enough, and is beginning to blot it out. That makes me think I am drawing nigh the gates; for in the heavenly city the sins are not remembered any more, not by oneself nor by any one. That's good to think on,' said Alick, with a long breath, ' not to have to remember them any more.'

He closed his eyes, but presently opened them again and said, less dreamily, ' Nannie, I would be glad to think you could forget them too. Thou wilt think kindly on thy poor Alick, and forget that ever he presumed on the grace of God, ay, and loosed his hold of the guiding hand, till he followed Satan astray—him who was a liar and a murderer from the beginning.' The veins were standing out now like ropes upon his brow, and his voice shook. Nannie, a little frightened, glanced at Vincent, tapped Alick lightly on the hand, and said—

' You know, Alick, I let you say all you chose last night on condition that you dropped that tone for the future. Have no fear that Nannie will not remember you kindly. All your friends will do that, and she has loved you more than has any one.'

' Ay, Alick,' said Nannie, tearfully.

' I would I could recompense thee, lassie,' murmured Alick. 'I will ask God to recompense thee, and to bless thee, and them thou lovest; and to fulfil all thy mind.'

'Oh, Alick, don't talk of recompense for love!' moaned Nannie; 'was it not a joy to help thee? I would have borne the trouble for thee, lad, if I could.'

'Thou wilt stay with me now, Nannie?' said Alick, quietly; 'I'd like my last sight on earth to be thy sweet face. I cannot think among the redeemed I'll find many sweeter than thine.'

'Dear Alick, I will never leave you! And shall we not meet again?'

'Ay,' said Alick, dropping his eyes, and with a ring of hopeless disappointment in his voice, 'where there's neither marrying nor giving in marriage, but we'll be as the angels of God in heaven.'

Vincent moved abruptly from the sick man's side and took a station by the window. Nannie, looking after him, saw that his eyes too had filled with tears. And Alick saw how her glance followed Vincent, but he said nothing. His hand was lying on hers, and round it his fingers closed appropriatingly.

After a long time, he asked her to sing their old hymn, which spoke to them both of summer days by the Everwell waters, and tender thoughts, and mystic faith in things unseen.

'My Father's house on high,
Home of my soul !'

Nannie's voice was broken and quivering, but the clergyman, lingering in the background, joined in to help her, and the attendant also, who had learned the hymn from Alick; and Vincent hummed the tune and tried to catch the words from Nannie. And on the dying face of the forgotten prophet was the rapture and the triumph of his hope's near fulfilment.

CHAPTER III

ALICK lingered for more than a week. Nannie was put up in the house, and was seldom away from him. Vincent lived at a hotel near, and came in and out. And daily he took Nannie for a short quiet walk in the fresh air, or to look at the wonderful Roman remains in the Museum, or to a service in the stately Cathedral, which came to have a special significance and association for them, from those sad days of waiting.

For the first day or two Alick was cheerful, and, it seemed very doubtful that his strength might not after all return. He liked to lie smiling at Nannie, her hand in his and his eyes fixed on hers, while she told him long pleasant stories of his mother and

Lizzie and the children and her own life during the years of their separation.   He gave her all his pictures, but without much seeming interest in them, and he talked himself sometimes ; chiefly in the old pietistic strain, ' so it was like heaven to hear him,' said the nurses.   Vincent he was always glad to see, and it was to him he gave any little directions about the disposal of things or people belonging to him.

' I'd like to have lain at Everwell,' he said one day, wistfully, ' among the folks for whose souls I have often striven with God.   I never had the reaping, but maybe the sowing was not all for nought.'

' It shall be as you wish,' said his friend.

' And she will pass by sometimes, and maybe pluck a blade from the grass that covers me.'

' She will,' said Vincent.   And Alick was silent again, seeming satisfied.

The only other friend to come to see him was Dr. Verrill.   He had never succeeded of late years in getting much out of Alick, and Alick did not talk to him now.   He just asked a few questions about the great work on vegetables, and seemed pleased when the little man said the illustrations would be its making.   Then he bade Nannie do the talking for him.

' A lightening before death,' said Dr. Verrill to

Vincent, as he went out; 'it's the way of nature, and would, I believe, be universal but for mistaken medicinal practices. If men would only recognise dissolution as a natural process! The lightening before death is, I believe, specially designed to allay panic. Now man does all he can to promote it. It's very bad. Shocking for the patient's friends, and disturbing to the moribund, whose nerves above all things should be left calm. In a state of nature, I believe, that poor man would go off quiet and happy, as he is now; but mismanaged by ignorant practitioners, I daresay he'll be kept artificially alive for several days, till every function has been disorganised by the thwarted desire to die; and the lightening is swallowed up in a hundredfold gloom. If it weren't for the law, which is perpetually interfering where it should have no jurisdiction, I'd have been inclined to put my fingers on his throat, and let him off gently at the moment nature intended, and had heartened him up for.'

'It is true, I am sure,' said Vincent, 'that we have mismanaged him amongst us. He was meant for better things than he has accomplished.'

Dr. Verrill was not altogether wrong. Alick was not permitted the triumphant departure which his friends had hoped for him. Not that he ever fell back into despondency; but the physical symptoms of his disease increased, and were at times distressing enough to witness. His memory and his consciousness failed gradually, till he had little desire or power for conversation. He lay silent and motionless, watching the people about his room, holding Nannie's hand, obedient to her in everything. When she sang, or read to him the familiar words from his favourite Scriptures, joy would light up his wan countenance; but by degrees stupor gained upon him, and speaking and listening became alike impossible.

Till the last night came; and then after a severe physical struggle, his friends anxiously waiting for his hardly earned release, there was one short interval of consciousness. He had no power of speech, but intelligence returned to his eyes, and his feeble hand drew Nannie to him, that he might for the last time press his lips upon hers. She spoke a few tender, valedictory words, and he smiled an answer. Then his eyes wandered round the assembled group till they had found Vincent. He groped till he had found his hand also, and then he joined it with Nannie's, looking from one to the other with eyes fast glazing again, his cold hand gradually relaxing its grasp of the two warm, living ones. After that he did not move again, but lay with closed eyes and peaceful brow till the death-rattle had changed into quiet sobs, till these grew fainter and slower, and at last came no more. At the hour of dawn—which for so many a soul, earth-bound in darkness, has brought an entrance into light—he stepped down into the river; which is the river of the water of life, and flows in the midst of the street of the holy city.

CHAPTER IV

LADY KATHARINE LEICESTER was a little surprised when, in the course of the morning, her son walked in at home. He did not explain himself at once, but sat with his head on his hand, as if weary; with an air of resolution too, like that of some battered warrior marching to the final combat, which shall bring in victory.

'Alick Randle is dead, mother,' he said at last.

'Indeed!' Lady Katharine had no wish to be unsympathetic, but she had neither understood nor encouraged her son's interest in that tragical fanatic. 'You were with him, dear?' she said, thinking she might be a little more expansive now that the miserable creature was disposed of.

'Yes, I have been with him for a fortnight. Nannie was there also.' Lady Katharine started inwardly. It was long, indeed, since she had heard that unpleasant name. But she replied with admirable composure—

'Ah, yes; she was engaged to the poor man, I believe. I hope his mother was able to be with him also.'

'No. Only Nannie and I.' A pause. Lady Katharine was feeling alarmed, and thinking of telegraphing for her father.

'Nannie has been living in London,' said Vincent, 'but, from what I hear, I fancy her home there is dissolved for the present. In any case she will not wish to return till Alick's funeral is over. I have come to ask a favour of you, mother. I want you to arrange for her coming here.' Lady Katharine's terror was beginning to show on her countenance.

'Why so, my dear Vincent?'

'Alick is to be buried here at Everwell, and Nannie wishes to be present; for one thing.'

'Certainly. I will interest myself in getting a lodging for the poor young woman. The baker's wife will take her, I daresay, for a few days.'

'That is not what I propose, mother.'

'What then?'

'I want you to invite her to the Heights as your guest,' said the son.

'Vincent!' There was a pause. The widow indeed, could hardly restrain her tears. After living in a fool's paradise with her son for so many years it was overwhelming to have the old anxiety sprung upon her all of a sudden in this manner. 'It is your own house, Vincent,' said Lady Katharine, very stiffly.

'Yes. But I cannot very conveniently invite Miss Randle into it as *my* visitor. The invitation must come from you.'

'I cannot prevent you, Vincent,' said Lady Katharine, dreadfully agitated, and falling into the snare of exaggeration, 'from inviting any person, man, woman, or child, into your house; but I am not bound to act as hostess. You and I have *never* agreed about our visitors, and I have already received a great many more of your friends than I could cordially welcome. There *is* a limit. I do not think you show much respect for your mother in proposing Miss Randle as a visitor. If you persist, I shall feel it my *duty* to go away at once to Henslow, and I am sure your grandfather will both understand and approve my reason.'

'Mother, dear,' said Vincent, rising and taking her hands, 'isn't that a foolish way of talking? You know perfectly that if you go away I not only cannot ask Nannie to my house, but must not allow her to come to Everwell at all at present. I think, mother,' he added, gravely, 'I am not rash in believing you will regret it, if you annoy me in that manner.'

Lady Katharine grew more and more alarmed;

and she had a painful recollection of certain unkind but emphatic assertions from the lips of Georgina Bryant, which had gained a sort of unwilling credence from her anxious maternal mind.

'You know, Vincent,' she protested, 'I neither understand, nor approve, nor can possibly assist your acquaintance with that young woman.'

'I thought you understood it perfectly, mother. It is simple enough. I have loved Nannie for years, and wished to marry her. So far my suit has been unsuccessful; but I have reason to believe that the main obstacles to our marriage are now removed, and so I hope Nannie will reconsider her decision. I wish to tell you, mother,' continued Vincent, 'that your objections cannot at this stage have effect in altering my intentions, but they may make considerable change in my relation to you. And I do think you will show your wisdom no less than your affection if you will refrain from any further useless opposition.'

'But I do not know Miss Randle at all!' said the poor widow, resolving to summon Lord Henslow at once; 'nor was I aware, Vincent,' she continued, rashly, 'that you were keeping up a secret acquaintance with her all these years, after she had been obliged to leave Everwell in consequence of the very unpleasant remarks passed upon her and you.'

Vincent was unprepared for this aggressive warfare on his mother's part.

'There has been no secrecy in the acquaintance I have kept up with Nannie since she left Everwell,' he answered, hotly. 'Common sense might show, mother, that I should not introduce to you, nor ask you to be responsible for any lady with whom I had kept up a secret acquaintance which I was unwilling to have investigated.'

'Vincent, *dear!* Only you know,' she continued, desperately, 'I do think it was foolish to continue the acquaintance, remembering what people thought and what was publicly stated in that horrid Uggle Grinby newspaper. Yes, dear, I know, I was *thankful* you denied it; but your grandfather said— And it is nearly five years ago, and *yet* you have kept up with the young woman! I am so afraid people will fancy that after all there was some truth——'

'I think it is highly probable,' interrupted Vincent, turning from her, 'as my own mother appears inclined to lead the way.'

'Oh no, dear! *dear!*' cried the terrified woman, detaining him; 'do you think I would doubt your word?'

'Very well, mother. But if you trust me and yet you consider Nannie's reputation in danger, it is only common charity for you to establish it.

Whether she is ever to be my bride or not, I repeat my request that you will receive her here openly, and confess your belief that she is unworthy of one breath of slander. In an hour I shall return to X——, and before I go, mother, I hope you will give me the message I want to carry from you to Nannie.'

Lady Katharine was left alone in a positive agony of perturbation.

Before very long she invaded the dining-room, where her son was reading the *Times* and dawdling over some cold beef. The gentle-hearted, perplexed woman was torn in two by maternal affection and her stern sense of duty. And the worst was that she had made Vincent angry—a thing which had not occurred for years. It had been most stupid of her. She kissed him now deprecatingly, and tried to refill his glass and to pile his plate—attentions which Vincent received coldly, but with tolerable patience.

'Well, mother?' 'said Vincent, pushing his luncheon away, and turning his chair.

'Dearest, I am so distressed that I hurt you, by appearing to doubt for one moment——'

'I don't want to hear any more about that. It offends me. Have you considered my request, mother?'

'Vincent, *dear*, if there was justification for your annoyance, don't let it hinder us from discussing quietly, and—and—good temperedly—this very serious step you are meditating.'

' Well, mother ? '

' I am quite sure that Miss Randle is a very good as well as a most lovely girl. I never really thought anything else *myself*. Knowing you as I do, and seeing what *she* was the only day I think I ever spoke to her, I hope you will forgive me if I gave you for an instant the impression that——'

' No, mother, I don't forgive you. If you had no doubts of any kind your remarks were pointless. But let it pass. I will think no more about it. Pray proceed with what you wish to say. It is what I have come here for—to talk the matter over with you.'

' Vincent, my dearest son, I am unwilling to further your wishes, because I cannot believe for one moment that a young person, however charming and excellent, of such a totally different rank and education and associates from your own, could make you happy as your wife or be happy herself. Dear, do pause.'

' I have paused for five years,' said Vincent. Then, as she remained silent and almost in tears, he continued, ' Mother, you need not enter into an argument. I have heard it all before, and I have thought it out myself. I know what you will say— that Nannie's grammar goes astray sometimes ; that she has not much learning to boast of; that she has no " accomplishments " (whatever they may be) ; that the ceremonies of a dinner-party or a ballroom are unknown, and even unimaginable to her. I know all that. But I know also,' said Vincent, ' that she is the most generous, the bravest, and the sweetest woman I have ever met ; that she has been a blessing unspeakable to myself and to every one who knows her. I do not say, mother, that under no circumstances could I possibly have married any one else—nothing is gained by exaggeration—but I do assert, and with the firmest conviction, that Nannie has been, and ever will be, the one only woman of my love.'

Lady Katharine, rather shaken, made no response, and presently Vincent resumed, ' I am not surprised, my dear mother, that you see objections to our marriage. You do not know Nannie, and it is natural and not unreasonable that you should think her deficiencies perhaps greater than they are, and perhaps of greater importance. They do not seem *altogether* unimportant to me even now; and for a considerable time after I was conscious of having given her my heart, the objections that you still urge, and the danger of causing her disappointment and suffering by dragging her into an unsuitable position, seemed to me also an insuperable impediment to any idea of marriage. But I learned to think differently.

Our attachment has been no sudden and romantic mushroom affair. It began, no doubt, in what you might call a flirtation between us, which, perhaps, from one point of view, had been better omitted. It was partly the result of circumstances which threw us together once or twice, partly the result of a careless and meaningless enough admiration on my part. Nannie was then a lively and innocent child, most beautiful, and with a nature far too refined for her surroundings. I have nothing to reproach myself with in our acquaintance, but I had no serious thoughts on any matter at that time, and it depended very much on the sort of girl she was, what the result of our acquaintance would be. Very soon I recognised that it must either be given up altogether or become a grave matter. I was as conscious of the position's difficulties as even you could wish. I was ready to retreat, if it were possible, and without too much—what shall I say ?— disappointment. You will remember that I exiled myself from Everwell for six months, and that I made frantic and singularly unwise attempts to rekindle my very transient flame for Georgina Bryant. It would not do. I could not avoid seeing Nannie, and to see her—oh, mother, yes !—to see her was to love her. Since then our attachment—and I very soon declared myself, and learned that she, my sweet Nannie ! was not indifferent to me—our

attachment has been steadily growing in seriousness
and in irrevocableness.   I have seen her in very
strange, very difficult, and very sad circumstances,
and I have never seen her anything but what she
is—pure, and noble, and lovable.   In addition, she
is very bright, and what I should call clever; in
fact, in every essential way,' said Vincent, laying
his hands on his mother's shoulders, and looking
down at her, smiling, but serious, ' superior to your
son, who is stupid and selfish and idle, who has not
set himself a very high standard in any matter,
and who has far too often fallen short of even his
standard, low as it is.   Do not, my dearest mother,
wish to deprive me of a companionship which I
know is to me elevating and ennobling as well
as ardently desired, and very dear; and which I
believe you will approve when once you are
acquainted with my darling herself.   Now I have
very little more to say.   Of course it would have
been easy to have married Nannie first, and to have
informed you of the step afterwards, when you
could recognise it as unalterable.   But I prefer
giving you full notice of my intentions, and if I
can, I mean to gain your consent.   Nothing but
Nannie's own refusal shall prevent my marrying
her, but it will make a considerable difference to us
all if my wife and my mother, both so dear to me,
are bad friends; if you, who might be such a help

in what she will at first doubtless feel a very difficult and trying position, are—not unkind, you are unkind to no one, but cold, obstructive, and unpropitious. I don't expect you at present to like my marriage; but I think you had better make the best of what you consider a bad job, and do what you can to have it turn out without the evil results you venture to predict.' And Vincent kissed her with affectionate ceremony.

Lady Katharine dried her eyes and returned the salute. There was a silence.

'Well, dearest, if your mind is quite made up, and your affections are so deeply engaged, I will say no more against it,' said the mother at last, slowly.

'Thank you. Thank you, my dearest mother. And I may bring Nannie here at once for you to make her acquaintance?' he urged, retaining her hand between his.

'Very well,' said Lady Katharine, with a sigh.

'Thank you most heartily, mother. It is a real kindness, for it will smooth our path and set us right in the eyes of the world. I believe you are mistaken in thinking outsiders have any evil surmise about us; but at any rate there will be an end to all that, if Nannie is seen under your wing.'

Whereupon he attacked the cold beef, and Lady Katharine lingered beside him, very loving and assiduous, but far from content.

'Mind,' said Vincent, looking up presently, 'I mean her to be welcomed. She must be treated by you and by every one exactly like any other young lady of our acquaintance.'

'Vincent, dear,' said the poor lady, 'I can't imagine what your grandfather, or indeed your own dear father, would say, if they knew what you were doing.'

'I shall probably write to my grandfather this evening; or I may wait till we are actually engaged. Then he can say his worst, and, I suppose, as he threatened, he will cut my acquaintance. I shall be sorry, for he has been very kind to me; but I cannot help it. The thing I shall not permit is that he or any one should bother Nannie with remonstrance. You, mother, will have to assist me in preventing that, and I beg that you will remember the hint yourself,' said Vincent, emphatically.

What more could Lady Katharine do? And he had no sooner finished his luncheon than he gave her no further opportunity for expression of her views at all. He had arrangements to make for Alick's funeral and other matters, and as soon as these were concluded he returned to X———.

The widow spent a most disagreeable afternoon. She cried from time to time. She explained about the visitor to the housekeeper with all the dignity she could command, and of course did not refer to her son's terrible intentions; but she detected a lurking smile in the corner of the good woman's eye, and she foresaw endless gossip, and the descent of Sir Vincent many degrees in public estimation. Nannie of all people! The very girl whose name had already been so unpleasantly mixed up with the family; about whom a madwoman had spun a silly story to make the scandal more sensational. It would be revived now. Horrible! One of the other girls would not have been so bad; but indeed they were all, *all* very loud and offensive. Oh dear, how *could he?* Simply, how could he? Certainly she had noticed that some of his men friends were a little *rough;* but she did think he would have appreciated a lady when he saw one. That dear, charming Georgina! That sweet, bright, girlish Victoria! Yet, now she came to think of it, he had once flirted quite hard with the fast, noisy, hunting Miss Chambers at Faverton, quite as much as with Victoria. Yet Lady Katharine would infinitely rather he had selected Miss Chambers than *this* designing girl, who had neither birth nor breeding, and who was a positive byword at Everwell.

'Perhaps I am wronging her,' continued the lady's confused and sorrowing thoughts, 'and she is a nice good girl really. Vincent says so. But then young men are so easily taken in by a pretty face. Certainly she seemed very modest the day I saw her. But she was a mere child then. Women of that class get so much worse as they age. Yes, *then* she was willing to admit she was no fit wife for Vincent. Now, according to him, she has changed her mind. It just shows she has deteriorated. Oh, my poor, dear son, what miseries you are preparing for yourself! Your career *ruined;* a wretched home; all refined society driven away, for of course only climbing flatterers will care to associate with a woman of that sort. Oh, how sadly different from my happy, happy, married life! And after having poor Mr. Bryant and his terrible wife for a living example before our eyes. Not to take warning! And it was even hinted that this girl was actually that shocking and disastrous woman's own daughter! But that was on the face of it untrue. Vincent said nothing about it. I am sure he does not think it could have been true.' Lady Katharine pressed her hand to her head, much agitated. 'Well, well, in no case could it make any difference. Her whole bringing up has been just that of quite a common girl—quite. Education does infinitely more than actual birth. Yes, I am glad that rumour was so utterly baseless. It would only make the whole matter more disagreeable than even it is.' Nevertheless Lady Katharine had an unacknowledged feeling that if her dear lost brother, whom she had tenderly loved despite his faults, had been responsible for

Nannie's existence, she would have regarded the girl with more interest than she could think of bestowing on the daughter of a mere coarse farmer, who had entrapped and victimised her son. As it was, she put the idea out of her mind and wrung her hands and said—

'It is miserable to think of. Poor, poor Vincent. Poor, dear boy. It is wretched to think of. I have been weak to yield. I ought to have opposed it to my very uttermost.'

CHAPTER V

'AND now, Nannie,' said Vincent, ' pardon me if I ask what you are going to do yourself?' She hesitated.

'I suppose I must go back to London to Lizzie,' she said; 'I'd have liked to have seen him laid to rest, but I don't see how to manage it.'

'Will you trust me to arrange it for you ?'

'Oh yes. I will do whatever you think best.'

'Thanks, Nannie. I was sure you would want to be present. Moreover, I understood that Lizzie was off your hands ? You want a breathing time to decide what you are going to do next, don't you ? Well, when I was at home this morning I arranged that you should come to Everwell, at any rate for a few days.'

'Oh, thank you! You are good!' cried Nannie, with tears in her eyes; 'oh, if you knew how I longed to be at Everwell just once again!'

'You are fond of the place?'

'Oh, I am! I am! There is no place I love so well!'

'Then I am very glad I have secured you a habitation there for a while.'

'Where is it?'

'I will tell you on our way thither this evening. You promised to trust me?'

Nannie was silent for a minute. Something in Vincent's gaze brought the colour to her pale cheeks.

'Do you really, really think, sir, it is best for me to go to Everwell just now? Please, I think you know what I mean.'

'I do think it best. I have considered carefully, and I think it is the very best plan for both of us,' said Vincent. She made no further objection.

The constant strain and fatigue of the last week had exhausted the girl. She was feeling nervous and agitated, restlessly anxious to be away from this dismal house. Her tears were not yet refreshing ones.

'You are not ill, Nannie, are you?' asked Vincent, anxiously.

'No—oh no. I am never ill. I am only so very tired. I did not know how tired till now that it is over.' She meant poor Alick's sickness and death, but had no sooner said the words than it struck her they might be imagined to have a larger reference, and she flushed painfully.

'Did you rest a bit, as I bade you?' said Vincent, drily.

'I tried. It wasn't very successful. Do you know I heard some one—one of the people here—screaming. It frightened me. It gave me dreadful thoughts. It made me wonder if Alick ever— One of the nurses came to tell me not to mind. I think she meant it kindly, but I did not like the way she talked. She told me stories—some about Alick. They were not disagreeable stories, but I don't want to talk of him to any one who did not know him as he was—who did not know all. It made me shiver. It made me hate the house. Then I went out.'

'Went out, Nannie?'

'Yes. I wanted to feel the air, and to see ordinary people,' said Nannie, 'working men, and wholesome women with babies—people who were happy, and not thinking of exile and corpses and madmen——'

'Dear Nannie!'

'Ah! It seems hard to you to have such thoughts, when he was alive yesterday. Oh, my poor Alick! When I think of the hopes we had for him once, I am glad—yes, I am very glad his disappointments are ended.   And now I want only to think of him as at rest, and at peace, and happy in the golden city.   I want to think that even his poor body is away from this gloomy place.   And I want, perhaps more than I ought, to get away from it myself.   That is why I went out and walked about the streets.'

'You shall hear the sea at Everwell to-morrow, Nannie,' said Vincent.

'I am afraid to let any one know how glad I am!' she said, under her breath.   Vincent was looking at her anxiously; he had not before seen her so overwrought.   She was clasping and unclasping her fingers restlessly, her eyes fixed on the sky. But she felt his gaze.

'I shall go to my brothers in Australia,' said Nannie, abruptly, with a ring of despair in her voice.   He answered, quietly—

'It is possible that will be best, Nannie, but you are not calm enough to make the decision now.'

'Go and get ready for your journey,' said Vincent, gravely and firmly.

Nannie obeyed, colouring with remorse for her agitation.

Vincent, left alone, smiled with measureless tenderness and a touch of triumph.

They started soon after.   Nannie had bought

herself in the course of her morning's restless wandering, a ready-made, plain, and rather rough black dress, which she wore with grace and dignity. She had the same simple but not dowdy black hat which she had worn in the London streets. Altogether she looked quite suitably dressed for a young lady in mourning and about to travel. She had schooled herself into outward self-possession again—was even cheerful under the influence of ' returning home.'

' First-class ? ' whispered Nannie, whose sense of humour rarely deserted her for long. ' I have no business here.' Sir Vincent smiled.

He gave her an illustrated paper and made a few remarks in the course of the journey, and took care of her generally in a way very delightful to her, and, in the eyes of their travelling companions, very natural and proper from a gentleman to a young lady whom he was escorting. But they were silent, on the whole—Nannie from her mourning and her great weariness, Vincent from suppressed and growing excitement. The people in the compartment with them thought they were rather shy, and evidently tired, after many hours' travelling probably.

' The girl in particular seemed knocked up, but one could see that when looking well she must be unusually beautiful. The young man evidently thought so. Engaged ? Oh no ; they did not seem at all intimate—were rather ceremonious with each other. Only it struck one he admired her, and one wouldn't say she had not a sort of admiration for him. We wondered who they were. They got out at Uggle Grinby, where they were to change trains, but we did not learn their destination.'

CHAPTER VI

'I AM not to get in here?' said Nannie, drawing back from the brougham at Tanswick station.

'Get in,' said Vincent, a little shortly, and Nannie obeyed, but without feeling comfortable. The first-class railway carriage had only amused her. Lady Katharine's brougham was different. She sat up very straight and did not look at her companion.

'Are you very tired?' he asked, in a low voice of irrepressible tenderness.

'Yes. How fast they go!' said Nannie, embarrassed.

'Still it is a long drive. Lean back and make yourself comfortable.' Nannie did not obey this time.

'Where are you taking me, please, sir?'

'I am taking you to my mother, Nannie.' The girl started and looked round at him questioningly.

'Why? You don't mean— Does she wish it?'

'Yes. I arranged it with her this morning.

We think it best, Nannie. It is reasonable for you to come to Everwell at present, and my mother is the most suitable person to receive you as a guest.'

' But——'

' Don't be frightened. You have not been taken prisoner. You are free in every sense. But we want every one to know you are a friend of ours.'

' Are you sure her ladyship wishes that to be thought ? '

' She knows, Nannie, that *I* wish it very much, and that makes her wish it.'

The girl was silent—still sitting up very straight, her hand on the window. The light was indistinct, but Vincent could see she was greatly troubled.

' Nannie,' he said, presently, ' do you remember that Alick bade me tell you the things he and I had talked of the day before you came to him ? '

' Yes,' said Nannie, panting. ' He did not speak of it again.'

' He left me to tell you at my own time.'

There was a silence.

' What was it ? ' asked Nannie, abruptly.

' Alick's mind was perfectly clear then. He knew that he had been insane, and that if he regained his bodily strength he would probably become insane again. I made him understand, or he said himself —I cannot say from which of us the words came first—that marriage between you and him was for ever impossible; and that that being so, he had no right to keep you bound to himself. He told you that much, Nannie, himself.'

She was silent, pinching her fingers.

'It was thought, then, that Alick might—in a measure—recover; but he guessed very well himself that he was dying. We spoke further, Nannie, of what was to become of you after he was dead; or, it might be, after he had recovered and had given you up.' Vincent paused. 'Subject to your own consent, Nannie, Alick gave you to me.'

A cry broke from Nannie's lips, and she put her hands before her face with a sob.

'It is too soon, I know, Nannie,' said Vincent. 'Neither I nor any one shall speak of it to you again until you wish. Nevertheless, dearest, it is best for you, and for me, and for my mother and a few people more, to understand, *if it is the case*, that you have come to Everwell as my affianced bride.'

'Do you mean,' said Nannie, with distress in her wide eyes, 'that I oughtn't to come here if it is *not* so?'

'I would not entrap you in that manner, Nannie. I have said you are perfectly free. You come in any case as our friend; you shall leave it there, if you choose. If you feel unable to face the decision now, tell me and we will defer it. If you are in doubt as to what your decision shall be, I think it will be better to wait, and to discuss it together when you are calm and strong. But, Nannie, can there be any doubt as to what your ultimate decision will be ? And if there is none, if you do intend to be my wife and my everlasting treasure, I repeat, it is very desirable to present you as my betrothed to my dear mother to-night.'

Nannie did not answer. There was a long silence, and Vincent ventured to put his arm round her and draw her nearer.

'She wouldn't like it, would she ? ' whispered Nannie, looking up with a perplexed, trustful air to his eyes, very near hers now.

'I cannot say she exactly likes it,' replied Vincent. 'She has promised not to oppose us. I put the whole thing plainly before her to-day.'

'Did you ? But your other relations ? '

'I have no other relations I am expected to consult.'

'Really ? '

'Really and truly. You, Nannie, have you any one's wishes to study ? '

'Only Alick's.'

'Nannie, Alick knew perfectly what he was doing when at the last he laid your hand in mine.'

'Oh, if I could think he knew ! '

'After what he had said to me I have no doubt

that he knew. Besides, Nannie, if he had never expressed an opinion,—death cancels all bonds.'

'No, no, do not say it. It may be true! I cannot bear to say it.'

'Then I will only repeat that his last and his dearest wish was for your happiness.'

'It is not that I am thinking of,' said Nannie, simply. Presently she added with a sigh, 'And you know there were so many other difficulties. It never seemed necessary to go into them before. But there they always were.'

'Believe me, Nannie, I know them all, and have considered them thoroughly.'

'Have you?'

'Yes. They might have been enough to separate some persons; they might have been enough to separate us when we loved each other first. They are not enough to separate us now.'

'Are they not? Are they not?'

'No. We have waited five long years and our love has endured. We have known each other in the sun and the rain; in ease and in perplexity; in joy and sorrow. We can trust each other. And we are quite aware that we shall have difficulties. There is no life without difficulties; ours will be a little different from other people's, that is all. We have both had experience in overcoming diffi- culties, and we shall have love, which conquers all, to help us. Moreover, Nannie,' said Vincent, smiling, 'I don't know what you have done to yourself, but you are somehow not exactly the little sun-bonneted damsel I fell in love with five years ago. I don't think it struck those people in the train, for instance, that there was any marvellous incongruity between us.'

'Are you glad or sorry?' whispered Nannie, with a touch of her old merriment.

'You are much the same to me whatever you are,' replied Vincent, 'but I think my relations would probably be glad. *I* can't, under any circumstances, Nannie, make much alteration, so I suppose it is better for you to come nearer to me. Husbands and their wives ought to be like each other.'

'*Oh!*' said Nannie, her cheek getting very hot, as he spoke so calmly of their proposed relation. However, she said no more, and gave no distinct assurance of her intentions. She even returned his embracing arm to himself with a little air of independence, and sat up straight again, without looking at him or seeming to feel his gaze. Vincent held his peace.

CHAPTER VII

'OH, I am frightened!' said Nannie, when at last the carriage stopped at Everwell Heights and Sir

Vincent got out.   He looked at her pale face and trembling form with slight anxiety.

'Come!' he said, encouragingly.   But Nannie shrank back in her corner, gazing at him with terrified eyes, as if the sudden rise on the social ladder was impossible.   'Come,' repeated Vincent, 'summon up all your dignity, my dearest, and march in courageously, like the lady you are.   If you knew how proud of you I am!'

Thus adjured, Nannie descended, and with a firm resolve to do him credit, with head well erect, and with all the stateliness of her natural grace, she was led by him across the Elizabethan Hall, down three steps and along a short vestibule, till she was in the presence of the high-born lady, her hostess.

'Here she is, mother.   Here is Nannie!' said Sir Vincent; and Lady Katharine advanced—at her stateliest also, and with a vague intention of anni-hilating her humble guest by sheer superiority of appearance and deportment.

She had dressed herself carefully and with as much solemn magnificence as her very quiet widow's garb would permit.   Vincent should not complain that she had not prepared for the girl with respect. And she deliberately intended to overpower Nannie; advancing with a step and a smile quite in keeping with the length of her sweeping train.   She looked, and she felt a queen; and she expected—vaguely—

to see an unkempt, dishevelled, excited creature, one-third the shrinking child of her recollection; one-third bouncing country lass, smelling of the hay; one-third London dressmaker, pert and forward and giggling. Lady Katharine was not a clever woman; she had no great insight, and when she prophesied she generally prophesied wrong.

But the pale young lady in the black, correct, unnoticeable dress, who came forward with quiet composure and the unaffected dignity of perfect simplicity, was quite as surprising to Lady Katharine as to old John, and to the young footman, a newcomer, who had heard with avidity all the gossip in the servants' hall that afternoon. The widow had a moment of bewilderment; a feeling that she had been under some extraordinary delusion, that she had mistaken her son, and that the Nannie to whom he had referred was not the person she had known by that name at all. And meanwhile the girl was advancing up the long room, which seemed boundless to her weary and agitated gaze; and Lady Katharine was stepping forward mechanically with the ceremonious and frigid greeting which she had prepared.

Vincent was just about half satisfied; but he put a chair for Nannie, and tried to still his ruffled thoughts with the reflection that his mother, whom he knew well, would thaw presently.

'My lady,' said Nannie, in her clear soft voice,

looking up fearlessly into the kind eyes of the queenly woman, 'Sir Vincent told me you *wished* me to come here.'

It is not too much to say that Nannie's words, and the manner with which they were uttered, cleared away from Lady Katharine's mind the idea that this girl could be assuming, or presumptuous, or in any sense forward. And as she looked at her, the widow realised how very, very sweet and lovely she was; refined looking too, with delicate features and a graceful carriage. Lady Katharine took her hand. 'Certainly, my dear, I am glad to see you. Come and sit down. I can see that you are very tired.' It was not what she had meant to say, but she said it; and already Vincent's frown had begun to give place to a triumphant smile.

All this had required a desperate effort from Nannie in her weakened condition; and the comfortable room felt hot after the cold autumn air outside. She sank abruptly into the chair her lover had placed for her, resting her hands on the arms and closing her eyes, while for a moment the room swam round her, and all her energy was required to ward off an attack of faintness. Lady Katharine had turned to the tea-table, but Vincent lingered beside the girl; and in her struggle against this mere physical weakness she cast one frightened, appealing look at him.

'Sugar, my dear?' asked the widow. It seemed a very kind and simple question, but Nannie started as if she had been struck, and when she opened her lips to reply, not a word could she utter. Alas! she had come in like a conquering heroine, but now she burst into tears like any frightened child; and she leaned back in her chair and covered her face with her hands, and felt that she was disgracing herself and disgracing Vincent, but that even for his sake she could not, could not help it.

It was too much for the lover altogether. All day, nay, for much longer, while Nannie had been under his care, and without any recognised relation between them, he had repressed any warmth of gesture or expression which could give her uneasiness. But now, if only because in his mother Nannie had a visible friend and guardian, the necessity for this reserve and restraint was over. And he had after all tasked her beyond her strength; and she had looked at him appealingly! his dear little Nannie whom he claimed openly now. Vincent knelt by her side, and drew her in his arms, and murmured every tender name, every comforting, protecting, loving word he could invent over her; and pressed her hand to his heart, pillowing her head on his breast, and kissing her pure forehead and her weeping eyes, and the sweet lips of which the *disiato riso* had been tasted long ago and long forbidden.

Nannie made no resistance, but it was not exactly the best way to restore her composure.

Lady Katharine stood by the tea-table, and for a few minutes watched the pair silently. And another illusion took its quiet and unnoticed departure from her gentle heart. From that moment it never occurred to her that there was possibility of separating these two. Vincent's eloquence had not convinced her that his passion for the girl was irrevocable, but the wild kisses he was showering now on Nannie's pale and suffering face were more potent reasoners. Very likely Lady Katharine was a foolish woman, and the only thing kisses recalled to her memory were those of the only lover she herself had ever had, which had ushered in for her a wedded life unstained by one unpleasant memory. Lady Katharine watched, and she did not know why, but her own soft kind eyes filled with tears too.

Nannie, however, was getting almost hysterical; rescue was imperative, and Lady Katharine came gently forward.

'Vincent, you foolish boy, get up. You are upsetting her, don't you see? Get up, and be quiet, and go and drink your tea. Nannie, dear child,' she continued, taking the girl's trembling hand, ' you are quite worn out. Wouldn't you like to come upstairs to bed at once? Come with me. I will take care of you, dear; don't be afraid of me.'

And presently she led the weeping Nannie from the room with as much tenderness as if the girl had been her daughter all her life.

'Oh, thank you,' whispered Nannie, later; 'I did not think you would be so kind as this. It has been such a strange, long day—such a strange, sad day! I cannot think. I can only feel sorrowful and yet so happy, so very happy, and that you are so good to me. And that he is here,' she murmured, 'and has kissed me again, and that we may stay together.'

Vincent was left by himself for more than an hour, very restless and lonely and excited, Lady Katharine's maid came with a tray, and carried off a meal for Nannie, but she volunteered no information, and Vincent tried to look interested in the *Saturday Review*, which he had snatched up in self-defence.

At last his mother reappeared. She came and stood by her son's chair, with her hand on his shoulder and her kind eyes beaming.

'She is asleep already, Vincent. I never saw any one so tired. Poor young thing, what suffering she must have had! But a good sleep is exactly what she wants; and I coaxed her to eat a little bit first, and then stayed with her till she slept.'

Vincent put his arm round Lady Katharine's waist and looked up at her.

'You dear, good mother!' he said, passing off his emotion with a laugh. 'Henceforth you "may command me anything!" Oh, mother,' he added, 'you can have no conception how I love her. She is the best—the dearest——'

EPILOGUE

NEARLY two years later, one sunny August afternoon, two people, an artist and his wife from Sir Vincent Leicester's Hotel, had walked to Tanswick to change a book at the railway stall. There were few persons about, and consequently a bronzed, handsome, showily dressed young man, who was taking a ticket, was the more noticeable. His voice was loud, and his whole appearance expressive of an excessively well-to-do personage, who thought, and had reason to think, decidedly well of himself.

'A colonial gent, I take it,' said the artist, 'come to see the old folks at home, no doubt. He looks as if there was good beef in the place he hails from.'

A little man without a coat, and who was carrying a plant of beetroot and a pestle and mortar happened to be passing, and overheard this remark.

'The sanguine temperament, sir,' he observed, 'becoming carnivorous, succumbs at last to a plethora. I see Death written in blood-red lines on Mr. John's countenance.' And he passed on without waiting for a reply.

The 'colonial' had by this time taken his ticket, and he stalked into the little waiting-room, leaving the door open, so that the strangers could see in. There was a young lady there, who rose as he approached and stood beside him, her arm through his, smiling and looking up affectionately and intimately in his face as they talked.

'It is Lady Leicester, I do believe,' whispered the artist.

'My dear, nonsense,' said the wife, 'talking to that vulgar man? She looks like a lady, I admit; but Lady Leicester from that beautiful old house? It is impossible.'

The train was now coming into the station, and the lady and the vulgar man were making their adieux, and even kissing each other affectionately, and saying last words as if loth to part. It was really rather a strange scene, but the pair themselves seemed unconscious of anything unusual, and the station-master and the porters and the man without the coat, though they stared a little at the colonial gent, exhibited no surprise at the lady's demeanour.

When the train had gone, the young lady drove

away in a pretty pony carriage, taking the queer coatless man with her, and the strangers consulted the station-master as to who they were.

'Well, I declare!' cried the artist's wife, 'I have lost all interest in Sir Vincent, now I have heard such a shocking thing! I thought that girl, pretty as she is, had an unrefined look!'

'No, my dear,' corrected her husband, 'you did not think so, till you heard she was a farmer's daughter.'

Later, when the pair were sketching in Everwell churchyard, they perceived Sir Vincent and his wife quite close to them, strolling up the steep slope together, and they even caught a word or two of the talk between the ill-assorted pair.

'Do tell me, Vincent,' so Lady Leicester was saying, 'how you got on with him?'

'Oh, very well. Upon your principle, Nannie; neither of us trying to seem different from what we are. His motive in coming was a very proper one.'

'All the same I think you are a little glad he lives in Australia.'

'I think it prevents friction. Fortune has favoured us, Nannie. Confess now, the difficulties we feared have not been so very bad after all.'

'I have often thought,' replied Nannie, 'it has been easier because we live in a place where every one knows us. I was not expected to be like a grand lady, or to have grand relations. It was so simple to be just natural with everybody. But if we had gone away to Devonshire or Essex— Don't you think so ?'

'I think the chief reason we have got on well is because you are an exceptional person, and have had no need to assume anything, since you are all right as you are. But probably it is as you say. I am sure Bryant's difficulties arose largely from his finding that people did not recognise in him the son of a grocer. It is the old story ; the frog who tried to swell into an ox, burst. You, my Nannie, wisely restrained your ambition to being a large and beautiful frog. I detect in you no symptoms of bursting.'

'I hope John won't burst,' said Nannie, laughing; 'he has swelled a good deal, I think.'

'Oh, I have great faith in John,' replied Vincent.

Nannie never passed through the churchyard without lingering by those graves of her kindred, where were interred so many broken hopes and ended sorrows. She paused beside them as usual to-day.

'Poor thing !' she said, reading the short inscription over Emma Bryant. 'No, she never was like a mother to me. Dear Lady Katharine is that ! But since I have had my own child, I have understood so much better what that poor woman wanted.

'Another instance,' said Vincent, 'of one who heaped unto herself damnation by trying to seem

other and greater than she was. But one pities
her, because it was so little her own doing.'

'And our Alick?' said Nannie, a little reproachfully, moving over to the cross-crowned grave by
itself, where the deposed Everwell prophet slept,
resting in hope; 'when you think of him, do you
think that he, too, aspired too high?' She knelt
on the grass, leaning her head on the white cross
and looking up at her husband with sweet eyes full
of memory.

'I suppose so, Nannie. But his chief fault was
ignorance; and his punishment was greater than he
deserved. So was Mrs. Bryant's. So is the
punishment of all the ignorant, stupid, harmless
people, whom we see arrive at failure. It makes
one doubt the moral government of the universe;
that because persons are weak, or stupid, or helpless,
they should be degraded and disgraced, ruined in
soul and mind and body.'

'But—are they?'

'By the hundred. You yourself, Nannie, if you
had by nature been a little vainer, a little sillier, a
little less strong, a little less pure, a little more
selfish and ambitious and incapable, might you not
easily have had Mrs. Bryant's history?'

'If you had been different too,' said Nannie.

'I say you might have had Mrs. Bryant's
history if you had been as feeble as she. I say you

might have come to far greater grief than ever she did, and I ask—mind, I don't assert it—would not your doom have been heavier than you deserved?'

'You never can tell that a person's soul is ruined, and nothing else matters in the end. Think, Vincent; eternity is so long, and a whole lifetime here is only a moment of it. Perhaps God does not expect too much out of a moment. Alick may have been sent into this world to learn some *one* virtue only! And if amid all his failure he learned *that* perfectly, would he not have had " Well done " said to him when he reached the golden gates, before he was sent to some other world to learn his next lesson? It is only a fancy; but of this much I am sure—we know very little of each other's souls; and what looks like failure and ruin, and even degradation, may not be so in God's sight —will not be so in ours, when we know as we are known.'

'I cannot say, Nannie; these things are very mysterious. I am half afraid Nature doesn't trouble her head about individuals at all, and only thinks of the whole. Man, too, Nannie, to compare great things to small, if he is to effect any social improvements, can only do it by following Nature's plan, damning the trees to save the wood.'

'Yes,' said Nannie, 'because he is only man. God can care for the wood and the trees at the

same time. And I am sure He does. If nothing
is too great for Him, why should anything be too
small? It is only because we are blind that we
need microscopes.'

'It is a cheerful creed, Nannie, and possibly
true. Only, the evidence is obscure. Two happy
people like you and me are more likely to subscribe
to it than one of the dreary failures we spoke of
just now.'

'No; it seems to me people generally learn it in
suffering. I am sure even Alick felt it. He never
got far enough to think about the whole, and the
race, and the survival of the fittest, and all the wise
things you and Dr. Verrill.talk about; but he knew
—in his heart—that God cared for *him*. Oh,
Vincent, I am sure it is true! I should not enjoy
my happiness as I do if I thought it had come by
chance, if I did not believe that God, who num-
bers every hair, did not know it to be the very
best thing for me; and that as I had received evil
—ah, how little it seems once it is over!—out of
His hand, so I should receive good when He
wished it.'

'Eloquent little preacher!' said Vincent, kissing
her; and then they strolled on, his arm round her,
as in their courtship days. 'It restores my faith
in Providence, Nannie,' said her husband 'to hear
one so dear as you confess to happiness. May you

ever be happy, my treasure, and may all other well-deserving folk get their deserts some day as well! But look down there, Nannie, and tell me who is driving in at our gate at this late hour?'

'Oh dear! What an exciting day this is!' said Nannie. 'That is Victoria. How nice! Lady Katharine will keep her till we get in, won't she? But oh! I did not want to hurry in from our walk, Vincent!' .

'Who is the elderly man with my cousin-in-law, Nannie?'

'I can't think. Her husband can't have grown so old as that since we last saw him, can he?'

'If he has, it's a serious look-out for me, seeing we were born on the same day. Walk quickly, Nannie, for my mother will reproach us for every minute we lose of that visitor's society. Shall we say, Nannie, that it is not altogether unfortunate that our brother John has this afternoon moved on to Faverton? That old, old man driving so affectionately with his heir's pretty wife (who isn't a quarter as pretty as mine, by the way) is none other than my irrevocably offended grandfather.'

'Oh, I *am* glad!' exclaimed Nannie, 'Victoria always said, poor man, he had made himself so lonely and discontented without you! Perhaps he'll forgive you after all, Vincent,' cried Nannie, 'if you point out that his great-grandson really, *really*, hasn't one single, ugly, red hair anywhere on the whole of his head!'

'Nay, that's certain,' laughed Vincent, 'but yet the pity of it, Nannie.   Oh, Nannie, the pity of it, Nannie!'

THE END

G. C. & Co

Printed by R. & R. CLARK, *Edinburgh.*

SIX-SHILLING VOLUMES.

Each Volume to be had separately, with the exceptions shown, in Crown 8vo, Cloth, Price 6s.

The Autobiography of a Seaman.† *6s.*
The Sporting Life of the Rev. 'Jack' Russell.† *6s.*
Mitford's Recollections of a Literary Life.† *6s.*
Brinsley Richards' Seven Years at Eton. *6s.*
Low's Life of Lord Wolseley.† *6s.*
Bishop Thirlwall's Letters to a Friend.† *6s.*
W. H. Mallock's Social Equality. *6s.*
W. H. Mallock's Atheism and the Value of Life. *6s.*
Arnold's Turning Points in Life. *6s.*
The Ingoldsby Legends.† *6s.*
Ashley's Life of Lord Palmerston.† *2 vols.* *12s.*
Stephens' Life of Dean Hook.† *6s.*
The Life of the Rev. R. H. Barham (Thomas Ingoldsby).† *6s.*
Sir E. Creasy's Fifteen Decisive Battles. *6s.*
Sir E. Creasy's History of the English Constitution. *6s.*
The Midland Railway.† *6s.*
Guizot's Life of Oliver Cromwell.† *6s.*
Mignet's Life of Mary Queen of Scots.† *6s.*
Barham's Life of Theodore Hook. *6s.*
Baker's Our Old Actors.† *6s.*
Phipson's Biographies of Celebrated Violinists. *6s.*
Havard's The Dead Cities of the Zuyder Zee.† *6s.*
Timbs' Lives of Painters.† *6s.*
Timbs' Lives of Statesmen.† *6s.*
Timbs' Wits and Humourists.† *2 vols.* *12s.*
Timbs' Doctors and Patients. *6s.*
The Bentley Ballads. *6s.*
Cooper's Coral Lands of the Pacific.† *6s.*
Wood's Cruise of the Reserve Squadron.† *6s.*
Wood's In the Black Forest.† *6s.*
W. P. Frith's (R.A.) Autobiography and Reminiscences. *6s.*

† These Volumes contain Portraits, Illustrations, or Maps.

TO BE OBTAINED AT ALL BOOKSELLERS.

LONDON
ICHARD BENTLEY & SON, NEW BURLINGTON ST.
Publishers in Ordinary to Her Majesty the Queen. *L.*

Lightning Source UK Ltd.
Milton Keynes UK
UKHW011025271218
334506UK00012B/750/P